the Dream Thief

ALSO BY SHANA ABÉ

the Dream Thief

Shana Abé

BANTAM BOOKS

THE DREAM THIEF
A Bantam Book

Published by Bantam Dell
A Division of Random House, Inc.
New York, New York

Book design by Karin Batten

Bantam Books is a registered trademark of Random House, Inc.,
and the colophon is a trademark of Random House, Inc.

ISBN-13: 978-0-553-80493-5
ISBN-10: 0-553-80493-6

Printed in the United States of America

For beautiful, amazing Stacey, who had the strength to pull me through. I love my sister.

Shauna Summers, Annelise Robey, and Andrea Cirillo: boundless gratitude for your patience and kindness. It made all the difference.

Mom and Dad, Ted and Jen, Bob, Mandy, all the kids, the rabbits and the crazy dog: you make my life better. Thanks.

the Dream Thief

PROLOGUE

Once, there were more of us.

Once we roamed the skies unfettered, masters of the four winds. We chased the sun and devoured the moon, sprinkled across the heavens like fierce, relentless stars. That was our right and our destiny, and none could survive our bright-eyed devastation.

We were splendor and smoky death. We were *drákon*.

Our home was the raw, misted mountains, and then a castle, built with hands and claws and laboring hearts; frosted white, wreathed with sky, it rose into a snow-crystal reflection of our might. We had no need of Others. We had no need to conquer. Already we ruled every realm of true worth.

Clouds pillowed our slumber. Stones sang us ballads from deep within the earth, begged us to gather them in our fists and keep them close. We pressed diamonds into the walls of our castle. We dined on plates of jasper and drank from goblets of quartz. Copper and gold graced our hair, warmer and more lovely than sunlight after storm.

And at night, in the sparkling dark, we would fly.

But such glories cannot long go unnoticed by the lesser beings. The Others looked up and envied us our castle and our wings. They swarmed our forests and mountains, determined to steal what was ours. Base and coarse and made of mud, they possessed one single, terrible weapon that we did not: ambition.

They burned the trees. They scorched the fields. They riddled our bodies with arrows.

And we fell apart.

Our *once* was taken from us, and we split into two peoples: those who remained in the castle, and those who fled for safer skies.

For generations, we who remained suffered the fate of those who choose to survive at any cost.

For generations we plotted, learning to blend in with the Others, using our wealth and Gifts to devise a new method of devouring the enemy: that of slow, inexorable seduction.

We became them. We walked among them. We wrapped ourselves in their scents, their habits, their small lives. When they invoked a human word for our mountains—*Carpathians*—we adapted again and whispered to the wind a name for our castle—*Zaharen Yce*—and then ourselves.

The Zaharen.

We pretended to be of mud instead of stars. We pretended not to fly.

And the people below us pretended to believe.

In this fashion, over time, we began to prosper. We unearthed new diamonds for the walls of our castle. We discovered new ways to bend the Others to our needs. Eventually they even accepted us as the dread leaders our blood and our hearts demanded we be; we commanded their armies and reclaimed our lands.

We made towns and mines and the finest of vineyards. We became *my lord, my prince, beloved grace.* Once again we shone with copper and gold.

And all was lush and good, until the loss of the dreamer's diamond. Until the loss of *Draumr.*

EXCERPTED FROM

*Dr. Hansen's Encyclopedia of Eastern Fables,
Derived from His Travels Through the Lands of Hungary,
Romania, Transylvania, and the Empire of Russia*

Published London, 1794

... and, in fact, one of the most enduring legends among the peasants of the Carpathian Mountains is that of the supposed "dragon-people." It is a testament to the overwhelming dread spawned by these imaginary beasts that it required a good fortnight and a hefty sum from my purse to discover a shepherd who would even mutter the proper name of the monsters into my ear: *drákon.*

The *drákon*, then, are magnificent, terrifying creatures who have the ability to exist as humans but may transform into dragons at will, especially at night. The popularity of these tales may be observed from hearth to hearth across the Carpathian range, where they are recounted with either fear, scorn, or admiration, but always with heartfelt sincerity. To the credulous, simple folk of these alpine villages, the dragon-people are real. Indeed, as I traversed farther into the mountains, I found the steeper the elevation of the hamlet, the less likely I was to observe any man or woman at night with eyes lifted above the ragged edge of the horizon. It is believed by the serfs that to observe a dragon in flight is an omen of extreme ill fortune.

By piecing together this and that of the various anecdotes, I was able to deduce several facts regarding the *drákon*:

As humans, they are dangerously convincing. The only physical aspect that betrays them is their extraordinary beauty, said to bewitch even the most jaded of rogues.

As dragons, they are fearsome hunters and fighters, reigning supreme over all other beasts.

And as both humans and dragons, they are easily entranced by gemstones. The finer the stone, the deeper the spell it will hold upon these creatures. A very many of the serfs I met carried with them white chunks of the native quartzite, believed to deflect the evil dragon eye.

The best-known legend of the *drákon* involves a medieval dragon-princess, a fair damsel spirited away by a clever, brutish peasant boy and forced to wed him. One might indeed wonder how a peasant would handle a bride who was destined to turn into a beast each evening, and the answer involves a mysterious diamond given the name *Draumr* [rough translation: the dreaming diamond], a magical stone with the unique power to enslave the *drákon* and leave them, essentially, at one's command.

I was informed over a meal of *gulyás* and sweet red wine that *Draumr* belonged once to the dragon-people, who—most prudently!—guarded it from mankind, but it was stolen along with the princess. With the magical diamond in his pocket, the peasant was able to keep his bride and defy her family, who perished one by one as they attempted to steal the girl back.

In a suitably tragic ending, the princess at last freed herself by murdering the peasant in his sleep, but then, alas, leapt into a watery grave in one of the many mine shafts penetrating the mountains, taking the diamond with her. Thus neither the princess nor *Draumr* was ever seen again, although there is some debate regarding the few souls who claim they "hear" the diamond "singing" to them, usually around twilight.

Apparently there is no shame in declaring a hint of "dragon blood" in one's family tree.

The central locality of these tales, everyone agrees, revolves around an actual castle by the name of *Zaharen Yce* [Tears of Ice], belonging to an actual noble family, the Zaharen [princes and counts], none of whom condescended to an audience with the Author of This Book.

But perhaps the most intriguing notion of all the tales of the *drákon* is one very rarely mentioned. It concerns the idea that once, long ago, a greater family of dragon-people existed than do now, and that this initial group was somehow forced to divide, leaving one family behind in these mountains whilst the other was sent flying out into the wilds of the world, searching for a new home.

One is left only to ponder over the agreeable comforts of tobacco and a tankard of the fine local brew where such infamous creatures might have deigned to touch back to earth....

CHAPTER ONE

Darkfrith, Northern England
1768

In the dream, she was always blind.

That's what would come first, the utter darkness, settling over her like a soft, soft blanket. But it wasn't a hopeless or desperate kind of blindness. In fact, it always seemed absolutely normal. Because the dream was never about what she could see, but all about what she could hear.

"Lia."

"Yes," she would answer.

It was a man speaking to her in the dream. A man's voice, one she knew as well as she knew the flow of water over the rocks of her favorite streambed, dark and familiar and smooth.

"Lia," he would say, an imperative.

"I'm here."

"Come to me."

And she would, because in the dream there was nothing she wanted more than to obey that voice. It was her only ambition.

"Tell me about today," the man invited, still so smooth.

"The peaches are ripening. The wheat is hip-high. The Dartmoor ruby has a buyer in Brussels. He wants the emeralds as well."

"Good."

And, oh, how it pleased her, that one single word. How it shimmered through her like warm, sunlit honey, filling her with sweetness.

"Where is the marquess?" the man asked.

"Kimber is in the drawing room, awaiting you."

That part was wrong. Even in the dream Lia knew it was wrong, because Kimber wasn't the Marquess of Langford yet. Their father was. Kimber was just a boy. But the man never noticed.

"And tonight, my heart?" the man asked, his voice stroking.

"Tonight is the Havington dinner party. The viscountess will wear sapphires and silk."

She did not know anyone named Havington. She did not know how she knew about the sapphires, or the silk. But she knew that it was all true.

"Which sapphires?"

"A necklace of one hundred thirty-two stones, set in gold, the center stone round, twenty-nine carats, with a spray of opals all around. A bracelet of thirty-five stones: twenty sapphires, fifteen opals. An anklet of eleven sapphires, twenty-one opals—"

"Very good. That's enough."

In the dream, she expanded with that sweetness once more.

"What time will the viscountess be removing her jewelry, Lia?"

"Twelve thirty-seven. Eleven minutes after the last guest leaves. The necklace is heavy," she added. *"And you're going to have to kill the second footman. He sees you on the way out."*

The man said nothing. His presence broke the darkness around her like a prism of pure, humming joy. Like a song. Like a reverie.

"Lia."

"Yes?"

"Twelve-thirty isn't late. Wait for me in bed."

"Yes, Zane," she would always answer. And then she'd wake.

❧

She wasn't ready.

Kim could see that she wasn't ready, even though they had waited the requisite fifteen days and sixteen nights for that one perfect June dusk without sun or moon or even stars. The sky above them was smoke and purple-blue, framed by the black cathedral of oaks and willows that made a rough enclosure around their circle of five.

Her face was still visible, pale, elfin-sharp, very clear to him even through the fading light. Lia didn't share the famous beauty of their sisters, Audrey's regal walk or Joan's silver-bell laugh. Fourteen years old, both earnest and shy, the essence of Lady Amalia Langford was all contradictions: elbows and a bumpy grace, wheat-gold hair and almond dark eyes, and a face that appeared close to ordinary until she smiled. Even then, she wasn't beautiful. She was, he considered, trying to be fair . . . arresting.

In fact, despite her powerful bloodlines, Lia didn't look like anyone else in the tribe. She was all corners and angles, always too tall, too thin, even as a little girl.

He'd been back from Eton only a few days. Kim would have thought that by now his youngest sister would have

11

grown into her heritage, but to him she still seemed like a changeling stuffed into someone else's shawl and lacy pink gown.

She felt his stare. From her seat on the forest floor her head turned. She met his look—her braids fraying loose from their pins, her cheek smooth with the last glow of twilight, no cap—then glanced quickly away. The corners of her lips pulled back into a faint, unhappy line.

That was how Kim knew she wasn't going to finish the ritual. She returned to watching the pair of wrens in the scrolled metal cage near her feet. They fluttered from bar to bar, breathing in small, impassioned notes. It was the only noise that broke the forest silence. There were no crickets sawing. There were no mice or badgers or moles rummaging through the fallen leaves.

This was Darkfrith, after all.

One of the wrens slammed too hard against the wires. Kim caught the flicker of emotion that crossed Lia's face, so fleet he doubted any of the others noticed.

But he was the eldest. He'd had the most experience reading hearts. That flicker had been pain, and sympathy. She'd always longed for a pet.

Hell. She'd be useless tonight after all.

Something dark scored the sky above their heads, something serpentine. None of them bothered to look up. The highest fingers of the oaks shivered in its wake.

"Daughter of the tribe," Kim intoned, going on with it anyway. By God, the carriage ride alone back home had taken over a week; he wasn't going to let her off easily. "What dare you offer us?"

But his sister was distracted again. This time her head cocked, her chin lifted, as if she could hear something the others could not.

"Lia," muttered Rhys, the third oldest, from across the circle. "Pay attention. This is your part."

"I, daughter of the tribe," said Lia, her chin lowering obediently, "bring unto you...bring unto..."

The wrens flipped back and forth and back in their prison.

"...this dire offering," hissed Joan, prompting.

"This dire offering."

"What is the offering?" Kim asked in his gravest voice, because it was ritual, and because he'd been practicing that voice for some while.

Lia lifted her hand to the cage. The birds pressed back against the far side.

"Heart and feathers," she said, but turned her head again—and then broke the circle by climbing to her feet.

"*Li*-a," said Audrey, exasperated.

"Doesn't anyone hear that?"

"No," answered Rhys. "And neither do you. Sit down, so we can finish this. It took me a bloody fortnight to catch those wrens."

"Wait," she said. "Listen. It's a carriage."

"It's not—" Kim began, but then he stopped, because, actually, he heard it too. Not just a carriage, a post chaise, rattling down the graveled drive from the distant manor house. He sent his sister a new, keener glance. "You heard that from here? It's at least a mile away."

Audrey had come to her feet as well, brushing out her skirts. "Who's expected?"

"No one." Rhys shrugged. "Just Zane, and he's leaving."

All three sisters swiveled to face him, and in that instant they looked remarkably alike.

"What?" he said, scowling.

"Zane?" echoed Joan. "Zane's here?"

"Not any longer. Apparently."

"Why didn't you tell us?"

"I beg your pardon. I didn't realize I was employed as your majordomo."

Lia dropped her shawl. It slipped to the ground with hardly a whisper, a white curving ghost against the brown leaves and dirt.

"Hold up." Kim caught her arm before her third step. "You can't leave. We've only just begun."

She glanced up at him but it was darker now, so he couldn't quite read her face. But he was irritated to have come so far for naught; he tightened his grip and gave her a shake.

"Oh, let her be," said Joan. "She's too young for this anyway. We all knew it."

"I did it younger than she," Kim countered.

"Yes, and you had something to prove, didn't you?" This from Audrey, his twin. "Eldest son, future Alpha of the tribe. You wanted to impress us." She lifted a shoulder, nonchalant. "Don't poker up. I would have done the same if I were you. It was clever to think up a ritual."

Rhys sighed. "Might as well let her go, Kimber. The moment's gone. They're right, you know, she's just too young. She's *always* too young. And she hasn't shown any of the Gifts, anyway."

Beneath his hand, Lia twitched. But Audrey had reminded him of who he was, and who he was someday going to be, and so Kim said, "You know what this means, Amalia. You won't be one of us, truly one of us, until the ritual is complete. Your Gifts won't come. Or if they do, they won't be as good."

"Yes," she said flatly. "I know."

She shook free of his grip, turned to the birdcage, and snapped open the door. There came a flurry of peeps and rustling; when she straightened again, there was a dark lump in her fist.

"To the *drákon*," Amalia said, and broke the wren's neck.

Her fingers opened. The little bird landed beside her shawl, one wing arced in an angel fan across the tassels.

"You have to do both," managed Rhys, into the sudden hush.

Without a word, Lia stuck her hand into the cage and retrieved the other wren.

Another rush of invisible wind sliced over them, clattering the leaves. She flung the second bird up after it, where it flapped and fluttered and skimmed off in a drunken line, vanishing into the night.

Lia shot a look at Kimber, chin tilted. "I suppose I'll only ever be half as good as you, after all," his little sister said, and with her skirts in her hands she pelted down the path that led back to Chasen Manor.

Changeling, Kim thought, watching her go. *Definitely.*

❧

Once, years ago, Lia had asked her mother if she heard the song.

"The supper chime?" Rue Langford had asked, tucking her daughter into bed.

"No, Mama. The other song. The quiet one."

"The quiet one. The music box from your father?"

"No. The *other* song."

And Mama had gazed down at her with her lovely brown eyes, her head tilted, a smile on her lips. She and Papa were hosting a *fête* that evening for the members of the council and their wives. Her skirts were ivory and cream; she smelled of flowers and soap and the silvery dust of hair powder. She wore pearls that thrummed with a low, gentle melody, simple, like a hymn. Lia reached out and ran her fingers over the bracelet.

"I'm afraid I don't know what song you mean, beloved."

"That one..."

Audrey was already out of the nursery, but Joan was in the bed against the other wall, sulking because she wasn't yet old enough to attend the *fête*.

"She says she hears a song all the time," said Joan in a very bored, grown-up voice.

Mama's look sharpened. "What sort of song?"

"A quiet one. You know...like the wind in a meadow. Like the ocean."

Rue's expression relaxed. "Oh. Yes, I hear that sometimes too."

"You do?"

"I do. Nature plays a wonderful symphony for us."

"No, not *nature*. It's a *song*."

Rue placed the back of her fingers upon her daughter's forehead. Her skin felt very cool. "Can you hum it?"

"No."

"Does it bother you? Does it hurt your head?"

"No..."

"It's not even real," said Joan loudly in her bored voice. "If it was real, we'd all hear it. We can hear *everything*."

"It is real to your sister," answered Mama, firm, and looked back at Lia. "You must tell me if it ever starts to fret you. Come to me, and I'll fix it."

Lia sat up in her bed, wide-eyed, interested. Rue was powerful, the most powerful female of the tribe, but Lia had no idea her mother's Gifts were that strong.

"How, Mama?"

"Why, I'll love it away, just like this," said Rue, laughing as she caught Lia by the shoulders and pressed rose-petal kisses all over her cheeks.

That was how Amalia knew that her mother didn't believe her either.

When the dreams began to surface a few years after that, Lia didn't bother to tell anyone. The song, for all its persistence, held a certain sadness and distance that made it seem almost innocent. But there was nothing of innocence in the blind dreams. In them she was another person...older. Enigmatic. She woke from them flushed and panting, guilty and excited and miserable at once. She wouldn't share those feelings with anyone, not even her mother.

At first they were fragments, just voices and sentences that seemed strung together without reason. She could hear herself speaking in them, but what she said made no sense. She could hear the man's voice, but it was as though he was far away from her, talking through a rainstorm. She caught only snatches of words.

Yet the dreams had grown clearer. And clearer. And with them, a rising sense of danger, a warning that pushed down on her chest and prickled the hair on her arms.

Nothing truly terrible ever happened in the blind dreams. At the same time, she knew that somehow they meant everything terrible. She spoke of stealing and killing and the loss of her parents as if reciting a list for the village market. It was not pretend. But in that humming, welcome dark, Lia felt nothing wrong at all.

A few months past, in the gray morning hours of her fourteenth birthday, the dream had revealed for the first time who the man was.

Zane. Zane the Other, Zane the criminal. Zane, former apprentice of the Smoke Thief herself, now the tribe's hired hands and eyes and ears in the real world, the world beyond Darkfrith.

And tonight, even though she had run as fast as she could in her hoops and heels, she had missed his carriage. By the time she'd made it past the forest break and onto the front lawn, she couldn't even see the smudgy glow of its rear lanterns. There was only the faint squeak of metal and wood and the *clip-clop* of hooves fading off into the hills.

That—and the song. Thin and eerie and sweet, it beckoned from the farthest thread of the eastern horizon. It always beckoned.

Deliberately, she turned her back to it. It haunted her days and nights; it haunted her soul; and the fact that no one heard it but her was something Amalia never liked to consider.

She found herself gazing at the warm, handsome windows of Chasen Manor, set back against the forest and lawn like a perfect painting of country peace. At the figures moving inside, supper being laid, beds turned down, evening fires stoked, everything as ordinary as could be.

Something new flashed in the sky above her head, twisting, bright as a scythe with the rising moon; it dropped swiftly into the woods.

With her arms hugged to her chest, Lia watched it fall.

She'd be called in soon. She needed a plan.

⚜

The London air hung heavy with soot and a wet, cool fog, clinging to his face like an unpleasant skin, dampening his breath. But he was used to it; in fact, he usually welcomed it, because foggy nights meant fewer shadows. In his business, light and shadow were as important as picklocks and poison and knives.

The only thing Zane truly disliked about the fog was what it did to gunpowder. He'd never found a brand that didn't lump into muck in humid weather.

From the hours outdoors, his hair had worked loose from its queue, unfashionably long, distinctive. It would be dark against his skin and the dull white of his cravat. He should have worn a wig. A wig, a cheaper hat, a plainer greatcoat: it would have been more anonymous. But what was done was done; he wasn't a man to linger long in regret. The people he'd cornered these past few days were paid too damned well to remember his face, anyway.

At least tonight was over. Tomorrow he'd start again, but right now he was hungry, he was tired, and he was very much looking forward to a meal and his bed—and what awaited him in that bed.

The candle lantern just past his house burned sulfur-yellow, a very dim sun choked with mist. None of the small, neatly spaced houses he passed were even visible through the gloom. He found his way because he'd always known it, because he'd lived here since he was a child and had mapped the streets and pavements and gutters in his mind so well he knew every alley, every door, every possible route of escape.

He made himself part of the night. He made his footsteps silent, his breathing imperceptible. He listened to the dark so intently it sounded like his own heartbeat, familiar and calm.

This was his realm, for better or worse. This was the place he claimed and defended, a tiny, ragged patch of safety in the midst of chaos.

And so in the back of his mind, past his awareness of the fog and the candle lantern and the muffled thumps and groans of the city, Zane was counting off his steps.

Twenty-two, twenty-three...there would be an oil lamp flickering in the front window of Madame Dumont's two-story, for the wastrel son who whored away half the night.

Thirty-seven, thirty-eight...step over the exposed root of the elm that had finally cracked the pavement into halves.

Forty-five. The black cat watching from the roof of Lucy Brammel's.

Forty-seven. The loosened trellis the cat used to climb to the roof; Zane had pulled it free of the chimney last January to see if it would hold his weight—it wouldn't—and Lucy still hadn't noticed.

Fifty-one.

He paused, another reflex. Fifty-one marked his first step onto his property. Too many men relaxed when they reached their own doors. It was one of the easiest places to make a kill.

But Zane was not like other men. He wasn't like anyone else on this clean, comfortable street, and it was one of the things he appreciated most about Bloomsbury. Despite being a neighborhood of actors and artisans, the truth was that everyone here was rigorously, predictably, church-squeaky *good.*

Another advantage to a man who lived in disguise: it made his sort stand out all the more.

He slipped around to the back of his house, evading all the traps he'd set, finding the short rise of stairs through the clouded darkness and then the keyhole to the kitchen door.

Joseph was waiting inside. He was seated at the side table, eating a bowl of something that smelled like very bad eel.

"Late," he grunted, by way of a greeting.

Zane removed his cocked hat, running a hand through his hair. "Whatever it is you are consuming, I do not want it served at my table tonight. Or any other night."

The man's brows arched; past his scars and badly mottled skin, he looked pained. "It's me mum's recipe."

"Then she is welcome to my portion." He bolted the kitchen door closed once more, had worked the top buttons of his coat free and was heading for the hall, for bed, when he was halted by his front man's voice.

"Got a visitor."

"I know."

"Not Mim."

Zane slanted a look back at him. Joseph shrugged. "A girl. Put her in the parlor."

"A girl," he repeated slowly. "Are you certain?"

"Aye," answered Joseph, with exaggerated care. "I'm certain."

Zane turned again and silently left the kitchen.

His house was dark. He'd grown up with it this way and kept it as a useful habit. A house ill-lit on the inside revealed much less of its inhabitants; he nearly always preferred to see and be unseen. But Joe had apparently felt the girl in question required a great deal of illumination. When Zane stopped at the arched doorway to the parlor, he saw that every lamp was burning, plus the pair of candelabras from the dining room. The contrast was almost like daylight: the reds and blue-greens of the Peshawar rug searing bright, the carved corners of the paintings rubbed with gilt, the gleam of the satinwood chairs eye-wateringly sharp.

The child slumped aside in one of them, head back, eyes closed, lips apart. There was a half-filled cup of chocolate tilting precariously on her lap, her fingers still curled around the handle. Her frock was girlish blue sprigged with daisies, her pumps were dirty, her hair was mussed. Limp ringlets of darkened gold fell softly against her cheeks. She looked pale and gaunt and remarkably plain, despite the beauty of that hair. Everything smelled of hot wax and honey.

He stood there and felt, to his distant surprise, none of the anger he had expected but instead a profound sense of relief.

To manage it he took the cup from her fingers and gave the chair a hard kick.

She came awake at once, straightening, her hands fluttering across her skirts.

"Lady Amalia. I wish I could say I was happy to see you, but I've already endured the pleasure of the Marquess of

Langford's company thrice in the past two days. What the devil are you about?"

"Father's here?" she asked, looking around them.

"Not at the present. No doubt it won't be long before he returns. I don't believe he's fully convinced I haven't hidden you away somewhere in the house. Imagine my joy," he added silkily, "at walking into my parlor tonight and discovering it to be true."

"I'm sorry. I..." She trailed off, shaking her head, then covered her eyes with one hand. "I haven't been sleeping well."

"Perchance it has something to do with the fact that you've been riding in a public coach for—let me see—almost a fortnight, isn't it? That's about how long it takes to travel from Darkfrith to my door by stage. Unless, I suppose," he paused, "you flew here."

He hadn't meant it as a barb, but she grimaced, just a little. Then her hand lowered; she gazed at him steadily.

"I didn't fly. You know I can't. And that's not why."

Zane didn't like that look, long-lashed, brown-eyed, direct. It reminded him too much of her mother. They stared at each other in the growing silence. Amalia's lips slowly compressed into a thin, stubborn line.

With a sigh he gave it up, lowering himself into the opposite chair. He glanced down at her cold chocolate and then tried a taste, feeling his stomach rumble. Hell was going to cut loose sooner or later, and he'd already missed supper.

The *drákon* did not take kindly to losing one of their kind. He knew that too bloody well.

Lamplight glinted silver along the scrolled edge of a tray beside him. Saints be praised, Joseph had left her food. Scones, orange cake, a dish of honeyed nuts and dried fruits—he leaned forward and helped himself to half an apricot and a sliver of cake.

"Bad dreams, snapdragon?"

"Yes." It was a miserable whisper.

"How unfortunate. I'm certain it was worth fleeing your home without a word to anyone—without, I am equally certain, permission from your almighty *drákon* council—to come here to tell me."

But she still didn't avert her gaze. She didn't even seem abashed. All her initial, drowsy confusion appeared completely vanished. She looked cool and composed and very much older than her years, even in her wrinkled skirts. Whatever it was that had compelled her halfway across the kingdom was well hidden behind that mask of mulish calm.

Very well. He knew how to wait.

Zane downed the apricot and crumbled the cake into pieces, consuming each mouthful with purposeful leisure. Joseph was thick-witted and slow and strictly as loyal as his next paycheck, but the true reason Zane kept him in his home was this. Cake. Scones. Fresh berry pies. He was the best hand at sugar pastries this side of the Channel, and the starving child Zane had once been fully appreciated his skills. By the force of his nature Zane remained a hammered blade; fat men never made good thieves. He survived on bites and water and potfuls of bitter coffee. But he was on his third slice before Amalia rose, taking back her cup from his hand.

She made a slow circle of the room, not drinking. "This doesn't seem much like the residence of a notorious criminal."

"No. That's rather the point."

"Is that why Mother gave it to you?"

"Pardon me," he retorted, brushing the crumbs from his waistcoat, "she did not *give* it to me. I purchased it from her, and at a damned premium price. It was all extremely legitimate."

"Oh."

"Yes, *oh*."

She set the chocolate on the windowsill. She lifted a hand to the iron bolt holding the shutters closed.

"Do not, if you please," he said curtly, unmoving. "I'd prefer not to invite your kith and kin inside at the moment."

"It isn't sealed?"

"The molding around one of the panes has come loose. I discovered that the hard way two days ago."

Her fingers jerked back as if burned. It was only one loosened pane, nothing very helpful to the ordinary men and thugs who usually haunted him, a mere breath of space between the solder and the glass. Yet it was all Christoff Langford had needed to breach all of Zane's careful defenses. Because Langford, of course, wasn't a man at all. He wasn't even human.

And neither was his daughter.

"You love my family," Amalia said now, her back to him, rubbing her palm up and down her rumpled blue-and-flowered skirts.

He did not reply.

"Some of them, anyway." She glanced at him from over her shoulder. "You do love some."

"If you say so."

"You know what we are," she persisted. "You've helped us, over the years. You're . . . close to my parents. You've aided the tribe."

"That wasn't for love, I assure you."

"What was it, then? Only money?"

"Money is a subject very dear to my heart, child. Do not underestimate it."

"And what of power?" she asked, softer. "Is that dear to you as well?"

"Did you venture all this way for an examination of my character, snapdragon?"

Lia turned and looked him fully in the face. She didn't like his pet name for her, and never had. It sounded whimsical, childish, when everything inside her felt strong and cold.

But she knew what he thought of her. She'd always known.

He was the only mortal tolerated by the tribe. He was the only one suffered to keep their secrets. While she and all her kind were kept trapped in the green heaven of Darkfrith, Zane was the sole living creature allowed to come and go at will. Even her father, the Alpha, tended to inform the council when he meant to travel.

It was their way. She knew it was how they had survived all these centuries. The Others raised livestock, or crops. The *drákon* raised silence, year after year after year.

Lia was the daughter of a lord. She lived in a mansion of glimmer and light; she looked out her bedroom window every day at open skies and wild, wooded hills and sometimes felt so suffocated it was a wonder she didn't open her mouth and start screaming and never stop.

The council gave lectures to the children in the village:

Of all the world, we are the last of our kind.

It is our duty to remain safe.

It is our duty to remain here.

We protect the earthbound: the young, the women, the weak.

We are drákon. *Duty to the tribe above all.*

Rhys and Audrey and Joan—even Kimber, who at least got to leave to attend a proper school—moved through the hours as if there could be nothing finer than what had been placed before them. Their lives were planned out, their hopes and futures would be forever confined by the boundaries of their land. They were born there, they would find mates there, and they would die there. To them, the world beyond the mist and bracken was of little consequence.

Lia understood why her mother had run away, all those years ago. If she thought for an instant she could truly do the same—

But she couldn't. She wasn't Gifted like the rest of her family. She couldn't Turn to smoke, much less to dragon. She wasn't beautiful, she wasn't brave, she wasn't any sort of reflection of the magnificence of her kind. It had taken all her meager resources just to get this far, and Lia knew her time here would be short. They'd find her soon.

There were only two things about her that set her apart from the rest of her tribe—two dark, disturbing things. And one of them was seated before her in this chamber.

Zane had not stirred from his chair. The lamps were bright and the shadows were harsh; he was sketched in charcoal and light, studying her with a half-lidded gaze she recognized from years of watching him pretend to relax at Chasen Manor, every line of his body casually elegant, his coat unbuttoned to drape the cushions, his waistcoat a satin gleam of pewter and taupe.

His eyes were paler than amber. His hair was very long and thick, honeyed brown. He was poise and muscle and as tall as her father; Joan and Audrey used to keep her awake at night for years in the nursery, just giggling his name, until at last she was old enough to realize why.

Because of this. Because of his hands, so strong and tanned. His fingers, gently tapping the wooden arm of the chair in an easy, steady percussion that belied the wolf-watchfulness of his gaze. Because of his jaw, and his brows, and the handsome curve of his mouth. Because when he stretched his legs and crossed his ankles and lifted his dark lashes to fully see her once more, she was as pinned as a deer in a dragon's clear yellow sights.

The flames from the lamps smoked oily black. Outside the shuttered window, the eastern song softly murmured.

She remembered the blind dream of him. She remembered the stroke of his voice—

"Forgive me if I interrupt your contemplation of my cravat," he said now, in a very different tone. "No doubt it's adorned with all manner of fascinating stains, as I've been out the past two days and nights straight, searching every inn and tavern and coach yard in the city for one thoughtless, wayward miss. I find I'm a shade impatient with all these heavy silences. Why, pray tell, have you landed in my parlor?"

Lia blinked. "You—you were searching for me?"

"Your father seemed to require it."

"Oh."

"Yes, *oh*," he repeated, this time clearly mocking.

She took a breath. "If I tell you something, will you promise not to mention it to anyone else?"

"No," he said bluntly.

"What if it's important?"

"In that case, absolutely no. Look," he said, leaning forward to prop his elbows on his knees, "if it's something so dire you can't share it with your parents, then I want nothing to do with it. I'm not courting that sort of trouble. Sorry, my heart. That's the way of things."

And tonight, my heart?

"Do you think," she asked carefully, "that it is possible to—to tell the future?"

His eyes narrowed. "What, like tinkers and star-casters, that sort of thing?"

She shrugged. "Or like dreams."

"Certainly."

"You do?"

"Aye. In fact, I've a carnival soothsayer on payroll who'll read your runes and spin you as fine a future as you could wish—especially if you're so accommodating as to leave your reticule unguarded."

"I wasn't jesting!"

"Neither was I. He's bloody good at what he does. Only been locked up twice. Much better average than most of my blokes. But then," he added mildly, "I suppose he's able to see just when the constables will be turning the corner."

Lia crossed the rug to stand before him. She felt calm, removed, after all the days of worry and heat and dread, rocked to sleep and awake in that wretched excuse of a carriage, the stench of people and old horsehair clogging up her nose. She felt a thread of her dream-self, smooth and mysterious, flowing through her veins.

With Zane still seated, she leaned forward and pressed her lips to his.

When she drew away again, his eyes had taken on a harder glow.

"Passable," he said coolly. "Feel free to try it again in about ten years. Until then, don't waste my time."

"Oh, dear," came a light, feminine voice. "Am I interrupting?"

"Not in the least." Zane rose from the chair; Lia was forced to step back. In the parlor doorway stood a woman, hooded and cloaked, the slit in her mantle revealing skirts of dove silk and a stomacher of white threadwork and moonstones.

With a turn of her wrists, the woman pushed back her hood. Red hair, gray eyes; her every movement carried the fresh scent of night.

Lia felt a flush of exquisite shame begin to creep up her throat.

"Who is this?" asked the woman, sounding amused.

"No one. Merely a little lost lamb."

"A lamb," said the woman, still smiling, entering the parlor. She touched a gloved finger to Lia's chin, lifting her face. "With those eyes? I think not. Rather more a windstorm descending."

Amalia pulled away. She glanced up at Zane—wolf-eyed, stone-faced, despite his languid tone—then grabbed his hand and held it hard.

"I want you to know," she said quietly, "that I will do anything to protect my family. Now, or in the future. I'll do anything at all. Remember that I warned you."

His mouth flattened into a smile. "How charming. Perhaps you'd care to inform your father as well." He disengaged their hands. "I believe that's him at the window."

And the locked shutters blocking the broken pane began to rattle and shake.

CHAPTER TWO

September 1773
Five Years Later

Before his eleventh year on this miserable planet, the street urchin known simply as Zane would have scoffed at anything that even hinted of the supernatural. He was a being of bones and flesh; so was everyone else. It was what made them so vulnerable. It was what had left him flat on the cobbles in a welling pool of his own blood one cold, cold winter evening, a knife wound to his ribs and the world pulsing blue and gray and snow, his back warm, his face numb.

By all rights, he should be dead. He'd known plenty who'd died from less, and good riddance.

But then, that night, Rue had found him. And the urchin had lived after all.

THE DREAM THIEF

He'd never had a family, not that he remembered. For a precious few years, he'd had only her.

She sat comfortably on the settee, the sunlight from the tall windows behind her picking out the silver in her chestnut hair, her hands slim and steady as she poured tea into the paper-thin china cups that they used, for some reason, here in the deep countryside. She looked relaxed and perfectly at home in the magnificence of the room, at one with the delicate furnishings and velvet draperies, the crystal chandelier silently sparkling just over their heads. She did not look at all like what he knew her to be.

"Sit down," the marchioness said, without glancing up from her pouring. "You're making me jittery. You pace like a cat."

"As if you would know."

"*Touché.* Sit."

But he didn't. He went to the windows instead, gazing out at the view that rolled and spun autumn forest and hills as far as he could see. Empty forest. Empty hills.

Darkfrith had no wild animals. It was perhaps the detail that bothered him most about this lush and cloudy shire. There were no hidden burrows in the woods, no small lives struggling for survival, celebrating the dusk or the dawn with mating or tussles. There were insects, and a scattering of birds. Once he had spotted a lone gray mouse skittering nervously along the edge of the stables. But in all the years he had been visiting the Marchioness of Langford and her husband, Zane had seen naught beyond those few pitiful creatures.

Little wonder. Even the smallest of beings surely sensed what dwelled in this place.

So Darkfrith was shining and barren. It was occupied purely by a people who moved without brushing the air, who watched him from shadows with gleaming eyes, who smiled

31

with sharp teeth and bowed in false acquiescence. He felt the creeping chill of their looks every moment, every second he stayed in this place.

If it weren't for Rue—and what she offered—he would never come.

"Lemon?" she asked, into the silence.

"No."

There was a flock of sheep speckling a nearby hill, an effective decoy for anyone truly curious about the affairs of the farms or fields. A pair of young boys were loping toward them, slowly but steadily; the sheep bunched, then scattered like minnows into the trees.

"Sugar?"

"No."

"Acquire anything of interest lately?"

He smiled to the glass. "Nothing to interest you, my lady. A few baubles here and there."

"From anyone I might know?"

"You might," he said, and left it at that.

"I heard a rumor the other day," the marchioness continued, serene. "It seems the Earl of Bannon is preparing to sell his collection of Trojan gold. Do you know the one I mean? Coins, diadems, I believe even a sword said to belong to Hector, as it were. The entire set should fetch a tidy sum."

"Have you an interest in Trojan coins, my lady?"

"I have no interest in anything beyond my family and my simple, humble life here, as you know," she answered smoothly. "I understand that the earl, however, plans to use the monies to purchase a mare. A very fine one. I believe he intends to breed her."

Zane cocked his head.

"He beats his horses," she said, casual. "I've seen it. Beats them raw. His maidservants too," she added as an afterthought.

He turned. "Is that why you summoned me here?"

"No. It's merely a bit of information I thought you might wish to have." She took a sip of tea. "I would certainly never mean to imply that someone should go and relieve the son of a bitch of his gold before he has the chance to profit from it."

She smiled at him over the rim of her cup.

"Ah, Lady Langford. Sometimes I do miss your wisdom."

"I am gratified to hear it."

He accepted the drink she offered, taking his seat in a chair. Rue Langford leaned back against her silk-striped cushions, both old and young, ever lovely in her dark and glittering way.

"And how *is* the family?" Zane asked.

"Excellent. Rhys and Kim are off examining wheat fields and rye. Audrey's with her sister—you missed the wedding, that was very bad of you. Joan was looking forward to having you there."

"Was she?"

"I believe she rather hoped you'd ride up on your stallion and sweep her from the altar."

"I haven't got a stallion," he pointed out.

"More's the pity," Rue sighed. "It definitely would have livened up the affair."

They shared another smile, this one far more wry. Even if he had been so inclined—which he definitely was not—the mere thought of a romantic entanglement between a daughter of the leader of the *drákon* and a human male would send these animal-edged creatures into a frenzy. Zane knew their boundaries and respected them, if for no other reason than he preferred his hide intact.

The tea in his hand was hot, aromatic. He gazed down into the steam. "And Amalia?"

"Amalia," echoed Rue, in a slightly less easy voice. "Yes. She's in Scotland."

He raised his eyes, astonished.

"I know," said the marchioness. "It took a great deal of effort to convince the council to allow her to go. But she wanted it very badly. She's at the Wallence School for Young Ladies, in Edinburgh. It's most respectable. We go up and visit thrice a season."

He set the tea aside. "After what the council did to *you* for leaving—"

"Yes," she interrupted, hard. "After that, you may be certain I took good care that my daughter would be well protected from them." Her nails clicked against the china cup, restless. "But she is Giftless, so she matters to them less. I suppose the odds were at least one of my children would be. My own Gifts came late, but Lia hasn't displayed even the most rudimentary signs of the *drákon,* not strength, not heightened senses or stealth or any hint of the Turn—" She broke off, drawing a slower breath. "It's not so unusual for a female of the tribe to be born without Gifts. These days, it's rather more normal than not."

Her skirts rustled. She shifted on the settee, and he realized she was not quite so comfortable as she first appeared.

"We thought it best if she got to have a taste of the world before being fixed in her place back here. This is her final quarter, in any case."

"I'm sure it pleases her very well," he said, after a moment.

"Yes," agreed Rue, composed again. "French and Latin and court manners. I'm sure it does."

He did not hear the double doors behind him open—the footmen here were as silent as the rest of them—but the air grew cooler, and the chandelier sent out a fresh rainbow of sparks.

The marquess entered, golden-haired, unsmiling, walking to his wife and bowing over her hand; he slanted Zane a shorter look.

"Langford," Zane greeted him, without bothering to rise.

Christoff Langford inclined his head. If Zane had a surname, no doubt the other man would be pleased to snarl it, but as it was, they only ever exchanged nods.

"Have you told him?" he asked his wife.

"Not yet. I was waiting for you."

The marquess dropped down beside Rue, draping an arm around her shoulders, examining Zane with a banked, green-eyed hostility.

"Pilfered anything recently?" his lordship inquired, freezingly polite.

"Yes. Abducted anyone?"

"We'd like you to take a journey," said Rue, as if neither of them had spoken. "A rather long one."

"To where?"

"To the east."

"East of what?" he asked.

Rue rose from the settee, crossing behind it to the expanse of windows. She wore a gown of blossom pink seeded with pearls, a French train that hissed, very faintly, against the maple floor. With the bright, wide panes of glass stretched beyond her, she seemed very small and slight.

"Somewhere out there," she said, lifting a hand to the glass, "east of England, east of France. Somewhere as far east as you can imagine is a stone. A diamond, we think. A very powerful one." Rue turned her face to his; the backlight devoured her expression. "We need you to go and get it."

"One diamond," Zane clarified.

"Yes."

"How big is it?"

"We don't know."

"Where is it?"

"We don't know."

"To whom does it belong?"

Rue smiled, apologetic. "We don't know."

"Well," said Zane, "won't this be jolly fun."

She stepped forward from the shadows, pink and white again. "About two years ago the first of us began to hear it. Just a few of us. It sounded like something from a daydream back then, soft and lovely. Nearly not there. When you tried to listen too closely, it would vanish entirely."

"Back then?" He lifted a brow.

"Yes. It has...changed. Grown stronger. More compelling. More of us hear it now too, nearly every member of the tribe." She lifted her hand once more, made a small, almost helpless gesture. "It's difficult to explain. You know we connect to stones. You know how we are. This one—calls to us. It's insistent and very clear. We need it."

"Why not go fetch it yourself? Send one of your vaunted hunters out to the wilds? Surely it would be quicker."

The marquess and marchioness exchanged a fleet, laden glance.

"It is impossible," said Rue finally. "The council will not permit it."

She was lying. She did it well, unflinching and cool and without the barest hint of regret, but he knew her well enough to register the tiny, tiny rise in her voice. And at the same time: the subtle shift in Langford's bearing; even seated, he became more taut, more hostile, if that was possible.

Interesting.

Zane fully believed that the council of old men that helped govern their so-called tribe would forbid a journey beyond the Channel; the deep distrust the *drákon* held of anyone beyond themselves wrapped tight as python coils around this place. What he did not believe was that Rue Langford— or her grim-jawed husband—would let that stop them if the matter was vital enough. She'd broken all their rules, all of them, for years, just because she could.

But she wasn't going. And she wanted to. It was clear as daylight across her face.

Zane looked past her, out the windows again, blue sky, bright clouds, the woods dying off in a glory of crimson and pumpkin and gold.

"You want me to travel to a place unknown, to find a diamond unknown, and secure it from a person, or persons, unknown, all at the edge of winter." His gaze drifted back to Rue. "And if this person does not wish to sell me his unquiet stone?"

She regarded him in silence, her lips gently curved.

"I see." He returned her smile. "Don't misunderstand. We've had some pleasant dealings in the past, highly profitable, by and large aboveboard. But I am surprised. In all these years, you've never asked me to steal anything for you."

The marquess spoke at last. "You will be paid sixty thousand pounds sterling."

Zane felt the air leave his chest. He felt his hands go cold. Out of instinct, out of survival, he held absolutely still until his senses lined up again.

Sixty thousand—

It was a fortune—more than that. It was damned near bloody unimaginable, and he had a very colorful imagination indeed. If it had been anyone else in the world saying such a thing to him, *anyone,* he would have jeered and walked away, because there were few things more perilous than dealing with madmen.

"Done," the thief said, and pushed to his feet to shake Rue's hand.

⚜

"Did he suspect anything?" Kit Langford asked his wife, watching from their bedroom window as the carriage containing their human guest rolled away down Chasen's drive.

Rue was standing behind him; he heard the shrug in her voice. "He's Zane. He always suspects something."

"But he'll go."

"Yes." She walked up and brushed her fingers to his, a soft, fleet intimacy that warmed him, just as her touch always did. He turned to her, taking up both her hands.

She was beautiful. Cool and dark, the night to the stars, she was always so beautiful. A smile hovered at the corners of her mouth.

"I dislike this scheme. Intensely," he added when her smile only deepened.

"I failed to hear you devise a better one."

"Actually, I did."

"We cannot both go," argued his wife, reasonable. "We cannot both vanish without word for months on end, no matter how urgent the cause. The entire tribe would be in an uproar. The council would have our heads."

"That is why—"

"And if it were to be only one of us, you know it should be me. I'm the one with the most experience at stealing away."

"If you think for a moment I would let you travel alone—"

"No," said Rue. "I didn't think that."

It was a delicate subject, one he didn't feel like exploring at the moment. But her eyes had grown stormy; to distract her, he bent down and pressed his lips to her temple.

"Imagine how lonely I'd be without you," he murmured. "Tottering around, a doddering old man weeping into his shirtsleeves..."

It earned him a laugh, low and musical. "You're far too vain for that. You'd use a handkerchief."

He folded her into his arms. They were silent a long while, her head against his chest, rocking slowly together as the clouds outside lapped vanilla cream against the horizon. Finally Rue sighed.

"It can't be either of us. It can't be *any* of us. We can't risk it. The lure of the song is fearsome enough at this distance. Even the elders agreed it could be irresistible up close. Whoever has that diamond now might understand its power. Might realize what we are and use it against us. That's why it must be Zane. He won't be susceptible to the song, and he won't think twice about handing it over to us once he has it. Especially since he doesn't know what it can do."

"Unless someone sees fit to tell him. What then, little mouse?"

She stilled a moment, then tipped back her head to see him.

"He's still our best hope."

"Aye," agreed Kit reluctantly. "I know it."

Their gazes locked. The heat began to build, that deep, burning craving for her, for her body and her voice and her heart.

Rue's lashes lowered, very demure. He felt her fingers tighten over his arms.

"Will you come to bed, my lord Langford?"

It was barely past teatime. Neither of them cared.

⚜

Paris was wet, a cold, gray city with even grayer people, the scent of decaying vegetables and clay and cattle everywhere. The sky remained leaden all the way from Avon to Strasbourg, but it didn't truly start to snow until he reached Stuttgart, when the raw winds tore through the clouds to embed a layer of ice crystals upon his rented coach, and the road, and his coat and the gloves on his hands: every inch of the world glistening with a sly, glassy enchantment beneath the weakened sun.

The horses struggled with the frozen muck. Zane had been riding atop the diligence until then, squeezed into the driver's perch alongside the German coachman until the cold seared his eyeballs and bit his skin to frost. He had never cared for the cramped interiors of carriages, no matter how stylishly done up. He needed the open sky, and open views.

But the horses suffered. So they traveled a great deal more slowly than he would have liked otherwise, stopping at inns, at taverns, even farmhouses, whenever the weather grew too dismal. He became used to the round-eyed looks of the country ostlers, their noses red with the wind, as the sleek new coach rolled into whichever godforsaken village arched next into view along the roads. He became used to the smell of hay mixed with sludge, and the shiny wet gloss of melted snow tracing lines along the black spokes of the wheels.

The entire rig had cost a great deal to rent. Few companies wished to hire out as far as he was going, and fewer still drivers. But hard gold always managed it; the Paris company had found a fellow with cousins in Munich. He would get that far before starting over again.

Strapped to the back of the carriage was a single trunk holding his garments and shoes and a very decent bottle of sherry. Inside the carriage were the more valuable things: his picks, his spare pistol, and bullets and powder horn. Three daggers, a dirk, and a single sheath of rice paper, tucked thin and small into the lining of his valise.

In Rue's neat, slanted writing, the paper read:

Pest

Oradea

Satu Mare

Carpathian range? No farther.

No more than twelve carats, no less than one-half; a cast of blue; uncut. Heavy in the hand.

Draughmurh? Drawmur? Drahmer?

It was precious little to go on. It was precious little to tie up his life and his establishment for an entire season, no matter how competent his associates or how satisfying his reputation. There had been nights he lay awake in the lice-ridden pallets that passed for beds in most hotels when he'd wondered when, precisely, he had lost his reason. There could be no other answer to this journey. Rue's imploring eyes and careful lies be damned: he had no true idea of where he was going. He had nearly nothing to go on, guesses and dreamwork from a clan of creatures who could answer only, *It sings* and *It calls* and *You must bring it back to us* when he asked for clearer directions.

Merde.

Too often he'd just settle back against the squabs and watch his boots drip. He'd been traveling over a month now, well versed in his guise as an English gentleman on the Grand Tour. He'd patronized so many tea parlors and coffeehouses and card rooms that the mere thought of downing another cup of tepid liquid amid the chatter of foreign tongues made his skin crawl.

He spoke French well, German tolerably. After that, he was no better off than the role he played, a bored English sophisticate with a taste for legends and gemstones.

The land passed by his window in depressing sameness. France, Germany, Austria: all gray and dun and somber skies.

Sixty thousand pounds.

He'd buy a castle in Tuscany. There'd be no bloody ice there.

❧

Despite fresh horses and his new coachman's best efforts, they could not cross the Danube to reach the city of Pest before the sun sank into a thick red and purple horizon, ending the final day of October. Zane settled for Óbuda instead, across the river, smaller, and, from what he could tell, slightly more stylish. The Hungarians here sported wigs and buckled heels he had last seen in the heart of Paris. The women were hooded and painted and walked the cobblestone streets in dainty, mincing steps, never far from their escorts. He'd garnered more than a few glances just checking in to the hotel—scruffy, unshaven, his trunk and greatcoat spattered with mud. The King's View was a veritable palace of plasterwork and imposing marble angels, but after three straight days without a good night's sleep, Zane reckoned the Marquess of Langford could afford it.

From his balcony he watched the skyline begin to illuminate, yellow flames that gradually connected into pictures through the dusk, outlining buildings and steeples and streets, the indigo emptiness of parks checkerboarding the glow. Pest glimmered and the river glimmered with it, its banks edged silvery white with the last dusting of snow.

The Danube was a wide, gray line between the two cities, dotted with fishing boats and ferries and great flocks of crows; their high-pitched cackles bounced back at him across the waves.

The balcony curtains swelled and folded, gently tapping his legs. The breeze lifted his hair. He'd already undone his waistcoat and settled in with his sherry to watch the birds when the floorboards outside his room squeaked, and stopped, because someone had paused at his door.

Zane had his pistol primed when the knock came.

"*Monsieur? Monsieur Lalonde?*"

He placed his foot against the door, held the pistol down at his side, out of view, and turned the knob. A lanky man with watery blue eyes looked back at him.

"*Oui?*"

"My deepest regrets for disturbing you, sir," said the hotel clerk in French. "You were left a missive at the front desk just now."

The man held out his hand. A cream-colored envelope rested on his palm, Zane's name—his *real* name—and room number inscribed in lavish script upon the vellum.

For a moment he only stared at it. The clerk waited, his narrow face betraying nothing. Zane closed the door, stuck the pistol into the waistband of his breeches at the small of his back, then opened the door again and took the envelope from the man's hand.

"Merci."

He found a coin in his pocket—God knew which country it was from—and flicked it to the clerk, who smiled and bowed and retreated down the sconce-lit corridor.

When the door was bolted again, he broke the wax seal.

Veuillez nous joindre pour notre célébration le samedi, 31 octobre, à neuf heures du soir.
Le dîner sera accompagne d'un orchestre.

Le Comte du Abony

Zane looked up from the invitation, frowning. *Samedi* was Saturday, today. Tonight.

Someone knew of him. Someone knew he was here; he'd never heard of a Comte du Abony; he could not imagine how the fellow had heard of him. Unless the *drákon* had somehow managed it, had figured out where he was going to be and when . . .

But they would not know his room number. And Rue would never make the mistake of revealing his name.

He glanced once more at the river outside, then quickly drew the curtains. He stood motionless against the silk-papered wall, fading into shadow with the falling night while his thoughts bled into theories and conspiracies and extremely improbable coincidences.

Through the sheer organza he saw a crow land atop the stone rail of the balcony; it peered at him sideways with fiercely black eyes, then shoved into the air again.

❧

The Comte du Abony lived in an actual palace. Zane had walked to it, because it turned out not to be far from the fashionable King's View, and the clerk had made it politely clear that even an Englishman could find it if he kept to the main boulevards. To guide him, he had the address and the surprising brilliance of the street lanterns, which dangled from fanciful iron posts twice as tall as a man.

He supposed only a very great fool would openly respond to the cordially worded card in his pocket. And anyone who knew his name would also know that Zane was no fool.

Yet he was going. He was walking. He had his dirk and his rapier and his wits; he had his best court clothing; whoever the hell this comte was, Zane meant at least to get a good look at him. And then, should the man wander off alone— too much wine, a willing woman—perhaps they might exchange a few words. . . .

In any case, he wouldn't risk spending the night in the hotel, not now, and for that alone Zane felt a particular urge to inflict a bit of pain upon someone.

His walking stick tapped the pavement very lightly. His gold-buttoned tricorne was tipped aslant over his wig, rakish, but it was only so that he could keep his sights clear. He nodded amicably to the passersby who nodded to him, studying their faces, following his senses and the clerk's directions, and the growing line of coaches crowding the streets.

Sedan chairmen hauling high, teetering boxes passed him

at a trot. Horses gleamed fat and glossy beneath the oil lanterns, snorting plumes of frost. The crests on the coaches—on the doors, on the hubs of the wheels—were painted in gaudy reds and greens and yellows, vivid blues. By the time he could hear the orchestra playing, Zane's saunter was getting him to the comte's dinner ball more quickly than any of the fine nobles trapped in their carriages.

He had meant to approach the celebration the way he did all unknowns, in a circle, from behind, where he could watch and judge from a prudent distance before stepping into commitment. But half the city seemed to be headed there, and from three blocks away he could see there would be no furtive arrival into this place; it was gated and fenced in tall, serious spikes, and there were liveried guards at every corner.

Very well.

At the gatehouse he handed his square of vellum to a footman, who accepted it stoically, bowing him up the raked drive. The massive bronze-studded doors of the palace entrance were already open. As he climbed their steps, a wave of heated air pushed past: paprika and perspiration and the musky confusion of too many perfumes.

Zane entered the atrium—more footmen, blazing candles, a mosaic of high, stained-glass windows glowing azure and saffron above. The music grew brighter, the heat more intense.

He'd been in many of London's finest homes; he'd seen ballrooms by both candlelight and the useful darkness of the new moon. One dead summer's night as a boy, he'd even gotten as far as the drawing room in the town residence of the Princess of Wales—only on a dare, and only because deep down he hadn't really believed that he could.

The princess had lived in a splendor of pink alabaster and baroque furniture. She drank tea from tiny silver-trimmed cups; her linens were powder blue embroidered with real gold; her hallboy snored. Zane had been thirteen, barefoot, a dark intruder who had not touched a thing. He'd never thought to see a more make-believe place than that, and it had only been the royal antechamber.

But this comte, it seemed, had outsplendored the princess. Here were columns of warm ocher marble inlaid with turquoise and panels of citrine. Oil paintings of bearded men and doe-eyed women draped in furs and velvet and crowns of jewels reached as high as the second floor. Enormous vases of fresh flowers—orchids, in October— guided the guests toward another set of doors; Zane slipped behind two lords and a trio of ladies, close as a shadow as they crossed the threshold into the ballroom. When the butler moved to announce them, he glided off, swallowed in an ocean of satins and lace.

For all the grandeur of the chandeliers, it was darker in here than it should have been. Slices of moonlight washed visibly through the far windows, gleaming pale along the shoulders and wigs of the revelers crowded there. The orchestra labored away in a box set high above the crush. They had their own branches of candles to play by, an uneasy glow that cast shades of fiddles and horns and flutes against the dark red ceiling.

In the center of the ballroom, a wide X of couples were performing the quadrille, slow and stately movements that seemed at odds with the hectic prattle of the room. Someone laughed very loudly in his ear; Zane angled away.

He worked his way to a wall so there could be no one behind him. He set himself to searching faces again, because he knew what the *drákon* looked like, and he knew what his kind looked like, even if he did not know the features of this comte.

Bobbing into view was a short, plump woman in a wig

teased high with feathers and swaying droplets of diamonds. She started, staring straight at him, hard and focused—his fingers grazed the handle of his dirk—and then, abruptly, her face cleared. She broke into a delighted smile.

"My dear! There you are! There you are indeed!"

She spoke not French but English, heavily accented but perfectly intelligible. Zane remained taut where he was as she swept toward him, champagne in one hand and the other reaching for him.

"Come along, come along! This is the way!"

He made an instant decision: she didn't appear to have a weapon; her breath reeked of alcohol; her delight seemed genuine. He allowed her fingers to close over his and she led him across the floor, over to a corner particularly dense with people . . . no, he saw, coming closer, not merely people. Men. Dandies and lords, beaux in lawn and ruffles and long-skirted coats, surrounding a solitary woman.

This one was younger, white-skinned, garbed in ruby silk cut very low across her chest. She was laughing at something one of the beaux whispered in her ear, her chin down. Her gloved hands clasped her fan across her lap.

"*Chérie,* only look!" exclaimed Zane's escort, presenting him with tipsy satisfaction. "Here he is!"

The lady in ruby glanced around, pleasure still teasing her lips and lighting her face, her eyes sparkling dark, her hair powdered into heavy curls. Her skin was pearled, her cheeks brushed with pink; she wore no patches for beauty, no jewelry, and very little paint—and he grasped at once how she had managed to draw so many moths to her corner. He had never seen a woman so exotically luminous. His mouth actually went dry.

But . . . surely he knew her. Aye, he knew that he did—

"It *is* he, is it not?" insisted the tipsy woman, now hanging on to his arm. "I recognized him right away, just as you said—those eyes, *mais oui,* such a color! I have the chills! I said to myself, who else could it be?"

The lady in the ruby gown lifted her chin and fixed her gaze directly to his.

"Yes," she said in a velvet tone. "You're quite right, Marie. It is he."

And with a jolt of profoundly unpleasant shock, Zane realized he was gaping at Lia Langford.

CHAPTER THREE

She had known precisely how it was going to be. It was strange that she did, because she'd never actually seen any of it, not the composition of the dancers and chairs, not the colors, not the chamber; none of the dreams that came to her offered sight. But Lia had known.

The moment she'd glimpsed the red silk in the bowfront window of the mercer's that rainy evening in Edinburgh, she'd thought, *This one*.

And the hair powder, from the Parisian salon: *Yes, this*.

The music, a Viennese piece still new enough to stir a scandal at the school when one of the girls picked it out on the pianoforte: *That refrain*.

The bottle of scent, a gift from her sisters.

The lace fan.

The city.

The hotel.

His face, because that was unchanging: carved and wary, glorious in the way a feral predator could be glorious, too far beyond human touch to be tamed, severe and beautiful even in its ferocity. His skin was marked with candlelight. His eyes burned animal bright.

He wore ebony when everyone else was done up in pastel flowers. His wig was a simple tye when all the other men sported curls upon curls. He was the only male nearby who wasn't even attempting to ogle her chest.

That was Zane. That was his expression as she glanced up at him, and it was so familiar to her that for a moment she only sat there, admiring him, forgetting all that he was and all that she had done to get them both to this strange and exquisite place. For that instant he was only Zane, the very dark man of her dreams. And because he was there with her, her heart expanded with bittersweet pleasure.

Stupid.

He was still Zane. She should have known he'd be an ass.

❧

He watched the corners of her mouth lift. Part of him—the part that was still dazed by her magic, by the shape of her eyes and the contrast of the crimson silk against her milky chest and arms, and the swan's curve of her neck, and the mass of smoky-thick locks that fell to her shoulders, half pinned, half not, like she'd just tumbled out of some very soft bed—part of him only stood there and stared, as dumb and dazzled as all the other fools encircling her.

But the other part of him was still a bastard outlaw in a room full of unknown risks. It was this part that snapped his jaw closed and sent the blood back into his heart. He leaned forward without a word to anyone, took her hand, and yanked her to her feet.

The dandies fell back, agog. A few of the younger men began to protest, but Zane only offered a nod to the woman she'd called Marie and pulled Amalia with him to a small, uncrowded space by a side table laden with plated raspberries and crystal bowls shining with punch.

He glanced around to ensure they were alone, then glared down at her.

"What the hell are you doing here?"

She'd made no protest to his forced march across the ballroom; when she answered him, her voice was calm. "The same as you, I imagine."

"You're supposed to be in school!"

She tipped her head and smiled—another shock, because it was definitely a woman's smile, both sensual and faintly amused. "It was finishing school." She freed her hand from his and slid it slowly down the cinched curve of her waist. "Well . . . I'm finished."

"Good God," he said at last, for lack of anything better.

"Merci," she murmured. *"C'est très gentil."*

A maidservant approached the table, bobbed a curtsy at them before beginning to ladle the punch into cups. Zane took Lia by the elbow and turned her away again.

"Was it you who sent the invitation?" he demanded.

"Yes."

"Then who is this Comte du Abony?"

"He is the gentleman hosting this very fine ball. I'm having such a splendid time." Her smile widened, just a little. "We never have balls at home. I can't imagine why."

"Well, you can bloody well ask them yourself when you get back there. Let's go."

"No," she said, still very calm, and put a step between them. "I'm afraid I'm not leaving yet. Not the ball, and not

51

the country. And if you wish to be so imprudent as to force the issue, Zane, you'll discover I've made quite a few friends in my time here. Do release my arm. People are starting to gawk."

He felt it without looking up, the pockets of whispers beginning to rise around them, the many eyes. He dropped his hand, returning her smile with a razored one of his own, and at least had the satisfaction of seeing her confidence falter, a swift lowering of her lashes before she gazed back at him again.

"I want you to understand something," he said, his lips barely moving. "I don't know why you're here. I don't care. I'm not going to be responsible for a chit of a girl who takes it in her head to run off whenever the moon is blue, or the stars align, or whatever your reason this time may be. I've come for a very specific purpose, and I don't like surprises. I find your presence here—offensive."

"I'm not a chit of a girl," she said, her smug expression vanished. "Not any longer."

"No, you're a *lady* now, clearly," he sneered, with a deliberate glance at her décolletage.

The pink of her cheeks began to darken. He pressed his advantage.

"So now, if you don't mind, we'll be departing. We will return to wherever you are staying and pack your things. In the morning you can start home."

"Actually," she took another step away from him, "I do mind. I'm not going home."

He regarded her for a long, tense moment, just long enough so that her blush deepened another shade and the pulse in her throat began to quicken. By the dim light of the ballroom she was truly beyond lovely, ruby and snow and those amazing dark eyes. Five years had passed since he'd last seen her, five years and a world of experience, it seemed. She looked like her mother and her father and no one else on earth, a being of clouds and stone-cold sorcery, poured into a very tight gown.

Against his will he caught the scent of her: not perfume but something more subtle, the air and the sun and winter roses.

"Fine," he said brusquely, and moved away. The musicians were playing something new, a jig. Amid the jangle of strings and festive bells, he went back to the punch table—because it was nearby, because it was where his feet took him—and allowed the maidservant to hand him a brimming cup. Beneath her starched cap she was young and homely. When he nodded to her, she smiled shyly back.

He lifted the punch in salute and downed the entire thing. Sweet cloves and brandy, the fumes searing his nose. As he was accepting a second measure, a sweep of crimson skirts came into view.

"I don't know how you found me at the hotel"—Zane acknowledged the maid once more before turning around—"but I won't be there much longer. Pray do not trouble yourself to search for me again."

Lady Amalia was quiet.

"I have no doubt there's a pack of your kinsmen on your heels, and damned if I'm going to be the one who takes the blame for this." He glanced at her coolly. "You're on your own, my lady."

"You need me."

"Highly unlikely."

"No, you do. You're looking for *Draumr*. And I know where it is."

He lowered the cup of punch, staring again.

Her lips pursed. She gazed down at her fan.

"Well?" he said.

"I'm not going to just tell you. You need to take me with you."

"Dearest child. Get it out of your head. You're not going anywhere with me."

"I am not a child!"

"No," he agreed, losing patience. "You're really not, are you? You're something far more ominous than that." He set the cup upon the table behind him and leaned down to put his mouth to her ear. "I wonder how all these good people would feel if they knew a monster walked in their midst?"

Amalia stiffened. A powdered gray coil of hair trembled against his jaw. "We stand at the brink of the Carpathians," she replied under her breath. "With woods and wolves and a thousand different legends. You'll find monsters aplenty in these lands. None of these *good people* will thank you for naming them. For all their fashion and French wine, they're a superstitious lot. And I will, of course, deny everything. You'll be just a mad foreigner."

She sent him a sidelong look, challenging; someone new came near. Zane was already pulling away, but Lia had turned and aimed a swift, glittery smile at the aristocratic couple now lingering before them. "Ah, Lord Miklós, Lady Eliz. *Jó estét.* Have you met my husband, Zane Langford?"

For the second time that evening, Zane—Black Shadow of Mayfair, dreaded Whip of St. Giles—was too astounded to speak.

❧

"They will not miss me until after Christmas," she said, twirling the quill in her fingers to draw slow, slow circles upon the paper on the hotel desk; the paper was thick and fine-grained, but her hand was never very good. The ink from the quill made blotches across the page. "They won't be chasing after me, because they won't know I'm gone until then."

"And how did you manage that?" Zane was standing with his back braced against the door to his room, his arms crossed. Lia envisioned him turning the brass knob and simply stepping backward, vanishing instantly into the darkness of Óbuda.

It was late, very late. The east-facing windows of the room showed a faint green rising in the sky. She glanced up at Zane. For half a second she almost hoped he'd do it, just open the door and go. He'd been quizzing her the entire night, and all she truly wanted to do right now was sleep.

But sleep wouldn't come, anyway. Or if it did, she'd wish it had not.

Her mantle and reticule were still draped along the foot of his bed where he had first tossed them, a jet-beaded glimmer against the patterned duvet. His own cloak had been flung over hers, careless, lamplight slipping along a thin flash of emerald satin from where the lining had flipped over. To anyone else in the room, it might truly appear they were man and wife, returned together from a long evening out.

But he'd only brought her here because she'd offered him no alternative. Lia was painfully aware that—right now—the man she'd called *husband* wanted nothing to do with her.

"I sent a letter to the headmistress from my parents, noting I would be absent this final quarter due to family concerns. I sent a letter to my parents from the headmistress, full of marvelous praise of my skills and diligence, and of how I had very graciously volunteered my last Christmas there to help tutor the parish girls."

"My heavens. I had no idea they were teaching forgery at young ladies' academies these days."

She twirled the quill a little faster.

"And theft," he went on. "I presume you did bother to steal the official stamp of the school."

Lia lifted a shoulder. "It wouldn't have been very convincing without it."

"Quite. And the marquess's seal?"

"I had a copy made Easter last."

"Cunning."

"Thank you."

"You're most welcome. It's always a pleasure to acknowledge the talents of a fellow delinquent."

She propped her cheek upon her fist. The quill was pheasant, she thought, striped and spotted. Perhaps quail. She frowned down at it, because it was easier to contemplate than Zane.

He'd also removed his wig and his elegant black coat. His waistcoat was silver brocade, a pattern of willow leaves and vines just barely visible in the weak early light. He'd raked his fingers absently through his hair until it fell into a sheen of tawny, sun-tipped gold; it was brown and blond and longer than she'd ever seen on any man, nearly half as long as her own.

She wondered that he'd never cut it shorter. She was glad that he never did.

He left the door to prop a foot up on the cushion of the armchair beside hers—shoe and all—and bent his head until his hair spilled forward again, sliding over one shoulder. Without looking at her, he began slowly to plait it.

"Expenses?"

"A saved allowance."

"Papa is generous indeed."

She let him think it. Until this month she hadn't spent more than a guinea on herself in three years. Half of those nose-in-the-air ninnies at Wallence thought she herself was on the parish.

"And of course, *Madame* Langford, I am most curious as to which aspect of your former curriculum covered bald-faced lies. Everyone back home seems to be under the impression that you are a sad, sad case. Not a hint of any of the old family traits."

"That part is true," she said, pausing her circles with the quill.

"Then how is it you know the whereabouts of this fabulous diamond?" he inquired smoothly. "When no one else does?"

The quill made a series of scratchy dots across the page. "Mostly true."

"*Mostly.* How awfully intriguing," he said, in a tone that indicated it wasn't. He abandoned the plait, nearly done, to prowl across the chamber, pausing at a decanter on the marble-topped *secrétaire.* From the corner of her eye, Lia watched him pour a glass of dark liquid. It was claret. She could smell the dry spice of it from here.

He held it between his palms, staring moodily at the surface. He did not offer her any.

"I don't see how it concerns you how I got here," she said, throwing down the quill. "All that matters is that I'm here to assist. I would think you might appreciate that. I don't want any of the money for myself, you can have the whole pot. Any other thief in the world would be overjoyed to have a beautiful woman offer to show him the way to a valuable gemstone."

"Alas. No lessons offered on modesty, I suppose."

She made a motion with her hand. "I only meant—that is—" A sigh escaped her; she swiveled in the chair to see him. "I'm well aware of my face. It's part of what happens to our kind. You were quite right." She swallowed. "We are monsters. But . . . I could be the monster who helps you. At least in this."

His eyes lifted to hers. They gazed at each other as the

light behind him warmed to pearl. After a moment he set the claret back upon the *secrétaire* with a snap, untouched, and moved to the four-poster, tugging at his jabot until it fell into folds.

"Where are you staying?" he asked, his eyes averted again.

She only watched him. He shrugged out of the waistcoat, tossing it over a chair. The lawn of his shirt stretched taut over his shoulders as he moved; his braid ended in a silken fan down his back. He perched upon the edge of the bed and kicked off his fine buckled shoes, one at a time.

"Actually..."

"Not a chance, my heart."

Lia rose from the desk with as much dignity as she could muster. "I am posing as your wife. It would be most *bourgeois* to share the same room with you."

She swept to the bed for her things and then to the connecting door, oak-framed, modest amid all the glory of the rest of the chamber. The key was at the very bottom of her reticule.

"Lia," Zane said softly, a perfect echo of her dreams. She glanced back. He had stretched out atop the covers, propped against the pillows, his fingers laced over the flat of his stomach and his ankles crossed. With his plait and the loosened shirt, he looked like nothing so much as a corsair, tanned and rough and perilously unknown. She was granted half a smile.

"How *did* you know which hotel I'd be in?"

"King's View is by far the best in the city. It wasn't hard to conjecture."

"And the room?" he asked, softer still.

"I paid the clerk to put you here," she lied. "Honestly, I'm surprised you didn't figure that out."

His smile never changed. Lia busied herself with unlocking the door.

"Think twice about refusing my help," she said, to cover his silence. "No matter what else you think of me, I do know how to get to the diamond. Since I'm not returning to Darkfrith without it, you need to consider the very real possibility that I will reach it before you do. Do you truly think you'll get any reward from my people without handing them *Draumr* yourself?"

She closed the door quickly behind her, before he could ask her anything else.

Then she locked it again.

She'd already ensured that he wouldn't have a key.

"Lia."

"Yes?"

"Come to me."

"Yes, Zane."

His arms around her. His lips upon her cheek.

"Tell me of tomorrow."

"Tomorrow the Duchess of Monfield will wear a brooch of pink rubies shaped as a rose on her kerchief. She'll be alone in her garden picking lavender at ten."

"Very tempting. But perhaps we might leave the duchess be for the moment. I want to know, my heart, about your kin."

"They're in the hills. They're making plans."

"What plans?"

"Plans to kill you. Plans to steal me. They'll amass three days hence. It will be raining. No one will glimpse them in the sky."

His breath drew into a sigh. She shifted in his arms; the diamond on the cord around his neck was a dark endless poem, a song that never ceased. His voice was an echo of it, low and unbearably sweet.

"What to do," he murmured. "What to do . . ."

"Use Draumr," *Lia said to him. "They'll hunt two by two.*

Set them to fight one another when they come. The papers will report it as footpads. No one need know the truth."

"Hmmm." She felt his lips again, a caress, slow and silken along her throat. "Clever girl. You're full of plans yourself, aren't you?"

"I am full of you," she replied truthfully, and was rewarded with the pleasure of his kiss upon her mouth.

⚜

She came awake in a square of sunlight, hard and bright against her lids. For a moment Lia only blinked against it, her arms flung out, her fingers clenched in linen and the puffy down of the coverlet. The air smelled of feathers and river; she inhaled again and remembered where she was. And why.

She sat up in the bed, warm and tired and gritty-eyed, not even noticing the man seated by the door until he leaned forward in his chair, a slim metal blade twirling expertly between two fingers.

"Not even a challenge," Zane announced, dropping the picklock back into the pocket of his vest. "Still, don't do that again." He stood, looking down at her with a particularly empty expression. His hair was tied back; the buttons on his cuffs shone pewter in the morning sun. "I don't appreciate locked doors. And I won't wait downstairs longer than twenty minutes."

Lia was ready in fifteen.

CHAPTER FOUR

Ages ago, fairy-tale years ago, it was said that the Gifts of the *drákon* pulsed through the veins of every single member of the tribe, male and female alike. As certain as the phases of the moon, the children of the shire would grow into adults, would Turn into hunters and warriors and splendid beasts. Back then, all were equally blessed.

But over time, the Gifts began to fade. It began with the womenfolk first, those who were more naturally earthbound in any case, caring for the young. Females who could complete the Turn—human, smoke, dragon—became scarcer and scarcer over generations. They grew more used to roaming the woods than the skies. With a lack of wings, they transformed their ferocity and flight into fierce devotion to their children, into a love of jewels and wedlock and long, wistful glances at the moon. Darkfrith was rich with women who only ever dreamed of soaring.

Then the Gifts began to thin through the men as well. The birth of a male child who could not Turn was still rare enough, but the Turn itself was growing darker, more treacherous. That initial, violent moment that usually began around a boy's fourteenth year—that wild and frightening instant when the self first dissolved into smoke, when something new had to come in its place or nothing else ever would—became, for some reason, harder and harder to complete.

Lives were lost. Young men, promising, bright, vanished into screams and agony. And the women of the tribe would secretly wonder if they were the better blessed, after all.

Yet dragon or human, male or female, every member of the *drákon* still had an animal side. The taste for the chase, the longing for the sky, the power to hear the stones and metals of the earth singing ballads and chants and arias: none of these things ever faded.

There was a reason no other creatures dwelled in Darkfrith. It was hard enough to keep sane horses for the stables. Even the black-faced sheep ran wild.

So Lia was unsurprised when she walked out of the King's View—at the august and sophisticated edge of Óbuda; far, far from the hills of home—and every steed downwind of her immediately began to stomp and tremble.

At the bottom of the hotel's horseshoe steps, a foursome of grays hitched to a polished new carriage bucked against their restraints. Zane, standing by the carriage door, glanced up at once. His eyes found hers.

By and large she'd avoided the typical beasts of burden on her journey here. She'd sailed, in fact, from Edinburgh to Rotterdam, and that had been lovely. The clipper had been small and cramped and very swift. Every day she'd stood at the prow to let the wind tear at her. Her cheeks never burned. Her hair never tangled. But she'd never felt salt in her tears like that, and she'd never felt her skin smart quite so beautifully.

When she had closed her eyes and stood very still, Lia imagined she was flying.

Darkfrith had succored sixteen generations of her kind. Of the past five, only three females had managed the Turn: Rue. Audrey. Joan.

Lia had grown used to the veiled, speculative looks from her people as she'd aged. She'd grown used to the gossip, the subtle heartbeat of excitement and expectation that throbbed through the tribe whenever either of her sisters took to the air.

They were silver and gold and red and green, magnificent. With Rue a white pearl in the sky beside them, they were the best hope for the future of the *drákon*. Villagers would gather outside to watch whenever they left the ground; Lia could only gather with them, her face upturned, and try to pick out the glitter of her family against the glitter of the stars.

Her birthdays passed: seventeen, eighteen, nineteen. Whatever other Gifts she possessed, whatever else she took pains to hide from her parents and her people, this was the Gift she craved most: to be complete. To lift from the earth, to dance around the moon.

It had never happened. The heartbeat of expectation around her gradually faded. She was patted gently, and smiled at sadly, and told of her great good fortune to be the earl's daughter, after all. Amalia would always smile back and agree, while her chest ached and her nails clenched so tightly into her palms that her skin bled.

She supposed if she never had anything else, at least she had the memory of that clipper ship. The taste of tar and brine and freedom on the wind.

The carriages she'd hired once ashore were large and slow, so swollen with passengers that her scent was buried beneath everything—and everyone—else. Lia kept a veil across her hat to hide her features. She kept her hands stuffed beneath her mantle and tried not to move very much. Whenever she exited a coach she angled at once behind it, to get away from the other animals, and for the most part her tactic had worked.

Except for today.

She stopped where she was on the hotel stairs, surrounded by footmen and her trunks, the hem of her mantle whipping sideways with the breeze. The grays were not calming; the one nearest her began to scream, shrill and angry. Lia sighed and took a step back, glancing up the curve of marble steps as if searching for assistance. The head manager was already hurrying down.

The wind swept from the east, from the water. If she moved enough to her left—

A hand took her elbow.

"Oh, no, snapdragon, no turning back now."

It was Zane, escorting her down the final few stairs. With the horses bucking, she was half pushed inside the carriage, catching herself with both hands as the floor lurched, falling into the seat as the door slammed hard behind her. The abrupt lack of sun dazzled her eyes.

Her mantle had twisted beneath her, a slippery knot of silk and wool caught against the cushions. She twisted to free it as she heard Zane stride to the front of the carriage. The coachman was there too, swearing loudly in what sounded like Latin, but somehow it was easier to hear Zane, his pace swift and nearly inaudible under the great huffing squeals of the grays.

Her mantle came free. Lia settled back as the darkness began to melt into shape and textures and dull mustard squabs. Past the confines of the coach, past the wooden walls and the wind and the racket of the street, Zane began, very softly, to speak.

Because she was alone, because he wouldn't know, she closed her eyes and fully opened her senses. She allowed, for this brief moment, the relentless drone of her surroundings to sink into her skin:

The rough suck of air into massive lungs. The muffled, grinding *chink* of horseshoes pushed into gravel.

The creak of the leather harnesses; the straining joints of the walls and floor.

Sweet, my love, be still. . . .

The smell of the river. Of stale tobacco from the window curtains, the curl of pine resin in her nose, of walnut, and iron nails—and then, more faintly, of soap and spice. Of *him*.

Heartbeats, like thunder. Birds breathing. Water lapping. The breeze slipping through his hair.

The whisper stroke of human fingers down an equine nose, through a mane . . .

. . . good hearts, bravest souls . . .

. . . and she then lost the shape of his words entirely and followed only his tone, that low, soothing grace of his voice that somehow made everything better, that somehow took away the fear and anger and left in their place peaceful stillness. And nothing, not the water or the tobacco or the gathering thunder, mattered over that.

Amalia pulled back. She opened her eyes and pressed the heel of her palm to her forehead to fight the sudden ache.

She'd once overheard her mother say that Zane could charm the fish from the streams and a tiger out of a tree. Lia believed it. She believed he could charm a dragon, if he wished. It was one of her deepest fears.

The horses were quiet now. They smelled her, they sensed her, but the change felt like a balm in the air. The need to bolt was gone.

The carriage door opened a crack. Animal tamer, master thief: he wrapped a hand around the edge of the wood and held it in place, his sleeve and shoulder outlined with sun. The interior of the coach lit like a flame.

"Do me a favor," Zane said. "Don't come out."

And before she could answer, the door closed to darkness again.

⚜

It did not occur to him until that afternoon to ask her which way to go.

He'd held his peace up on the driver's perch again, keeping an eye on the horses and the road. Without discussion, the Romanian coachman had crossed the Danube and pulled them out of Pest. It was what they had agreed upon days earlier, to head deeper into the vineyards and woods, to head for the mountains. It was what Rue had suggested in her sparse rice-paper note, after all.

But he had within his grasp a living, breathing compass to what he sought. At least that was what she'd claimed.

For a very long while, Zane only stared at the rump of the horse hitched in front of him.

He did not want to ask her.

The entire business of Lady Amalia Langford made him uneasy. Despite what she'd said, he wouldn't be surprised if he awoke one night soon to a knife—or worse—at his throat from one of her exuberant family members. Clearly she'd been planning her escape for some while. It seemed unlikely not a single member of the *drákon* had noticed her behavior.

He studied the rough countryside just beginning to unfurl from the clutches of the city. Everything was cold and raw and damp, burnt colors that blended up into clouds and hazy sky. She did not belong here, just in the way a precious gem did not belong with dirt or stones. It put them both at risk. He'd seen it already in the coachman's face, in that of the hotel workers, even in her swains at the ball:

She was different. Her body, her face. The way she moved, as if the very ground did not exist beneath her feet. Different.

Intoxicating.

Dangerous.

God. It'd be a bloody miracle if the peasants didn't end up tossing torches at them as they passed.

The carriage jolted through a rut, and Zane thinned his lips. He was overreacting. Another bad sign. He was used to operating alone, in the dark, letting his spiders spin webs for him while he remained hidden in corners, directing, reaping. He'd let greed tempt him out into the open, greed and curiosity, and now it truly appeared he would suffer the consequences.

But he had come all this way. Damned if he was going to run home now with his tail between his legs just because some brown-eyed sylph had latched on to him and would not let go.

He did not want to think about this. He didn't want to think about her at all, with her primrose skirts and her trunks stacked over his and her hair glinting summer gold by the cool autumnal sun.

She had duped her people and broken away from Darkfrith, which meant she was crafty. She had journeyed alone all the way to Hungary, which meant that she was audacious, if not reckless.

She'd willfully ignored the rules of her kind—barbarous rules, ironclad rules—which meant she might be desperate.

She had found him at the hotel. She had lured him to the ball.

She had worn a dress that shaped her in ways he'd never dreamed a woman could be shaped; she'd tilted her head and smiled at him and sent a goddamned tremor down into the marrow of his bones.

She *was* dangerous.

And it would be foolish not to ask her.

He glanced at the coachman—bearded, wrapped in scarves, as fine a gypsy as Zane had ever seen—and then turned around in his seat. He opened the panel inset behind him, showing a metal-laced grille and the black interior of the coach.

"Lia."

She moved into view, a dim, pale shape, wrapped in dusk.

"We're headed east of Pest, for—Jászberény—"

His mouth twisted around the foreign word; he heard the Roma's subtle snort. But Amalia only nodded and sat back. From the depths of the carriage her voice sounded very sweet.

"That's good, then. Keep on."

She did not come forward again. He allowed the panel to slide shut, turning once more to stare at the horses.

It was his imagination. He could *not* smell the winter rose of her from here.

But the animals in front of him shivered and tossed their heads.

⚜

Reaching Jászberény devoured most of the day. They breached its outskirts just as the sunlight was beginning to slant into long, heavy rays, throwing shadows sapphire-rich across the buildings and roads.

It was an ugly place, with little of the airy glamour that had marked the cities dotted along the Danube; instead, there were boardinghouses and crooked streets and taverns belching smoke from their chimneys to cloud up the dusk.

People actually stopped and stared at the coach as the driver maneuvered their way through the troughs and potholes that pocked the roads. It wasn't difficult to find the better part of the city: a single wide square of pillared shops and businesses, flanked by a butcher's quarter and a park with a pond and a few November-dried trees.

Zane chose a hotel in the middle. He couldn't read the name on the sign, and he didn't care. He'd seen enough of inns to know that this one would have fleas and gilt and a chance at letting two rooms together. It was enough.

He leapt down and over a mud puddle, glad to stretch the ache from his unused muscles. A pair of doormen were already rushing forward, but Zane reached the carriage door first. He turned the handle and—without even meaning to—held his breath.

Skirts and petticoats rustled from within. She lifted a gloved hand to him and emerged cautiously, hoops first, a dainty foot forward, the hood of her mantle pulled low over her face and her hair. As soon as she was standing, the wind twirled between them; her hood flipped back and the horses let out a whimpering protest. Zane motioned the Roma to the back of the hotel. With a crack of the whip, the coach rolled away.

Lady Amalia stood unmoving on the sidewalk, one hand cupped over her mouth and nose. She threw him a short, distressed look.

"What?" he said, forced to exhale.

Her brows pinched together. "It reeks."

He angled his face away and tried a deep breath, relieved to smell only town and evening frost. "No more than any other place." He shrugged at her expression. "You said this would do."

Her chin lowered. He saw her gaze flit to the alley that led to the butchers' quarter, where a sign depicting a slaughtered pig swayed helpfully from a post. The alley entrance was narrow and already layered in gloom, a liquid line of runoff and water reflecting a silvery sheen down the middle of the flagstones. A pair of cloaked figures splashed briefly into view, shattering the silver into pools.

Ah. Zane knew what would be prowling in those shadows. He knew now what Amalia sensed, the death and hunger and those faceless, impoverished people. It was a stench that lurked in the blackest crooks of his memory, and always would.

He kept his home in Bloomsbury as clean as a monastery. He kept a maid, and Joseph to cook, and enjoyed the luxuries of delivered coal and ice and imported fruit from sunwarmed lands. He used his wiles to gain himself whatever he wished, be it silk or jewels or paintings, and he was cold and clear enough in his own heart to make no false apologies for any of it. Zane earned what he had, as sure as a baker earned coin for his bread; he had been raised to steal, and if he didn't do it, someone else surely would. He kept a careful order in his realm of shadows, made certain his people followed a strict set of rules, and culled anyone who either flouted them or challenged him. It was how he had reached his place today, and how he had kept it.

In his world of violence and sawdust and gin-soaked taverns, the scent of blood in the air didn't even raise his hackles.

But Amalia's world had been different. However bold she acted, however mad her schemes . . . she wasn't truly like him. Not in any way. She had been raised as a gentlewoman, in a manor house, by beasts disguised as men.

He watched her lips turn down as she gazed at the sign. Beneath the folds of her mantle, he watched her shoulders square.

"No, my lady," Zane heard himself say, and he moved to stand between her and that shining furrow of blood. His arm lifted to guide her the other way, toward the park. "Look over there instead."

Mist was rising from the sod, ethereal, sweeping coils that rose up to embrace the copper-leafed trees. It was blue and slate against the darkening horizon; the grass had blurred to lavender and emerald and brown. Far in the distance, past the town's steeples and spires, a jagged hint of mountains sliced purple into the sky. The moon hung white as chalk above them.

Her shoulders relaxed, just a little.

"Over there," Zane murmured, "are rabbits tucked into hollows, and blackbirds coming awake in the trees. Can you feel them?"

"No," she answered, soft.

"But they're there. And I'm quite certain they'd appreciate it if we moved indoors. What say you?"

And she smiled.

It was just as he'd thought: the interior of the hotel presented a surfeit of gilt and mirrors, peach-painted walls, and at least two footmen scratching at their wigs.

Zane sighed. It didn't bode well for the mattresses.

⚜

They took supper in the public room, amid country gentry and a handful of gray-powdered nobles, seated at a holland-draped table in a corner by a wide glass window. The skyline was fully dark now, broken only by street lanterns and a few lonely flames set beneath casements.

Lia kept her teacup in her hands when she could; the glass threw a chill, and even her cashmere shawl didn't help.

They dined in near silence, listening instead to the chatter of the room, the civil bustling of the waitstaff, the babbled conversations among the patrons in French and Hungarian and a few tongues she did not know. The chandelier above them flickered with the draft; colors danced along the table and dishes, and the steam from her soup became a fog upon the panes.

The thief sat across from her with a platter of creamed fish and parsley between them. She watched him through her lashes. He ate neatly, sparingly, his hands deft, his body relaxed. He'd undone his coat of fine biscuit wool and was gathering the glances of every woman in the room, from the pair of dowagers in amazing high wigs to the little serving maid, no more than thirteen, who fumbled the cheese plate when he smiled at her.

In the candlelight his hair shone burnished bronze. It fell long and straight in a tail over one shoulder, the blue velvet ribbon that held it in place knotted only slightly too loose. He lifted a section of soft white cheese from its tray and, without looking at her, began to slice it into quarters.

"You do that rather a lot, you know."

She blinked, coming out of her reverie. "Do what?"

"Stare at me. Have I a cinder on my nose?"

Lia took refuge in her tea. "Not at all."

"What a relief. No doubt, then, you're merely lost in thought, considering our time and distance to this all-important diamond—what did you name it again?"

His voice was light, and he still did not look up from his work, but she felt his attention fixed on her with all the familiarity of that dark, delicious hum.

"*Draumr.*"

"*Draumr,* of course. What does it mean?"

"I don't know," Lia said honestly.

"Where did you hear it?"

She did not reply. He slanted her a metallic-gold look.

"You're expecting me to take a great deal on faith, snapdragon. And for a man of my trade, faith is never free. If you wish me to believe you, if you wish me to trust you and let you haul us willy-nilly through all the mud holes of this bloody continent just on your say-so, then you're going to offer me something in return." He placed a cube of cheese upon her plate. "I don't want all your secrets, Amalia. Just the ones that set *my* arse on the line."

Lia said slowly, "I heard it in a dream."

His expression did not alter. "Is that so?"

She inclined her head.

"And is that how you know where it is now? From . . . your dreams?"

"You needn't sound so skeptical. It *is* true."

"Forgive me." He tipped back his head and smiled at the peach plaster ceiling. "I find myself astonished that I've actually thrown my fortune in with a girl who's willing to risk her life—and mine—over the visions dancing in her head."

She was used to the seduction in his voice, she was used to the soft-stated command; she was not used to his contempt. Lia leaned across the table until the edge bit into the bones of her corset. "You know I'm not a girl. You know what I am. I've dreamed it, and it's true. You may believe me or not, I don't care. But you asked, so I've told you. In the future if you'd like to me lie to you to soothe your nerves, pray inform me now."

His gaze returned to hers. From across the chamber a woman's laughter dissolved into giggles; the clatter of silver against china was very loud in her ears.

"Do you think you could? Lie to me, I mean?"

"Without the slightest of qualms," she snapped.

Zane picked up his knife again, examining the mother-of-pearl handle. "I confess the sight of you does appear to make my will a trifle weak. Perhaps a few lies, then. Small ones, I beg you, just to ease my missish nerves."

She stared at him, uncertain if he had complimented her or not. When he glanced up at her once more, his eyes were wolfish bright.

"We're to venture forth to the queen of the fairies," Lia said. "She'll welcome us with minstrels and tamed bears and all the caviar we can eat. The diamond's waiting for us on a pillow of purple velvet. We'll ride an enchanted carpet back home."

"And there we'll dwell, happily forever after," the thief finished, dry.

"Exactly."

"Wonderful. I'm much relieved. Where might we find this fairy queen?"

"In the mountains, I think. In the Carpathians."

"You think," he said, and the blade began to tap against his plate.

"I believe I've offered enough for one evening." Lia sat back, pulling her shawl closer. "You've told me your faith isn't free—well, I've decided neither is mine. It's your turn to offer me something."

As soon as she said it she realized how it sounded; heat began to climb up her throat.

"My protection?" Zane inquired, watching her with his mouth faintly curved. "My gallant company? No, no, I see you require something slightly more valuable. Fair enough." He used the flat of his knife to serve her another portion of cheese; she hadn't touched the first. "The gentlemen at the table square to our right—no, my lady, don't look. Good heavens, you're smarter than that. Drink your tea, move only your eyes . . . there. Do you see them?"

"Yes."

"Tell me what you think of them. Quietly, *s'il vous plaît*."

They seemed unremarkable: two young men in wigs and cravats, their coats cut too wide, watch chains dangling, their stockings not quite clean. They were sharing a jug of ale and a steaming pot of sausage stew, speaking in whispers and sending frequent glances to a pair of young ladies at another table not far across the chamber.

The ladies, Lia noted, were even more simply dressed, and accompanied by an older, scowling woman in a mobcap. The three of them ignored the men.

"Baronets, or squires," she said after a moment. "Or whatever such a title might be out here. Well-born, but not wealthy. Young." The two men burst into smothered laughter, ducking their heads. "Inebriated," she added.

"And credulous."

"Oh?"

"Before the night is over, our love-struck squires will find their purses quite a bit lighter than yesterday."

"Why?" she asked, suddenly suspicious. "Are you planning to lighten them?"

"I?" His brows raised in mock innocence. "I assure you, I have no such desire. For one thing, I doubt very much they're carrying anything worth pricking my interest. For another, it's a bit too unjust, even for me. It would be rather like plucking a rattle from an infant's fist."

"Then—"

"The women," Zane said, easing back in his chair, still with his faint smile. "The two comely maidens and their prune-faced matron."

Lia turned her gaze back to them, just in time to see one of the girls flash a grin at the men.

"They're really very good." Zane ran a finger up the stem of his wineglass, examining the deep red *Tokay.* "Just the right amount of coquetry applied over middle-class respectability. The old woman adds the perfect touch. Were we in London, I'd have a pleasant word with them all."

Amalia said nothing. She watched the two girls, their

practiced smiles. And the squires glancing back, still flushed, lifting their glasses, sending a sly salute when they thought the matron was not looking. But Lia saw now—now that Zane had told her—that beneath the ruffled lace of her cap, she actually was.

"Try the fish, why don't you?" the thief suggested. "It's better than you'd expect."

"Why did you show me this?"

"You wanted something of value from me."

She had. She knotted her hands in her lap and watched the red-cheeked squires, their shiny, unguarded faces.

"It's the way of the world, love," murmured Zane. "For better or worse, you're out here in it. It's my little gift to you: open your eyes."

The young men began to search for their money. They began to count out their bill upon the table, while the pair of girls pretended not to watch.

"It isn't fair," Lia said.

The thief turned his face fully to see her; she met his look.

"They're young and foolish. But they're only besotted."

"Aye. It will be a useful lesson for them."

She set her cup upon its saucer.

"Snapdragon," warned Zane. "Think twice."

"Perhaps what they have with them is all they have. Perhaps those watches belonged to their fathers. Perhaps there are people depending upon them, upon those meager coins in their purses. Servants. Children."

"Yes. Perhaps."

Lia threw him a heated glance, placing her napkin upon the table. Before she could rise, his arm snaked out; his hand pressed hers hard to the wood. His voice came very low.

"*Think,* Amalia. What would you say to them? We don't need that sort of attention. I only showed you because you asked. Have you forgotten why we're here?"

"I've forgotten nothing," she said with a level stare.

He returned it for a moment, his eyes glinting pale, his brows and lashes shadowed sharp against his skin. Then his fingers slid from hers; he shook his head. "What a pretty conscience you have. Knowing your parents, I can't imagine how you came by it. No, wait," he said, as she pushed at her chair. He came to his feet. "I'll do it."

Before she could respond he was walking away, not toward the table of the drunken young men but to the other one, where the trio of women were nibbling at the last of their meal. He wound through the room, by all appearances heading for the double doors that led into the hotel's main hall, tall and handsome and surprisingly unsteady on his feet: a man who had indulged in too much drink.

As he passed the women's table, something happened. She couldn't see it clearly, there were too many other diners between them, but Zane dipped and turned and the women erupted into stifled shrieks. She caught the sound of glass striking wood—he had knocked over their carafe of wine. The matron leapt up, saving her skirts with both hands; the younger women followed more slowly.

Conversation ceased. Everyone in the dining room turned to observe the commotion. In the echoing hush she heard Zane's urgent apologies in French, and the waiters converging, and the matron chattering words too swift to understand. But Lia could see the woman's profile now as she took two steps toward Zane, the anger etched around her mouth—erased the instant he lifted from his bow and she got a better look at his face.

The matron paused, then summoned a small, sour smile. She clucked at the two girls, drawing them nearer while the liveried waiters swarmed like green-coated bees around the table. In the midst of them all, Zane bowed again, bringing the older woman's hand to his lips.

Lia saw something new enter her expression. She saw her quick, darting glance to the younger two, a silent message exchanged over his bent head.

The dishes were cleared, the soiled cloth removed. Fresh bleached linen was whipped across the table, more wine was being poured—Zane very openly pressed a gold coin into the hand of the *maître d'hôtel*—and then he was bowing a third time, clearly preparing to back away. When he came up again, the older woman touched her hand to his arm and spoke. With his back to Lia, Zane leaned in close and turned his mouth to her ear.

What Lia saw best then was the blue-veined hand upon his sleeve. How the matron's fingers abruptly clenched, hard enough to pull the wool into puckers. How she let go of him very quickly as if repelled, her fingers spread.

Zane straightened. He nodded to the other two and walked on to the exit without looking back.

The woman turned her gaze slowly around the room. Lia dropped her chin and studied what was left of the fish, silently counting to ten before raising her eyes again.

No one was looking at her. The matron had gathered up her charges and was hastening them out of the chamber, their shawls trailing, their wineglasses still brimming—much to the dismay of the country squires.

Five minutes later, Zane returned. There was no hitch to his gait now; he moved as smoothly as a cat through the staggered tables.

"Dessert?" he inquired, flicking the skirts of his coat as he resumed his seat.

"What did you say to her?"

"Only that she'd do better elsewhere." He lifted a hand for a waiter. "With the dowagers, for example, at the table by the fire. Those appear to be real pearls at their throats."

Lia's jaw dropped. "You sent them to rob someone else instead?"

"Well, you could hardly expect me to warn her off without sweetening the deal. She looked frail enough, but she was a tough old mare, believe me. I think she bruised my arm."

Waiters appeared, silent and bowing, taking away the fish and cheese, bringing mints and hot coffee and a tray full of petite sugared cakes. Lia waited until they retreated out of range.

"How could you do such a thing?"

"Very easily. I can't imagine why anyone would wear pearls in this rustic backwater of a town unless they craved the attention."

"Zane," she hissed.

"Dearest wife, didn't you notice the foursome of men at the side door? Yes, go ahead and look. They're guarding the dowagers, and their pearls. I noted them when we first arrived; we were all in the lobby together. There's not a chance in Hades our little band of pickpockets will step anywhere near those women tonight, nor any other night. Trust me."

He picked up one of the pastel-sugared cakes, tapping it until the grains sifted down onto his plate. "So. Are they?"

"Are they what?"

"Real pearls," he said. "I'd wager my soul you can tell."

She didn't answer. His voice grew gentler, more insistent.

"Are they, Amalia?"

She closed her eyes. The scent of the coffee was a sudden heat in her head.

"Yes," she said.

He was silent. When she looked at him again, he was gazing out the window, his expression serene, the cake forgotten in the center of his plate. The light from the candles above them slipped bright and dark along the contours of his face.

He looked elegant and severe and very distant, a phantom of a man fixed in a roomful of gay strangers.

It was chance, and only that, that pinned his gaze precisely where the song of *Draumr* seemed to float from the hills.

"The rabbits and the birds," she said, inching forward in her chair. "Did you really feel them in that park?"

His lips creased in smile.

"When did you have time to wash your hair?" He glanced back at her, his hand reaching for her shoulder. His fingers cupped and released a falling, amber-lit lock. "It's most becoming. But I do wonder at your priorities. It would have been more practical to keep the powder in."

They stared at each other without moving.

"Do you know," said Lia at last, in the most even tone she could manage, "I find that I'm far more fatigued from the day than I first realized. I believe I'll retire now."

"Excellent," replied the thief, in exactly the same tone. "Let's."

CHAPTER FIVE

In the realm of the *drákon*, as in the realm of human men, there are hunters, and there are prey.

We, of course, excel at hunting. It is who we are: that hard carving wind, that swift and fatal talon through a hammering heart. We are the fog draped in circles around the forest pines; we are the golden eye of the sun, shining terrible and bright upon the earth and its lesser beings. We hunt because we breathe. Animal or mineral, diamonds or blood, if we desire it deeply enough, it will be ours.

This is nature. These are our Gifts, and we are entitled to them as surely as a lion is entitled to his roar, or a mouse to her hoard of autumn seed.

But the Others forever come and upset our balance and try to cheat nature. They lie and slink and steal from us, because they know in their bones they can never truly touch our splendor. They're weak and jealous—but not helpless. It is the most jealous of creatures who can blossom into the most dangerous.

On the unfortunate occasion when the *drákon* become prey, it is always the Others who cast us there.

This is what happened to Amalia and her consort as they drew closer to our homeland.

CHAPTER SIX

"Lia."

"Yes, Zane."

"Where is your mother now?"

"Behind the door to the blue parlor. The fire's gone out. It's darkest there."

"Weapons?"

"A pistol. A rapier. She'll use the pistol first. Before you can speak, she'll fire through the door."

"Wait here. Do not follow me. Do not leave this chamber, no matter what you may hear."

"Yes, Zane."

"I'll be back very soon."

"Yes."

But he didn't leave. A single, rough finger stroked fire along her cheek.

"Tell me you love me," he whispered.

"I love you."

"Tell me you'll do what I say."

"You know I will."

His hand lifted away. "Good. Stay here."

"Yes."

❧

He was up before she was, which didn't surprise him. Zane never needed a great deal of sleep; as a child he'd taught himself to drowse with his eyes open, to sink into a slow, stuporous awareness that passed well enough for respite when times were dire and he couldn't afford genuine rest. But although he was uncomfortable, and he was worn, the fact that the most disturbingly beautiful being he'd ever seen was warm in her bed just a room away didn't truly qualify as dire.

Not yet.

So he allowed himself a few hours' slumber, letting the night take him. The steel of his dirk remained a firm, familiar shape beneath his pillow.

He did not sleep well. The hotel room was musty. He'd cracked a window to freshen it, but all that did was add to the chill. The wallpaper was peeling at its seams and the rug badly needed to be beaten. The smell of dust and motes settled into a persistent itch in his nose.

Close to daybreak, when the door opened silently, he came instantly alert. It was only the chambermaid, creeping into the room with a broom and bucket of coals and his boots, which she placed carefully by the armoire.

He watched through slitted eyes as she stoked the fire in the grate and then swept up whatever small mess she'd made. She crept out again as quietly as she'd come.

To hell with it.

He dressed as the room began to illume to a faded grandeur, the cool, foggy sunrise softening all the rough edges. The little fire didn't come close to denting the chill; he was half tempted to linger in bed until breakfast...if it weren't for the fleas. And for the fact that past the wall against his headboard, there slept a woman who snored.

It wasn't Amalia. He couldn't hear anything at all from her room.

So he dressed, his buckskin breeches, his cleanest shirt, the Parisian dun surcoat that wore best against the grime of the road ready upon the bed. His boots had been polished; he shook them out upside down, one at a time. No hidden needles, no spiders, no poisonous scent rising from the freshly oiled gleam. He found a tie for his hair and crossed to the door that separated him from Lia, testing the handle.

Locked.

He smiled at that. She was game, if nothing else.

He bent down, took a look at the keyhole, and went back for his tools. The lock was old, just like the rest of the place, so clumsily antiquated he wondered why they bothered with it at all. He closed his eyes and let the pads of his fingers guide him, trusting the delicate edge of his pick, the hook, the turn, the tumblers releasing—

There was a time when the muted *click* of that release would bring with it a small, physical rush of satisfaction through his veins. It meant success: escape or invasion, wealth or information, or all of them at once. Before he'd reached his teens, before he knew about the particular pleasures of money or power or women, that rush of sensation had been the finest feeling in the world. He'd apprenticed to one of the best cracksmen in the business, had procured him cash and whores and whatever else the bastard demanded, up until the very night that Dirty Clem, stinking drunk, had stuck a boning knife into Zane's ribs—all because Clem had taught him this:

To turn a lock.

To open doors.

To slip in where he was not invited, and never would be.

Zane placed his palm upon the paneled wood, giving it a little push. At least the hinges were greased; the dusk of her room swept over his feet without a whisper. He stood there a moment, allowing his eyes to adjust.

The maid had been here too. The fire in Lady Amalia's grate glowed a cheerful orange, shaping color along the rug and the posts of her bed, nearly lost before it even reached the duvet. Lia was a beguiling lump beneath the covers, asleep in precisely the same position as in her bed in Óbuda: arms out, her face tipped to him. The blankets had dragged down until only a single sheet covered her chest.

She wore no nightgown. She wore nothing at all, as far as he could tell. She was fair as an angel in gloom, her hair a guinea-dark flame that spread in waves along the pillows. Her brow was peaceful, her lashes long and brown. Her fingers curled up into her palms to clasp the air; the rise and fall of her chest threatened the sanctity of that sheet with every breath.

In a flower of pretty sparks, an ember in the fire popped open.

Wife, he thought, unbidden.

He sucked in his breath. He turned his head and without thinking took a step back, away from her, away from the sight of her bare skin and her hair and her tranquil, uncanny face.

But he wasn't as noiseless as he should have been. His back bumped the door and Amalia stirred, coming awake.

She stretched. The sheet slipped at last, dragging down to her waist, and he could not look away, he could not, as she raised her arms above her head and yawned and turned, pulling her fingers through her hair until all at once it went to smoke—every tendril, to actual *fumes*—there on the pillows, silky gray plumes that lifted and curved about her face.

"Jesus Christ," Zane said, and hit the door again with his back.

Her eyes opened. She sat up and the smoke swept back into hair, a heavy blond tumble that bounced past her shoulders.

He was staring. He was frozen. She yanked the sheet up high to her chest.

"Get out," Amalia said.

"What was *that*?"

"Out!"

He reached behind him for the knob to her door. Without taking his gaze from hers, he closed it to solid wood behind him, sealing them together in the room.

"Goodness me," he said, managing—just barely—to keep the venom from his tone. "It seems last night you offered me a grain of truth, didn't you? You truly *can* lie to me without qualm."

She let go of a breath, pent up as if she'd been holding it. Her eyes were very wide.

He moved forward into the room. "How long have you been able to Turn?"

"You are mistaken," she said, deathly still. "I cannot Turn."

"Now, granted, it's rather dark in here. And I'm not at my best without my breakfast coffee, but there's nothing amiss with my eyes. I know what I saw."

"I don't know what you saw. But I swear to you, I can't—"

"Amalia," he interrupted, very pleasant. "Lie to me again, and I promise you that you will not enjoy the consequences."

Her mouth closed. He watched her fingers whiten around the sheet and took another step forward, nearly at the bed.

"Yes?" he said gently.

Lia felt her face begin to heat. He held motionless, waiting, looking down at her with a wintry, gleaming gaze.

She wasn't lying. She could not Turn. She was a woman with strange talents; she was a dreamer who heard music and horrors, and all of it was as beyond her control as the moon was to the tide. She woke up each day never knowing what new trick her body would perform, or when or where. It was like having a beast locked in her chest where her heart used to be, a beast that could wink awake at any moment and shred her hard-won facade to ribbons.

She hadn't known of it until that afternoon in Edinburgh two years ago. Out for tea with a group of younger students—in her second year Lia had been allowed to chaperone, a sweet morsel of liberty—strolling down Lawnmarket, she'd glimpsed a young man in an apron, a farrier, approaching from the other direction. His gaze had cut to hers through the black-shouldered people; he smiled as they passed. Lia had smiled back, warmed to her toes by just that swift, appreciative glance.

Her hat had settled low upon her head. She'd felt light and peculiar and happy, unusually buoyant, until one of the girls behind her caught up and tugged at her sleeve, *Lady Amalia, you've lost the pins to your hair.*

She'd reached a hand to her hat. And where before there had been a coiffure of perfectly respectable white-powdered ringlets beneath the brim, there were now long, golden curls falling free to her hips.

In broad daylight.

From just a man's shy smile.

That had been the first time. For a full six months after that, she would not meet the eyes of a comely man, young or old, servant or nobleman. She did not dare. When the *drákon* Turned to smoke, nothing remained on their bodies, not powder, not jewels or clothing. Nothing.

It wasn't supposed to be possible, to Turn in pieces, to vanish by parts. Her people were dragon or human or vapor: no one lingered in between. No one but she.

She'd wanted the Gifts. She had gotten this half-life, this dragon heart—and the song and the dreams.

Zane closed the final few feet between them, easing right up to the edge of the bed. There was threat in the stealth of it, in the very grace and silence of his stance. She'd never before seen him move like that; in all the years she'd known him, she'd never before felt him radiate true menace—but now the hair on the back of her neck began to prickle.

He is a criminal, she realized. *He is.*

"I cannot Turn completely," she said. "I don't have that kind of control. I don't have any control, really. The entire process is ... beyond me. I wasn't lying about that. Whatever you saw just now, I didn't do it. Not deliberately."

She couldn't tell if he believed her; she couldn't tell what he thought at all. His face had that cool, stony expression he wore so frequently around her. Then he frowned a little and took up a lock of her hair, studying it.

"It was this," he said, giving the lock a tug.

She nodded, unsurprised.

"Why are you here, Amalia?"

"To—to take you to the diamond."

"Why?" he asked again, combing his fingers slowly through the gold. "Serviceable as I am, a woman like you, a fiend of your particular skills, would surely do better on her own."

She opened her mouth, and closed it. She felt, very sharply, the blood rising again in her cheeks.

The thief smiled down at her, openly taunting.

"That was unkind."

"Some would say so is duping an innocent man."

"You are as far from innocent a man as I know! And *fiend*

89

or no, I came here to ensure you gain something valuable at the end—"

But he'd clapped a hand to her mouth, smothering the rest, his head turned to the door that led to the hall outside. She heard it then too: footsteps, running very lightly down the carpeted corridor. There were no other sounds, no wood creaking, no panting or rustling clothes—and then not even those steps.

A sudden odd chill crept across her skin.

Lia wrapped the sheet around her and followed as he padded to the door. He threw her a single glance of warning, reaching for the latch. She smelled the alcohol just as his fingers grazed the handle.

"Wait—"

The air beyond the door ignited with a *whoosh,* a flash of burning light that slammed against the wood and sent a bar of orange brilliance searing along their feet. In nearly the same instant, Zane had whirled and flung her with him across the rug, his arms tight around her, the sheet caught and torn away. They bounced into the bed and rebounded. She landed on her knees, winded, and he hauled her back up by one arm.

"Are you hurt?"

He didn't glance at her unclad body—he barely even waited for her to shake her head *no* before releasing her and sprinting back into his own room. Smoke was curling in fingers around the edges of the door; Zane had vanished.

Lia ran to the armoire, pulling out her chemise, her stockings and gown and stays and shoes—she tugged the chemise over her head, threw the circle of hoops to the floor and shoved her feet into her pumps as the fingers of smoke brightened into flame.

"What are you doing?" He was back, carrying his coat and

sword and valise. "Turn! Get out of here! I'll meet you outside—go to the park, I'll meet you there."

"I can't!"

The air was a swirling cloud above their heads. She could hear the happy crackle of the fire spreading and the paint from the door beginning to bubble. From somewhere very far away, people started to scream.

Zane had her again by the arm.

"Amalia!"

"I can't! I can't Turn!" She wrenched free of him, working feverishly at the hooks to the gown. "Can we get out through your room?"

As if in answer, a wall of smoke billowed from his doorway. The light behind it flickered and bloomed; from somewhere beyond came the sound of glass exploding.

He hauled her into him once more, pressing her face to his chest. For a brief, startling instant she smelled him instead of the acrid smoke, warm linen and man, his palm hard against her cheek. Against the thin silk of her chemise, he felt solid and taut and very real.

"You *can* Turn," he was shouting down into her hair. "This isn't the time for games. Just get out of here."

"I'm not lying—"

"Lia, goddamnit—"

She jerked away, her eyes beginning to sting. Two of the walls were already writhing with flames; ash from the wallpaper floated up to the ceiling in monstrous black flakes.

"I! Can't! Turn!"

He didn't bother to argue with her again, only grabbing her hand to pull her to the window. When the sash stuck, he used the valise to smash the panes. His shirtsleeves snapped in the sudden new draft, and the smoke pulled around them to funnel out into the cold.

The screaming swelled abruptly louder.

He leaned his head out the opening, looking down, then glanced back at her.

"It's two flights down. Can you climb? There's a gutter to the left."

She nodded, still trying to work open her gown. He made an impatient sound, snatching the mass of it from her hands and pitching it—overskirt, petticoats, and all—out the window.

"Follow it," he said, and pushed her up to the sill. "Mind the glass."

In her chemise, in the cold, Lia clambered out the window. A crowd of people had amassed on the street below, hotel workers and guests and passersby, everyone shouting and pointing. A line of men slopped buckets of water through their middle, snaking back into the hotel.

The wind was a freezing shock. She saw the gutter, a lead fluted pipe barely attached to the stone wall, and stretched a hand to it. The pipe was slick with dew; she tried twice to catch it, swaying back and forth as her fingers slipped across the metal. Zane held fast to her other hand.

"Hurry," he urged, very calm, as the ceiling above him rippled into flame.

Dragon heart. With a surge of desperation she dug her nails into the lead. The metal gave like wet clay, and the pipe began to bend.

"Let go!"

He did. She swung free for a heart-stopping moment, dangling, and the people below cried out. Quickly, before the pipe gave, before she lost her nerve, she shimmied down, half sliding, half falling, the chemise twisted up to her knees, the soles of her pumps slipping for purchase against the lead and stone. She landed in the arms of several waiting men, hands grabbing her, lifting her back to her feet. People were yelling at her, incomprehensible, but Lia was staring up at the smoke and the broken window, and the man there leaning out to see her, his hair a brown gilded streamer blown across the frame.

"Lia! Catch!"

He tossed down the valise. She caught it and staggered back, supported once more by the many hands. When she looked up again, Zane was halfway down the pipe. He landed with a nimble leap just as it detached from the building, the length of it tilting to the ground in a slow, smooth arc that crumpled against the cobbled street.

Zane pushed his way to her. He took off his coat and draped it over her shoulders, his arm wrapping around her waist. She set the valise at their feet. They stood there together with the rest of the people, watching the upper floor of the hotel—their rooms, their beds, their belongings—crumble into cinders.

Her hand hurt. She must have cut it on the glass; there was a gash across her knuckles, sticky with blood. She cupped her fist to her chest and closed her eyes against the smoke, turning her face to Zane's shoulder. The wind slashed like a blade around her bare ankles.

And then she felt it. That same chill across her skin, not from the cold but from something else—some*one* else. It was electric and thin and very, very familiar.

The beast in her heart stirred, fell and glimmering.

Lia lifted her head. It wasn't possible...but there was another *drákon* nearby.

She glanced casually around the swarm of people, scanning faces. She saw the dowagers of the night before, lined and haggard in the rising light, their guards flanking them. She saw the squires, red-eyed, their cravats undone and their wigs askew. She saw men in slack jackets and women in headscarves and a scattering of urchin children—and there—behind a pair of colliers gawking at the mess—

It was just a flash, a quick thrill of movement, white skin, dark hair. A set of oddly tintless eyes meeting hers. She pulled away from Zane, but it was already too late: the colliers were shoved aside by one of the men with buckets, and there was no one behind them.

Only a wisp of smoke, rising up to blend into the smudged, violet-tinged sky.

CHAPTER SEVEN

Against what Zane would have wagered were considerable odds, the water brigade was managing the fire. Smoke no longer poured from any of the lower-story windows; the unholy curtain of crackling yellow had vanished from behind the closed panes. People were still shouting and rushing about, but it seemed at least half of the hotel had been saved.

Half. All that was left of the upper floor, the attics, was a mosaic of broken rooftiles and black skeleton timbers, flecked with orange embers.

Zane turned to Lia. She appeared pale and very shaken. Her hair fell snarled over the sleeves of his coat, a sheen of rose lacquered over the guinea-gold, a gift from the rising sun. She was gazing away from him, distracted; a line of soot streaked from her cheekbone to her chin.

"I think," said Zane, bending down to her ear, "that perhaps I'm ready to concede that you cannot Turn."

Her look back to him was startled, as if she'd forgotten he'd be there. He offered a bow and handed her her gown, thrust at him by a man in passing. It was wet and trampled but undeniably what he'd thrown from their burning window. She stared down at the layers of cambric and coral-pink damask as if she'd never seen any of it before.

"Lia," he said, touching her shoulder, and she started again. He caught his cuff in his fist and rubbed the soot from her cheek, then tucked her arm through his. "Come along. Come with me."

Her lips seemed very red. Her eyes were dark. She held his arm like a dreamer, walking beside him through the throng of weeping and smelly people without glancing left or right, her breath clouding in the chill.

The people were not all that smelled. Zane reeked of smoke. He did, Amalia did, the sky did, the very atoms in the air. Sullage and cinders crunched beneath his boots like fresh snowfall; for an instant he worried for Lia, but as he looked down he remembered she'd found her shoes in time. She stepped mindlessly through a greasy puddle, the ruffled hem of her chemise flipping pretty against her calves.

Her legs were long and bare. Beneath his surcoat, beneath that slip of ivory silk, she was wearing nothing at all.

He looked up. He wished suddenly, fervently, for coffee.

Across the square was what appeared to be a tavern—perhaps it was a teahouse. It had mullioned windows and a door and a knot of people standing outside it gaping at the smoldering hotel, some of them holding tankards. He steered Amalia toward it.

It was a tavern, largely deserted. He settled for ale instead of coffee, ordered another for Lia, and led her to a table in the corner, well in sight of the door. He made sure she was seated, went back to the bar for their drinks, and turned around with his hands full.

She sat alone in the light. It wasn't much light, just the wan, murky rays that managed to pierce the panes of the window nearby. The beam itself fell drained of hues: everything around her was dusty and brown and dull. But Lia glowed. Her hair madonna-loose, the spare dress in her lap. She was pink and gold and soldier-straight in her chair, her expression pensive, faraway. He could still see the faint mark of the soot upon her cheek where he hadn't gotten it all off.

Something within him shifted. He felt queer, almost dizzy; the very world seemed to tilt to a slow, molasses stop, everything suspended. Dust motes. Voices. His heartbeat. Only Lia moved. She took a long, deep breath, her chest lifting, her lips parted, and he thought, sinking, *Oh, God.*

He wanted her. Not somewhat, not in passing. He wanted her deeply, and he wanted her now. Here. He wanted to touch her hair, and taste her skin, and breathe in the scent of smoke and roses he knew would rise from the soft sweet corners of her. He wanted to push his hands under the coat and feel the shape of her waist, and the weight of her breasts, and every creamy inch of her. He wanted to bite her lips and pin her arms and be inside her, and the hot, eager lust that scorched through him all at once was so strong, so overwhelming, that Zane did the only thing he could do to keep himself standing where he was, dripping ale from the tankards.

He closed his eyes and thought of her parents, and of what would happen if they knew.

He had seen what the *drákon* did to their own kind when they broke the tribal laws. He'd seen the place where they buried their forsaken; Rue had shown him one winter night when he'd been younger and much more reckless: the ominously bumpy field, the blackened earth.

This is where our outlaws lie, she'd told him, her face hollowed by moonlight. *This is where their bones are cast after the burning.*

The *drákon* lived by rules coiled within rules. Their society was ancient, feudal, and he had no illusions about his own place within that order.

He was suffered to live because of the marchioness. He was alive today, in this dank foreign tavern, because he was useful, and that was all.

You keep a great secret. You hold fates in your hands. She'd touched his arm then, lightly, deliberately. *You know our laws. Do not forget this place.*

And he never had.

The barkeep stumped past him carrying a platter of bread and butter and a thick steak of cold ham, all of which he set gently before Amalia. She looked up at the man and smiled.

"*Köszönöm.*"

"*Persze.*"

Zane felt his heart squeeze back to life. He joined her at the table.

The keep had brought knives and napkins too. He arranged them with ridiculous precision upon the battered wood, all the while stealing glances at Lia—her tousled hair, the chemise, that dreamy distraction—until he happened to catch Zane's eye.

Zane watched him blanch and back away.

He lowered his gaze, thinking of the dead and charred bones and the face of Lia's mother on that long-ago night, the only warning she'd ever offered him.

Do not forget.

"So," he said briskly, and lifted his tankard. "Who would want to kill us?"

Amalia's head swiveled around as he took a heavy draft. It was sour and cold and stung all the way down to his stomach.

"Kill us?" she echoed.

"You were there, child."

She blinked at him, at last awaking.

"I'd say it was grain alcohol poured in the hall, perhaps oil. Something like that, fortified or very pure, that burns hot. Anything diluted like cider or beer would burn too slowly. Saltpeter is swifter but too unreliable. Still, it wouldn't have taken much to bring down that claptrap of a tinderbox. But you tell me, m'lady. What was it?"

"Alcohol," she said, after a moment. "Not oil. It smelled distilled, but almost sweet. Definitely alcohol."

He nodded. The color began to return to her cheeks; it was a little like witnessing marble flush to life. He blew a breath through his teeth and looked away.

The tavern was filling quickly, the men standing outside filtering back in, other guests from the hotel, rumpled and stunned, drifting toward the last of the empty tables. Conversation echoed off the walls; he didn't need to speak the language to understand it. Everyone was talking about the fire, the sudden and devastating destruction.

Except for Lia, who was frowning down at her ale.

"Have you any enemies?" Zane asked.

He'd meant it more to shock her, to bring her back to this place and moment—he needed her thinking, not lost and beguiling in her daze—but she looked so instantly guilty his senses prickled.

Damn. He knew better than to ignore that sensation. He hadn't gotten where he was by fighting his instincts.

"What, from boarding school?" She was shaking her head. "No one who would follow me here. Of course not."

"Excellent," he said, pretending to focus on his drink.

"We may rule out young ladies desiring vengeance over borrowed hair ribbons or such."

Her cheeks grew more flushed. "Oh, most amusing. It's far more likely someone is attempting to murder *you*, my lord thief. I imagine you have enemies aplenty."

"True. For some reason I do tend to rub certain people the wrong way."

"People from whom you *steal*."

"My, how proper," he marveled, pausing over his tankard. "You've gotten your tuition's worth in grammar lessons, haven't you?"

She huffed and looked away from him, taking up the loaf of crusty brown bread, ripping it in two. She dropped both halves without bothering to eat either. He watched her, her fingers toying with the soft innards, her brow puckered. She was scattering crumbs all over her gown.

He took his share before she ruined it, reaching for the butter. It had been a long, long while since he'd allowed himself butter, but under the circumstances, he really thought he'd earned it.

He felt her gaze as he worked. She didn't speak again until he'd finished the entire half loaf.

"It might have had nothing to do with us. It might have been about someone else entirely. Or—it might have been an accident. Fires happen all the time."

He didn't answer. Her fingers destroyed more of the bread.

"Do you truly think it was meant for us? To kill us?"

"Yes," he said.

"But why fire? Why not—shoot us, or poison us, or run us down on the road?"

"I don't know."

"But—"

"Since we have entered this establishment, no one has shadowed us. No one has us under surveillance, save the" farmers near the hearth, and I imagine that has more to do with your attire than anything else. The ale came from a common cask; the bread from the back, so I suppose there is a risk there, but as I've had my half and still feel rather hungry, we may assume it's not been tampered with. The barkeep appears to have developed something of a *tendresse* for you, but that's only to be expected." She opened her mouth; he went on more quickly. "Whomever—whoever started that fire, they're not here now. We have a brick wall with no windows or doors at our backs and the entire room in plain view. The roof is tile, the floor is stone. This place, at least, will not burn easily. So eat your breakfast. No one eludes their enemy on an empty stomach, and it looks like, Lady Amalia, it is going to be a very long—"*journey,* he almost said, but finished with "day."

Her gaze had flown to the straw-haired keep behind the bar, his shoulders hunched, wiping the counter with a rag in endless, determined circles. Zane watched her watching him, then leaned across the table and lowered his voice.

"Haven't you noticed? It's the *good* portion of the ham. No bone." He speared the meat with his knife. "*Bon appétit,* fair wife."

But he did not believe they were to be let loose so easily.

He made good use of the barkeeper's moon-eyed infatuation, convincing the man Lia required the use of the private back room and paying heftily for the privilege.

Zane prowled through the chamber first, learning it—a cracked window, creaking floors, no fireplace, no other exits—then ushered her inside.

"Dress, and try to rest awhile," he said. "Bolt the door. Don't open it for anyone but me. Should anyone else attempt to enter, feel free to shoot them."

"What?"

"The pistol's in the valise. Do load it first."

"Where will you be?"

"Not far."

⚜

The lower level of the hotel was still swarming with people, most of them weary, robe-clad guests trampling soot through pools of spilled water. The scent of carbon and singed cloth was much stronger here; he held his handkerchief to his nose to hide his face and pushed his way through the people, slowly ascending the first flight of stairs.

The second flight was blocked entirely by a threesome of footmen, sans wigs, who stood with their arms resolutely folded behind a thin, bearded man who was attempting to explain, Zane assumed, why no one could pass. The argument echoed all the way back to the lobby. The dowagers of the pearls were becoming especially riled.

Gentry. Never thinking of the smaller ways to do things.

He skirted the edges of the unhappy mob and slipped down a nearly empty corridor, searching until he found the door he knew would be somewhere nearby: small, plain, and locked. The servants' stairwell.

He was not followed. No one saw him go in. No one saw him as he shut the door softly behind him, relocked it, and moved noiselessly up the cramped stairs.

Even the best of criminals could leave behind clues. It was a lesson Zane had learned early on in his years. A man too confident, too greedy, or simply too lazy was a man who made mistakes.

Mistakes could lead to Newgate, or a hangman's noose. Mistakes could lead to a name.

The top level of the hotel was demolished. It was open air and sunlight, and warm blackened beams that crumbled beneath his touch. He didn't trust the charred floor of what used to be the hallway; the wood was thin and splintered. By balancing his weight he was able to make his way nearly to where his room used to be, where he saw something odd. Something long and round, black and yet gleaming.

It was a bottle, the only thing glaringly out of place.

He crept closer. He hung by his hands from the empty doorways, swinging like a monkey from beam to beam. He managed to get just opposite the bottle, but there was a long, toothsome hole gaping in the floor between them.

Zane stretched. He was tall and purposefully limber; he leaned out as far as he could and with the tip of his finger managed to hook the bottle into a roll, catching it just as it was tumbling to the level below.

He swung back upright. He lifted the bottle to the light.

There had been a label once, but it had burned away. He didn't need to read it, though. Zane recognized the bottle's shape, the particular red cinnamon shade of the glass beneath the soot, the tapered neck and stoppered mouth. It had once held a very fine Spanish sherry.

His sherry.

Which had been secure in his trunk, locked in his room.

Zane glanced around him. The trunk was gone, the door and bed and curtains were gone. The only other recognizable thing left from his room was the graceful bow of the window, the sash still set where he had fixed it last night, trying to rid the dust from the air.

Everything else was charcoal.

Anyone sleeping too soundly this morning, he considered, would have been too.

Lia, he thought, and turned to make his way back to her.

⚜

He had, of course, saved the valise because it had all the money in it. Lia should not have been surprised by that; she

103

had no reason to feel annoyed or disappointed—but she did feel those things, all of them, even as the thief's brows arched and he murmured, "Yes, you're most welcome. Shall we discover a place to purchase some new clothing?"

But there were no dressmakers to be found, not even in the controlled chaos of the city square. By the time he had returned to the tavern, she'd washed the blood from her hands and knees and twisted back her hair into a loose, falling knot. But she was forced to walk the sidewalks of Jászberény with both hands lifting the skirts of her gown; without her hoops, the yards of extra fabric dragged like a wedding train over the ground.

They paused together near the hotel entrance, watching people sleepwalk in and out, as if the fire had hollowed their will as well as the building.

She knew this is where Zane had gone. He'd come back to her with soot on his breeches and hands.

Lia tipped her head to see where their rooms used to be, now simply windows framing sky.

The day was brightening into cerulean. There was no hint of clouds; even the last, thin smoke from the embers vanished swiftly into swirls.

And there was no other *drákon*. Not the faintest shiver above or below, in any shape or form—nothing at all since that instant in the cold violet dawn. Perhaps she'd imagined it. She was tired, she was frayed. Perhaps it had been simply her nerves....

Except for the glimpse of those eyes. She would not have imagined that.

"Did you dream of this?" Zane asked, surveying the ruins beside her.

"No," she admitted.

"What was in your trunks?"

"Clothing. Cosmetics. My scarlet silk," she realized, suddenly mournful.

"Any weapons?"

She turned her head to regard him. He met her look through lashes dark as the soot, then shrugged.

"Well, *I've* lost my best dirk. It will be easier to replace a few frocks than that."

It wasn't. The city square held banks and grocers and even a tobacco shop, but to find a seamstress they had to pull their coachman away from a dicing game in the stables. If the ostlers had been part of the turmoil of the morning, they had settled back into prosaic routine now. There was a group of about ten of them squatting in a circle in the dirt, quarreling over a pile of sticks, when Zane approached.

Lia lingered by the eaves of the entrance, as far from the animals as she could manage. She watched as Zane spoke with his hands to the gypsy, who listened and chewed on a hay straw and finally nodded.

"Zot," said the man, and left to harness the horses.

The dressmaker's shop fronted one of the smaller, crooked streets that made up the mass of the town, half up a hill that climbed and climbed. Lia followed Zane inside gingerly; the street was shadowed and the shop ill-lit. All she could see of it was rolls of cloth stacked against the window and a single branch of candles burning in the back.

It was unlike any place she'd seen. Not only were there bolts of bright cotton and woolens, there were strands of dried red peppers hanging from the walls, and scrolled looking glasses, and flower-glazed crockery dotting nearly every shelf. Broomsticks tied with bows rested in all four corners, and a single gown lay haphazard upon a counter, its lemon-yellow skirts embroidered with songbirds and ivy, draping down to the floor.

Beside the dress was a bowl of loose stones. She moved toward it through the gloom, following the faint, small music that tingled down her spine. The shop faded, the scent of peppers and smoke and spice faded; she dipped her fingers into their hard sparkling midst, stirring up psalms and canticles with just her touch.

Pleasure—instant, zinging. She closed her eyes. In the shadows of her mind *Draumr* picked up the melody, turned it sweeter and richer and bolder through her blood, made it a summons she couldn't much longer refuse. . . .

Distantly she heard Zane speaking, a woman responding . . . and a slighter sound right before her. Breathing. Lia glanced up. A shopgirl with china-blue eyes was staring at her from behind the counter, a cushion of pins and thread clutched in both hands.

Lia lifted her fingers from the bowl and smiled. The child smiled back, then glanced quickly at the *couturière* standing with Zane.

"This is your wife?" the woman was saying, in heavily accented French. "But of course—how sad, the hotel. Yes, we have heard. Come, Madame. Please come! Here we will find you something beautiful."

And so she was draped with the woolens, colors she would never normally choose simply because they did not exist back in pale, pastel-washed England: the fiery reddish-orange of poppies, wild peacock blues, buttercup, emerald. In her too-big gown, Lia held swatches and examined weaves and pretended not to hear the soft, steady chanting of the stones in the bowl.

"No," said Zane, from where he lounged by the counter. "We won't tarry here. We need something already completed."

The seamstress protested very loudly, but Zane was firm: they were leaving today. Whatever the woman had on hand would have to do.

"Impossible," announced the *couturière* in her tortured French. "What I have, she is commissioned."

"Of course." He sighed. "How very regrettable."

The thief bent his head and examined his left hand. He closed his fingers, opened them, and like magic a row of gold coins appeared, gleaming against his palm. The girl in the corner openly gasped.

Lia ended up with the lemon gown and three others—red, green, blue, as bright and primitive as the sunrise—as well as heavy stockings and stays and silk ribbons that ran like river water through her fingers.

"From Paris," said the woman, and showed a gap-toothed grin.

Lia left Zane to haggle over the payment, inching once more toward the bowl of jumbled stones.

"Do you like them?" The *couturière* was beaming with pleasure; no doubt she'd made a handsome profit on her country gowns. "A young lady so lovely, of course you do." The woman gave her a wink and picked up a pale, glinting shard, placing it carefully in Lia's hand.

"Diamond! Very rare." She addressed Zane from over her shoulder. "For your bride, good sir, I'll make you a fine price."

The thief pushed off the counter. He filled the shop in the way a lazing lion would fill a formal drawing room: his surcoat and breeches and shirt were drab amid the frolicking colors; he'd lost the leather tie to his hair, so it draped his shoulders in an uncivilized mane. He moved with something darker than poise, something that suggested nighttime, and silence, and feral-eyed vigilance.

His hand lifted. He drew his center finger slowly down the inside of Lia's wrist to the center of her palm, to the stone she held, a shocking soft touch that sent tremors through her arm.

"Does it please you, beloved?" he asked, smiling, and she knew all he really meant was, *Is it worth it?*

She wondered how much gold, exactly, he had brought with him in his valise; she herself had lost her bank vouchers with her trunks. But she returned the pale shard to the bowl, resisting the urge to rub her wrist upon her skirts. Instead, she picked out a different stone.

"This one pleases me."

It was a chunk of dull yellow, chipped and glassy. Even the seamstress lifted a brow.

"Madame does not want the diamond?"

"No, I think not. We'll take this."

It was presented to her wrapped in tissue, along with a series of boxes for the gowns and undergarments, the seamstress clucking under her breath all the while. Zane carried the lot of it back to their carriage. He waited until they were both inside before flicking open the tissue to examine the yellow stone.

"What was amiss with the diamond? I could have bargained her down to a song."

"Well good it would have done you. The thing was paste."

"Ah." His lips curved. He tipped the stone to his palm. "And what, if I may ask, is this?"

"It is a sapphire," Lia said. She took it from him and blew on it, then held it up to the window, to the flare of the sun that spilled through the glass. She glanced back at Zane.

"Yes?"

"Never mind."

With the light streaming into it, the chunk of sapphire took on the exact wolf tint of his eyes.

The carriage bumped and rolled. They plunged into shadow again.

"Lia," he said, abrupt. "What will happen to you when we

get back to Darkfrith? What will the council do to you for running away?"

"Nothing," she lied. "Or perhaps a very small something. Confinement for a month. Blindfolds, bread and water—I'm jesting. I'm the daughter of the Alpha. Once I explain why I did it, everyone will understand."

His brows lowered into a frown, his gaze brooding. She couldn't tell if he believed her or not.

"Thank you," she said, to distract him. "Thank you for—well, for everything."

It worked. He shrugged and turned to look out the window, following the buildings they passed. Lia curled her fingers around the sapphire, content to watch his face in the dark and shifting light.

CHAPTER EIGHT

Once there was a princess.

She was very fair indeed, no doubt the fairest princess of any princess who had ever been or ever would be. For she was not merely a princess but an actual dragon in disguise, and that meant she was beyond beauty: she had eyes that glowed and skin like a moonlit rainbow. When she spoke, the rivers paused to listen, and when she moved, the ground yielded beneath her feet in reverence to her greater glory.

She heard the minerals that sang beneath the mountains, pockets of diamonds, heavy veins of gold. She could vanish into wisps and bound across the sky with wings and scales and frightening beauty, because in her delicacy she represented the very finest of her kind.

It is well known that the *drákon* are the most lovely of all creatures. Their bodies are sinuous and slick; their eyes blaze and their claws are crystal daggers. They glint green and blue and red and gold, all the colors of all the jewels. And since this medieval princess was considered the best of even these beings—her walk, her face, the grace of her hips and legs and her slender, clever fingers—she was prized above all things.

Dragon-men from the four corners of the sky came to woo her. Human men laid flowers where she walked, and spoke of the music of her voice, or the color of her hair, or how her eyes would pierce their souls with a single, indifferent glance, draining their hopes and dreams.

It was not her fault she was like this. It was only who she was born to be: the precise, absolute pinnacle of her kind. She was a treasure, guarded in a mighty castle perched high in the Carpathian peaks, betrothed to a dragon-prince. Her life was a glimmer of gemstones and alchemy. Her future was writ in stone. She would marry and breed and bear superb children, and the *drákon* would reign for a thousand, thousand years above the earth.

If only that peasant boy hadn't shown up. If only he hadn't dared to seize what was not his own.

So:

Once there was a princess.

And once there was a lowly serf.

Their futures were about to clash. Destiny would shudder. Silver stars would fall. But nothing was going to stop that boy from stealing what he desired.

He was a real bastard, if you think about it.

CHAPTER NINE

For the next three days, the weather held. Zane was glad of it—far more than glad. The sky burned blue and the wind blew mild, so he was able to remain outside the carriage. Away from Lia.

If the Roma thought it odd that his English passenger did not wish to travel in secluded luxury beside his wife, he kept his own counsel. For three days Zane sat with the coachman, letting the sun sink into his bones, watching sunflower fields and meadows and darksome forests clip by.

And for three nights, they'd found refuge in inns, happily off-season inns. Every one of them had two rooms to spare.

The meadows slowly folded up into hills. Every evening he

would sit with Lia and discuss the next day's route; he could hardly ask her much else, not in the cramped, public rooms they found. She was usually quiet, which he supposed was natural to her. Of all Rue's children, he remembered that Amalia was the still one, always lingering alone behind her siblings when he saw her . . . laughing with them when roused, teasing with them when prodded, but somehow distant. Apart.

Brown-eyed, golden-haired; a skinny little daisy amid all the pretty gardens of dragon-children. Aye, he remembered her reticence.

But it left him to fill in the conversation, something Zane had never learned to enjoy. Before Rue had stepped into his life and steeled his manners into something approaching civilized, he'd used conversation the same way he'd used his picks—for skill, for information, and that was it. Social chatter was for nobs who didn't have to work. And Zane, one way or another, was always working.

So suppers in the countryside became the two of them dining in silence, with peasants in homespun offering stews and fried pork and steaming boiled cabbage, and Zane covertly following the play of firelight over Lia's face. Or the way her lips moved. Or how her coiffure never seemed completely tamed, but somehow always perfect, with wayward strands that curled against her neck and shoulders just like from a portrait painting, no matter how tightly she pinned the rest.

Country inns were drafty places. Someone would open a door, someone would unhinge a window, and the strands would lift and he'd find himself adrift in her scent, in cool winter roses, a fragrance subtle enough to raise the hairs on the back of his arms and sweet enough to drown out the stink of the cabbage.

She no longer wore hair powder. She hadn't even bought

any back in Jászberény with the rest of her toiletries; he almost wished he didn't know why.

But he did.

In a way the past three days had been a comfortable dream, because even though the sun shone warm and the pastures were picturesque, and no one followed them—another reason to ride above—deep in his gut Zane knew it couldn't last. Dame Fortune was never so accommodating as that.

He was a mongrel masquerading as a gentleman. Lia was a myth masquerading as a lady. Impossible as it seemed, he'd bet his arse someone knew where—or what—one or both of them truly were. And what they were doing here.

As they set out that fourth morning, winding deeper and deeper into the rising green hills that led into Transylvania, with the clouds behind them spreading thin and sparkling, Zane couldn't shake the feeling that this day—this cold, crystalline day—was going to be the end of their fair streak of luck.

Damned if he wasn't right.

❧

She was sick of riding inside the carriage. She was sick of the carriage itself. She was sick of the constant swaying, and of the horses curling their lips in fear when they saw her, and of the coachman smirking at her, and of Zane avoiding her eyes all the time, and of the bloody, *bloody* diamond singing to her across the heavens in a symphony that was *not* getting any softer the nearer they got.

Lia pressed her fingers to her temples and sighed. She wasn't sleeping again. Like the call of *Draumr*, the dreams were getting stronger. Sounds. Scents. His lips, his hands, stroking her body every night, kisses and whispers and she'd wake in a panic, thinking it was real. That it was already real.

But she still slept alone. How much longer, she couldn't

say. The future was looming, and she had yet to figure a way to avoid it.

She was going to be his lover. It might as well have been scrawled across the stars. In all the dreams, in all their outcomes, that part was always the same. And once that happened, Amalia knew the final threads of her safe, guarded existence would forever unravel.

The *drákon* mated for life. She could not sleep with him and then just slip away; she could not use her own body so lightly. Perhaps it was that there were so few of them left, but mating—marriage—was taken with great gravity back in the shire. The young children played games mocking love; as they grew older the games turned more sensual, and more serious. By the time marriage vows were exchanged in Darkfrith's lone and white-marbled chapel, all games were done. Husband and wife were sacred to her kind. No one divided them. No one even tried. To do so would be to risk the punishment of the tribe: imprisonment. Even death.

She was born to a world of harsh, shining rules. When she gave her body to Zane, she would be giving him her heart. And so her life.

He would never wed her. She knew from her dreams that wasn't what he desired; his hopes and ambitions ran far darker than that.

He craved power and luxury. He craved possession, not love. In the blind future she would bring him riches and pleasures he'd not yet imagined. She would steal and lie and twist fates for him. And for a mortal man who could not truly open his heart, it would be enough.

For a creature who had long ago lost hers to him, it would be an abomination.

She was trapped. She was stuck between worlds, too much a beast to become fully his, too much his to become fully *drákon*.

In Darkfrith she'd avoided the places she knew her peers went for stolen moments. She'd removed herself as far as possible from the hidden pockets of woods, and the old granary, the swimming stream, and the secret cave by Blackstone Fell that wasn't secret at all—not to young couples. Even her brothers and sisters thought her painfully chaste.

She wasn't. God knew she wasn't.

Lia sighed again and leaned forward to drop her head in her hands. Nineteen years old, a virgin who'd never even known an actual kiss—yet she knew all about making love. She knew a human man's taste, and his body heavy over hers, and the wild pleasure of him inside her, every night. She did whatever he asked of her, everything he asked. She did things she'd never known a man and woman could do together.

Touch me here. Like this.

Take me in your mouth.

Lie back.

Put your arms above your head.

Do you feel this, Lia? Tell me. Tell me how I make you feel.

Tell me what you want me to do to you.

No wonder she couldn't sleep.

And she was so *tired*, and so *cold*. . . .

She was cold. She sat up to push back the curtains of the window and saw that the clouds of this morning had caught up with a vengeance; the sky had bruised into heavy purple, swallowing the sun. They were winding through what appeared to be rows and rows of gaunt, woody grapevines, starkly beautiful, almost endless. At the blur of the horizon were blue-veined mountains with their peaks veiled in storm.

She drew the sheepskin around her knees a little higher. It was going to snow.

Even as she thought it, the first of the flakes tapped the window, holding its shape just a heartbeat before sliding away. The next three did the same, and the fourth stuck. In less than a minute the window was edged with white.

She kept her hands tucked under the folds of her new worsted cloak and watched the grapevines gradually vanish under powder. In all the distance there was nothing that indicated a town or a village, not even a farmhouse for all those grapes. The light was dwindling and the carriage bumped on.

The sound of hooves against packed dirt was a steady, even staccato...it was a rhythm she knew now down to her bones, in her sleep, thump-*thump,* thump-*thump,* like a lullaby...when she closed her eyes she could see it too, gray hooves, brown dirt...the outline of horseshoes and mud printing through the clean new snow....

And the grapevines were sleeping through the cold, and the wild geese had their heads bent under their wings, and the mice in the great house were silent against the baseboards, listening to the wind, eyes open, whiskers twitching....

She knew that house. She knew, suddenly, where they were.

Lia came awake just as the driver's slot above her snapped open, sending a wash of cold air over her face. Zane's fingers entwined with the metal grille.

"Amalia. There's what looks like an empty mill up ahead. We're going to have to take shelter there."

"No." She climbed over the seat to kneel just below him. "Keep on this road. There's a villa farther along. They'll take us in."

His fingers vanished; he bent down to see her face.

"A villa?"

"Yes. It's not far."

His tricorne tilted low over his eyes. Snow dusted his collar and shoulders.

"Are you certain?"

"Yes."

"Forgive me. Might I inquire *how* you are certain?"

"I—" she began . . . but it wasn't a dream, not really; it felt more like a spell. Like what happened *in* the dreams, when she saw things that should be impossible to see.

"It's ruddy cold up here, my lady. I don't fancy us being mired in a blizzard."

"Zane," she said, leaning up to him. "It *will* be there. Just another minute."

He observed her a moment longer from under the brim of his hat. She heard the coachman make an inquiring noise. The horses began to slow.

"No," he said, turning back to the driver. "We're going on."

She kept the curtains open, so that when they rounded the next curving turn she could see the lights shining through the snowfall and just make out the fuzzy, leaden shape of buildings, low-slung against the grapevine hills.

⚜

"The Grand Tour! *Most* romantic! My dear." István Hunyadi turned to his wife at his side. "Do you remember our journey to Vienna, all those years past? The boulevards! The food!"

"The dancing," said that lady, with a tip of her silver-wigged head.

"Yes, yes. You were graceful as a dove."

Hunyadi was a humble winemaker, or so he claimed. Zane doubted very much that was all the man did. Lia had been correct: this lonesome, twinkling place in the hills was nothing less than a villa.

They had been greeted at the gate by heavyset men bundled in scarves. The men spoke no French at all, so the gypsy had been the one to explain their situation, his voice rising when the gatekeepers had not seemed inclined to grant passage. The snow was falling thick and fast by then, and Zane was already calculating how long it would take them to slog back to that derelict mill, when one of the men held up a hand and barked an order to let them through.

The man had been looking at the carriage door, at the window. Zane had no doubt that Amalia was there looking back at him.

If his fingers hadn't been numb and his nose a block of ice, Zane would have had them turn about anyway. But the gypsy clucked at the horses, and they eased inside.

At the entrance to the main house, more men rushed to greet them—footmen, Zane had supposed—but once he'd gotten a better look at them, he realized they weren't. They wore no livery, done up instead in furs and plain wools in earthen colors, their hair shaggy and unkempt down their backs. He'd taken Lia's arm and kept her close as they ducked through the snow into the atrium, a wide, stone-lined mouth that seemed to swallow them whole with the closing of the doors.

The villa was made up mostly of limestone. The rugs beneath their feet were Persian. The paintings on the walls were oils. There was a series of pressed-glass lamps swaying gently from the ceiling; they were colored violet and burgundy and gave off a pirate's glow.

Zane put his lips to Lia's ear. "Do you know who lives here?"

She shook her head. But by then it was more than apparent who lived there, for he was coming down the hallway toward them, a short, wide man wreathed in smiles.

"God's grace, to be out with your lady in such a storm! Come in, come in! You are welcome here!"

Hunyadi was dressed in velvet, and he spoke fluent French. He bowed like a courtier and laughed like a bawd.

Zane was inclined to like him, if for no other reason than the man wore an immense gold chain around his neck studded with rubies the size of quails' eggs.

That, and he didn't serve cabbage at his table.

They had interrupted a pastoral *partie de plaisir,* it seemed. There were a dozen other guests present, every one of them done up in wigs and jewels, and painted faces with lips that curved politely at Lia and Zane's damp, bedraggled state. But as their host had welcomed them, the guests could do no less. Two extra places were set at the table, soup served, wine poured. Zane sat back in the soft candlelight and began his careful ravel of lies and truth of how they had come to the kind Monsieur Hunyadi's door.

Lia seemed to hear none of it. She sat clutching her wine-glass, gazing off into the shadows. She wore the best gown the *couturière* had to offer, a rich, deep green affair with black lace and ribbons that paled her skin to alabaster. Even with her cheeks scrubbed and her hair pulled back, she outshone every other woman in the room. They knew it too, these blue-blooded Hungarians. Under thinly arched brows the women exchanged whispers and glances and lifted their noses as they eyed her up and down.

For a moment—just a moment, a brief tick of time while the soup bowls were cleared—Zane allowed his gaze to linger on a necklace of cobwebbed gold and colored gemstones. He imagined how easy it would be to be a ghost in the hall. To wait until the wine was done, and the banter finished, and everyone was conveniently asleep in their silent, scattered rooms. There had to be enough trinkets in this villa to keep him in satin and Spanish oranges for years. No wonder István Hunyadi kept so many guards.

The necklace would be magnificent on Lia.

When he glanced at her again, she was watching him, her glass paused halfway to her lips. She looked slightly alarmed.

He tipped his head and smiled back at her, mocking.

"Do you enjoy the wine?" Hunyadi asked Lia, oblivious. "Please, I beg to know. There are few things more agreeable than the opinion of a beautiful lady."

"It is lovely," Lia said.

"Yes? Not too dry for your taste?"

"Not at all."

Hunyadi rubbed his hands together, his eyes gleaming. "We use a different process here than the Germans, you know. The fermentation alone—"

"Tell me, Lord Lalonde," said Hunyadi's wife, "what brings you to our land? You have said you are on the Tour, but I confess we do not see many English so deep into the countryside."

"No," said Zane, giving her an attentive look. "And you might not have seen us, by heavens, had we not had the good fortune to stumble across your generosity. My beloved bride, you see," he smiled once more at Lia, "has a very great fondness for wine and winemaking. Her family maintains a substantial vineyard outside Arcis-sur-Aubé. Good, hearty country stock, God bless her, but their Blanc de Blancs is entirely exquisite. She insisted we venture deeper into your land than first we planned. She's heard splendid things about your Riesling."

"Truly?" Hunyadi shifted in his chair, the rubies on his chain gathering the light. "We've had a very nice season, my lady. You will be interested to know the harvest was late and the juices concentrated—"

"But you, Lord Lalonde," purred the wife, taking a deep breath, "what is it *you* enjoy?"

"Ah," replied Zane, still smiling. "I enjoy diamonds."

Everyone turned to see him.

"All precious stones, really, but especially diamonds," he continued, gazing straight into the wife's avid eyes. "It's something of a passion with me, shall we say."

"Do you collect them?" asked a man down the table.

"Whenever possible."

"Fascinating," said the wife, showing a row of even, yellowed teeth.

"You have done well to come here, then," announced someone new, an elderly gent with white curls down to his shoulders. "The Carpathians are known for the quality of their mines. You'll find no better stones than ours."

"Yes." Zane lifted his glass. "So I've been given to understand."

Another course was served, pheasant and trout, the red wine whisked away and replaced with white. The servants here were dressed to match the dark, no paint, no wigs, just simple frocks and chapped hands. They moved in utter silence; their eyes never lifted from their work.

The wife stabbed her fork into the broiled pheasant set before her. Her fingers glimmered with rings. "A happy business for you indeed, Lord Lalonde. But where do you go from here? The best jewelers are back in Buda, I fear."

"We're down to chasing legends, Madame," answered Zane. "Fool's dreams, but amusing enough. I've pulled us all this way to find a stone named *Draumr*."

From the corner of his eye, he saw Amalia stiffen.

"Perchance you've heard of it?" he asked mildly.

"*Draumr,*" muttered Hunyadi, tugging at his lower lip. "*Draumr, Draumr.* It does sound familiar, I vow. A strange name though, isn't it? Not of our tongue."

"It is a diamond?" inquired the wife.

"Yes."

"A very...large one?"

Zane's smile deepened. "Assuredly so."

"What is the legend that accompanies it, my lord?" asked another woman, tilting forward into the candlelight so her emeralds sparkled with every breath. "Pray, do tell us."

"Alas, dear lady, I don't yet have all the details. But . . . it is a sky-blue diamond of uncommon beauty," he improvised. "So uncommon it haunts the dreams of any who've seen it. In fact, it's said to be so fantastically unique that, if one listens closely enough, the sound of its singing fills the ears, more dulcet than the music of the heavenly spheres. It is . . . ethereal. An opus so haunting it captures souls, grants infants their first tears, gives wings to lovers, and," he finished, inspired, "bankrupts the hearts of honest men."

"Singing," sighed the emerald woman, with another rapturous lift of her bosom.

"A treasure indeed," drawled one of the gentlemen guests.

"I've a mind to set it in a necklace for my bride." Zane leaned back and favored the wife with a look from under his lashes. "'Twould suit her well, I think. Since I've mentioned the notion, she simply won't let it rest."

"*Singing,*" exclaimed Hunyadi, with an air of triumph. "I do remember something now! Certainly I do! Wasn't there such a stone in those wild Magyar tales from the Carpathians? Serfs will believe anything, you know. I am nearly positive they have a saga about something of the sort, a singing diamond."

"Yes," said the elderly man abruptly, straightening with a creak of his corset. "Yes, I recall it too. I heard the story as a boy. I can't quite recall the details . . . but it had something to do with the dragon-people of the far mountains. It had to do with the *drákon.*"

Lia dropped her wineglass. It shattered like a bomb upon the stone floor.

⚜

"You knew," he said, standing with his back to her, gazing out the tall, glazed window of the bedroom chamber they'd been assigned.

"No," she said.

"Don't lie to me."

"If I had known," she said, very composed, "why wouldn't I have told you? Why would I have kept it hidden? It serves no purpose."

Zane did not answer. His shoulders were stiff beneath his new indigo waistcoat; she could not tell how angry he was. If he was.

He had seemed more surprised than anything else. He'd masked it well, had finished the meal with the suave, clever polish of a master of deception. A part of her had even admired his pretense, how he'd continued to flirt with the unbearable wife of their host. How he'd tried every dish, and complimented every drink, and meticulously fished out the last of the details of the *drákon* that he could from these sotted, smug aristocrats.

Diamonds, warfare, lost souls. The rough fable of her people, presented like a medieval parable with no bearing on actual fact. She could hardly comprehend it herself.

The dragon-people, yes. It's a very old myth. I recollect they're known for a few things, gemstones primarily. And like most wicked creatures, they wreak havoc among the peasants— stealing away the fairest virgins, poaching deer, switching babes in their cradles for mischief, that sort of thing. They hunt by night but look just like you and me during the day—just like your fetching young bride, my lord!—but they're said to have eyes that phosphoresce and smiles to freeze your very blood....

It had frozen *her* blood. It had kept her a lump in her needlepoint seat beside the laughing Hunyadi, unable to speak, unable to eat . . . because with every word she remembered the frisson of the dragon that morning in Jászberény, and the smell of alcohol that had ruptured into flame.

Zane turned his head and fixed her with a pale yellow look; the glass behind him reflected the fire in the hearth and her own shape perched upon the bed, her face and gown smeared into shadows. The bed itself was wide and plush, covered in mink. She'd retreated to it because it was the farthest distance she could put between them, and still she felt his heat. Still she felt the pleasure of his voice.

It was a small room, extravagantly furnished with burled wood and pillows and more of those dangling, colored lamps. They cast blue and turquoise along the length of his body, as if he stood at the brink of a dark, deep sea.

"How long have you known?"

"Precisely as long as you have," she retorted. "Approximately two and one-half hours. So sorry, it seems my timepiece was recently incinerated. I suppose it might be a tad longer."

"Amalia."

"I didn't know! I had no idea. You know my people as well as I. You know what they say in Darkfrith—we are the last. We are the only. I assure you that if anyone there had *any* idea there were others like us alive in the world, someone would have done something about it."

"Yes," he agreed, with a faint lift of his mouth. "I do believe that. But what, my lady, are you not telling me?"

"Why—nothing."

"Did you realize," he said conversationally, "that when you lie, the most charming spots of pink appear high on your cheekbones? It's really quite convenient. Oh . . . not for you, I suppose."

"I did not know of this. I swear to you, I did not."

"Very well." He crossed to her through the strange shifting light, took a seat close beside her on the bed before she could protest. The mattress tilted her toward him; she leaned hard away to keep her balance. "Why don't you tell me what you did know? What, snapdragon, you *do* know. I prefer not be led around like bear bait. It's really most undignified."

She dropped her eyes. The shadows changed; she felt his fingertips graze her cheek and suddenly couldn't breathe.

"Lia."

"You said you didn't want all my secrets."

"You'll discover that lying is just one of my many nefarious skills. We have that much in common. Lia," he said again, amusement threading his tone, "good heavens, must I torture you for an answer? It's a simple question, my lady: what do you know?"

"Every night," she said finally, very slow, "I dream. In my dreams...things happen. Random things. Things that come true."

His head tilted. "Is that a common Gift among the *drákon*?"

"No." Her lips pursed. "Apparently none of my Gifts are very common."

"Naturally not. What do you dream of this diamond?"

"That you will find it—that we find it."

"And?"

"That's all. We find it. You give it to my mother. You're rich."

His finger tapped her cheek. "That's the end of it?"

She pulled away from him, unable to bear his casual touch. "That morning in Jászberény, standing on the street after the fire...I thought I felt the presence of another *drákon*. Watching us. Watching me. I didn't tell you because I thought it wasn't real, that I was merely fatigued. I thought I was imagining it."

He sat back. "But you weren't."

"No."

"Dear me."

"Yes."

He was silent for a long while. Firelight licked up his

stockings in whispers and crackles and threw hot gold off the silver buckles of his shoes. In time, he heaved a sigh.

"This rather changes things, my heart. The stakes have been raised. If it is your delightful kinfolk who wish you harm, you've become quite a liability."

"Why would they wish me harm?"

"I've really no idea. All I know is it's bloody hard to fight smoke. Believe me, I've tried. Sixty thousand pounds won't do me a damned bit of good from the cold, dark beyond."

"I don't want you to fight them!"

"But then who will protect you," he asked smoothly, "the next time around? Who else knows their secrets as I do? Who else here knows that they must be able to see to Turn? Who else here knows the usefulness of hoods and blindfolds and a solid bullet to the gut? Who else knows how to steal through shadows, and capture singing diamonds, and share riddles with all the other animals? Who else is a mere human, a mortal man, with knives and pistols and blood on his hands, and the knowledge of how to defeat a mighty dragon in flight?"

She stared back at him, mute.

"Perhaps they wish to kill *you*," she said.

"Perhaps," he agreed, nonchalant. "But I really rather doubt it. You make a nice, shining target—a pretty maid, a dragon-maid, encroaching on their land and their traditions. Oh, yes, I also know how your kind admire their traditions. I'd wager you're shattering all *sorts* of worthy rules right now. It's not even England, it's middle Europe. We haven't seen a real water closet in days. I can't imagine the laws of the *drákon* out here are much more enlightened than your own."

"Do you want me to go?" she asked, very still.

"Not especially. But if you mean to stay, I'm afraid there would be a price. I don't work for free, love. Everyone knows that."

He smiled at her, a dangerous smile, a thief's smile, warmed by firelight and the dark timbre of his voice.

Her own voice came very thin. "What is the price?"

"Only this," he said, and leaned across the bed to cover her mouth with his.

CHAPTER TEN

It wasn't like her dreams. It was softer, and warmer, and tasted of the Madeira they'd finished with the end of supper, and of him. She kept her eyes open, because for the first time—this very first time—she wanted to see him. She wanted to see his face.

He'd gotten a faint sunburn from his days outside that crinkled color along the edges of his eyes; his hair had blown long and wild in a handsome streaked ruff down his shoulders. She knew his face, she knew his expressions, she knew the slow heat of his look whenever he turned his head and caught her studying him. She knew the squared cut of his jaw, and the shadow of his beard before he shaved, the pure lines of his nose and chin and those sensual lips.

But she did not know him like this: his brows a dark serious slash, every lash satin. His skin a golden gleam with the light, his queue a fall of shifting colors. He kissed her slowly, so slowly, as though he wanted to taste her as she was tasting him, as though they weren't seated together on the bed with only inches between them, and every man and woman in the villa believing they were wed.

His hand came up. She felt the brush of his palm sliding from her temple to her eyelids, blocking out the light.

"Close your eyes," he murmured. "Lia-heart. Close your eyes."

A thousand dreams, a thousand hushed commands. She did as he said, and his hand moved to cradle her cheek, her neck, his thumb stroking the line of her jaw as his lips stroked back and forth, making delicious friction. She felt the unhurried, familiar heat begin to pulse through her body. She felt her heart racing and the animal in her, the dragon, stretching and singing *I want* through her blood. When his tongue found hers, she dug her fingers into the mink. When he brought up his other hand to push his fingers through her hair, she took a gasping breath against his mouth, all she could inhale, and he stole it back from her with a low, masculine sound in his throat.

That was her hand touching his shoulder. Those were her fingertips discovering the angles of his cheekbones, the heavy rope of his hair, a plait that she held and used to bring him closer, because she could, because she knew he wanted her to.

He took her by the shoulders and pushed her back against the bed, his mouth never lifting from hers. With his forearms braced by her head he had her trapped, half of her at least, his chest to hers, pushing her into the glossy furs. His head tipped; she felt his teeth against her ear. He took her earlobe into his mouth, his tongue tugging, releasing. He traced his hands down her sleeves, her wrists, their fingers entwining, and raised them slowly into the tangle of her hair.

Put your arms above your head.

Lia turned her cheek to the bed, trying not to pant. "It ... hasn't been ten years yet."

She felt him pause, smiling into her neck. His heart beat a fierce tattoo against hers. "You remember that, do you?"

"Vividly."

"Hmm." With slow intention his teeth pressed into her skin, harder than before, a brief, stinging pain before he stopped; he let loose one of her hands to slide his arm under her waist. "Are you sure I said ten?"

"Yes ..."

"How rash of me." He shifted, using his arm to lift her closer. Even through her stomacher and stays he burned her, all heat and muscle. "I meant, of course, six."

"Five," she corrected him, as he trailed kisses along the crest of her collarbone, down to the starched lace ruffle of her bodice.

"Five," he agreed unevenly, rubbing his cheek against the rise of her breasts, turning his face so that she felt his lips, his eyelashes, respiration—sensations that lit through her like a torch touched to tinder. "Five long, very long years ... God, Lia ..."

When he found her mouth again they were both panting. Willfully she kept her eyes open, saw the wolf-hunger the fire illumed across his face, saw the ceiling, and the shadows, and the blue-green cast of the lanterns that danced along the blackened oak beams. The desire inside her was a beast of its own, throbbing just under her skin, poised to devour her.

"Is this enough for your price?" Lia asked, turning her head aside once more. "Have I—" She was forced to take a quick breath. "Have I met it yet?"

His head lifted. He gazed down at her without speaking.

"Do you require a whore?" she said deliberately, when he didn't move at all.

He didn't get angry; he didn't act offended or draw back. Instead, slowly, awfully, the corners of his lips turned up.

"Perhaps I do. Are you offering yourself for the position?"

"I wasn't in jest."

"Neither was I." Zane took her left hand and drew it down his body, pressing her palm over his breeches, the length of his arousal, holding her there when she tried to yank away. Above his cold smile, his eyes glittered hard and bright. "A man in my condition doesn't find this sort of delay very amusing. But—if it's what your ladyship wishes..."

He released her hand. She lay still, watching him. He rolled from her in one lithe motion, ending up seated back upon the edge of the mattress. His shoulders lifted; he took a slow breath and did not look at her again.

"Let us negotiate."

"Negotiate?" She sat up, wary. None of the dreams had included this.

"Aye. I assume you know the meaning of the word. You desire something. I desire something. Perhaps together we may come to an amiable...conclusion."

He began to unbutton his waistcoat. She slipped off the bed and walked to the hearth. It didn't seem wise to remain there beside him.

Yet from across the room she still smelled his skin, the wind-clean fragrance of his hair. Her skirts were still wrinkled from his weight.

"I don't suppose it would help to appeal to your sense of duty to my family, to ask that you stay with me out of respect for your agreement with them."

"No, it wouldn't."

"Or out of honor. As a gentleman."

He gave a curt laugh. "An interesting notion."

"A gentleman thief."

"You've been reading too many penny novels, my heart. There is no such creature."

"Then what is it you want?"

He was quiet for a very long while, so long her eyes began to smart from staring down into the flames.

"One night," he said at last, very soft. "One night with you. That's all."

She would have given him every night. She would have given him the stars, and the milky moon, and all the diamonds of the earth. Even if it had meant they lived as outcasts; even if it meant her own doom. Lia closed her eyes.

"Would you do that?" he asked.

Yes, the dragon in her heart whispered. *Yes, yes.* Her lips felt bruised, her body felt bruised. There was an aching inside her, a burning demand for him and what she knew he could do for her.

One night. It would never be enough.

"Yes," she said, and when he didn't respond she angled slightly to see him from over her shoulder.

His face held an odd look, an arrested expression, as if he'd just considered something deeply surprising. Then he scowled.

"I almost think you mean it."

"I do mean it." She turned to him fully. Her fingers worked at the ties to her stomacher.

"Lia."

She ignored him, loosening the tight draw of the ribbons, allowing the stiff green bodice to ease open. He waited until she'd unlaced the final tie, pulling the piece apart and letting it slip with its short, narrow sleeves down her arms, exposing her corset and chemise, the fine, translucent silk. Then he stood, crossing to her.

"Don't."

"All right." Her arms fell to her sides. She looked straight up at him, a clear, concentrated look, and felt something within her gather into storm.

Yes, whispered the dragon again.

Without even willing it she Turned, all of her, all at once, into smoke.

It was shocking. The buoyancy of that day in Edinburgh, the light, floating happiness swept her entire being. She was nothing; she was a cloud, a mirage, no body or heavy dark thoughts. There was none of the pain she'd heard accompanied the first time; there was only the feral, ferocious bliss of giving up her body for air.

She swept up and touched the ceiling, learned the pattern of the beams of wood, the cold stiffness of the white plaster and cream ornament. The air was heated and thick and held her aloft like a cushion. She stretched thin as paper through the lamp-colored light, then drew into a mass, churning, aware only dimly of the man below her standing immobile in his shirtsleeves, his face upturned and his hands at his sides.

Zane.

As soon as she thought his name, she felt the heaviness return. Again with no direct purpose, with no conscious resolution, Lia sifted down into shape and form and took breath as a woman standing before him, her hair long and free, her body completely unclothed.

Her empty gown lay on the floor between them.

She lifted her hands to him. He accepted them, his fingers closing over hers.

"That was new," he said.

She smiled in spite of herself, joyful. "I know." She blinked back tears. "I did it. I did."

"You did." His voice sounded different, emotionless;

his clasp was very light. "It was—breathtaking. Congratu-
lations."

She inhaled deeply, feeling her body again, feeling her
lungs. "Did I startle you?"

"Don't be absurd. I'm quite used to seeing half-naked
young ladies melt into smoke." He released her hands.
"Think nothing of it."

"Then what's amiss?"

"Snapdragon." He stooped to retrieve her gown, staring
down at the mess of it, and then shook his head. "Perhaps
you'd care to dress."

"Isn't this what you wanted?" She did not take the gown.
Elation still bubbled through her, the thrill of success. "Here
I am, Zane. Here is your night."

"Yes . . . I'm afraid I've changed my mind."

"You said I was pretty, before."

"Did I?" A new laugh escaped him, mirthless. "How un-
original. I must be the master of understatement. I think
you're goddamned radiant, and you know it. Sometimes I
think if I look at you too long I'll go blind, like a lunatic staring straight into the sun. No," he said in a savage undertone,
and let the gown fall back to the floor. "You're not pretty."

She walked away from him, to the bed. She drew down
the covers and ran her hands along the sheets.

"Stop it," he said.

"One night."

"No."

"It was *your* proposition."

"An instant of insanity. No doubt soon it will pass."

She climbed into the bed. She pushed down between the
sheets and stretched like a tigress, watching him.

"You're too young," he said, blunt. "We're too different. If
anything, dear God, you've just proven that. You—I tend to

lose my balance around you, and that's a dangerous thing. It would be a disaster." He shook his head once more, his mouth hardening. "We have enough to worry about as it is. I'll stay with you, Lia. If there's trouble ahead, I'll do my best to protect you. But that's all. We'll retrieve the diamond and hand it over to your mother. And then our business together is done. You return to your life. I return to mine."

His gaze dropped. Without looking at her, he grabbed a handful of furs from the bed, spread them before the hearth.

"You think I'm radiant?" she whispered.

"Good night, Lady Amalia."

"Good night, thief."

She could not see his reaction. He'd turned his back to her, a darkened figure surrounded by firelight. Lia settled back into the bed; Zane eased flat upon the floor, an arm beneath his head. His breathing was rigidly even.

Minutes passed, hours passed, before he spoke again, barely a sound above the hushed flames.

"One night. I'll take it later."

But perhaps she only dreamed it.

⚜

"Lia."

"Yes, Zane."

"Who is left to come?"

"Joan. Audrey. They'll say they want only to talk, to parley a peace. They'll bring arsenic for your sherry. Joan will distract you while Audrey slips it in."

"That would be your sherry as well," he said, thoughtful.

"I am now expendable."

"Oh, really?" He drew his palms up her bare arms, cupped his hands behind her neck. He kissed her cheek, lightly, gently, as Draumr *warmed into a prickle against her skin.*

"Come outside with me, my heart. The moon tonight is fine

and high, and I believe I fancy a ride on my favorite dragon. We'll meet your sisters in midflight."

For the first time ever, she hesitated.

"Amalia," he said, darkly soft. "I've two pistols primed and the diamond around my neck. No harm will come to you or our child. I promise you that."

"Yes, Zane."

⚜

She was not his to take. He knew that. He'd always known that. He needed no reminders, but it seemed they were all around him anyway:

The rose-cream clarity of her skin, unnatural in its perfection.

The pitch of her voice, low and magical, a blend of dusk and honey.

Her steady grace. The shy glance of her eyes, dark velvet brown beneath heavy lashes.

Her laughter at one of Hunyadi's ridiculous compliments, subtly infectious.

The blade-thin smile of Hunyadi's wife, watching them together.

The wife's jewels.

Gold.

Diamonds.

The smoke rising up from the chimneys, evaporating in threads.

The morning had bloomed brilliantly clear, everything visible strictly blue or white like the glaze on a new Dutch tile. Beyond the windows of the great hall where they took their breakfast, the sky loomed cobalt, frankly blinding against the blanket of unmarked snow.

"But you cannot leave today! Do not be so rash, I beg you!" Hunyadi seemed genuinely distressed at the news of their departure. "The roads will be unmanageable, and I've yet to show Lady Lalonde the tasting room!"

"Yes," said Lia, turning a cat smile to Zane. "And I was *so* looking forward to it. You *do* know how I adore winemaking, my lord."

"Indeed," said one of the other men, staring straight at her, "what a pity it would be to depart so soon."

"Lady Lalonde promised us the harpsichord this afternoon," announced the elderly man.

"And whist this evening," declared another.

In the space of one half a day—less than that—it seemed Amalia had lured every male of the villa into her luminous orbit. She laughed and sparkled and made an ordinary event like breaking their fast into something as heady as sipping ambrosia straight from the gods.

Zane gazed back at her, unamused. He thought of the bed in the chamber that awaited them, and of the furs, and the hard stone floor that had left bruises up and down his spine and a pinch in his neck. And of Lia on the soft mattress, undressed and waiting.

"My dear sir, we are unforgivably rude." Zane gave a nod to Hunyadi. "I cannot excuse our poor manners, except to say that we have trespassed upon your hospitality long enough. You were kind enough to take in such ragged travelers; we cannot intrude another day upon your festivities. We've appointments in Bucharest," he continued, louder, to cover the noises Hunyadi was beginning to make, "and I fear missing them, as several important gentlemen await us."

"But the roads!"

Zane lifted a hand to the windows, to the icicles dripping prisms from the eaves. "I perceive the day is warming."

"Yes," agreed Madame Hunyadi, abrupt. "I think it will be a fine day."

It was merely an adequate day, which was enough. It was

not so chilly that the horses couldn't manage it, which was his only real concern. But it seemed the storm that had tossed them here had left them with a smooth, blank canvas of a map. The gypsy shook his head and muttered to himself underneath his layers of scarves as Lia and Zane made their good-byes and climbed into the carriage.

The villa drive had been shoveled, all the way to the main gate and a few yards beyond. After that it was an ocean of white.

A collection of noblemen and -women had gathered to see them off, painted faces under hoods, powdered wigs and elaborate outfits contrasting garish against the plain simplicity of the cold outdoors.

"Farewell," Lia called, with a gay wave out the open window.

Hands were lifted in return. Zane touched his hat to them, ready to rap on the ceiling for the driver to start, when Hunyadi broke apart from the crowd.

He strode up to the window, squinting against the light.

"Good sir," Zane said, and took his gloved fingers.

"I've been thinking upon it. If you seek that diamond still—if you have the time, and the notion—you might visit the castle of the Zaharen, in the far reaches of the Carpathians, around . . . fifty leagues northeast of here. *Zaharen Yce,* it's called. It's said to be the ancient stronghold of the *drákon.* There is a prince who lives in it now. Perhaps he knows where your singing stone may be found." The man grinned, jolly once more. "Come back when you have it, why don't you, and show it around. I'd give a bottle of my best to see it in a necklace."

Hunyadi stepped back with a bow, still scintillating with his rubies. "God keep you both. *Viszlat.*"

CHAPTER ELEVEN

"Fifty leagues northeast." Lia drummed her fingers nervously against her knees.

"I cannot help but notice," Zane said politely, "we're already headed that direction."

"Yes." She closed her eyes and listened to the music of *Draumr,* trying to gauge how far away it still was, how many roads, how many mountains. But it was like trying to follow the wingbeats of a hummingbird; all she had was the perception of life, of soaring distance, the urgency of its song like a grace note that beat over and over through her skin.

"Does he have it? The prince in the castle?"

She opened her eyes. "I don't know. I hope not."

"As do I." Zane crossed his ankles and his arms, his body

rocking lazily with the sway of the coach. "It really does seem like rather the last place on earth we should venture."

"I agree."

Minutes passed, and they did not speak again. The air kept a brittle bite; she tied the curtains back on the window beside her to let a patch of sun pick out the nap of the sheepskin and the weave of her skirts. It was the first time Zane had spent any amount of time confined in the carriage with her, but even though they had passed beyond sight of the villa, he didn't seem inclined to leave. His legs stretched all the way to the baseboard of her seat, his boots a brown polished sheen that gave off the faint, pleasant aroma of fine leather. His thighs were taut and well muscled beneath the folds of his cloak and his doeskin breeches—the same breeches, she realized, that he had worn last night.

On the bed with her.

Her eyes drifted up to his. He was watching her, impassive.

"Amalia." He held her gaze. "If *Draumr* is there in this castle, or anywhere near there, I'm going in alone. You will wait for me in whatever village or town we find nearby."

"No," she said, startled. "You can't find it without me."

"Your parents thought otherwise."

"You don't know what it looks like. You won't even know if what you see is real, if whatever this prince shows you will be real."

"True. It's a risk I'll take."

"Zane—"

"Listen, love. In a convenient, happy world, *monsieur le prince* fully and faithfully believes the legend of the *drákon* is merely a quaint little fairy tale that was once associated with his home. He's kindhearted and feeble-witted and happens to have our diamond all right and tight in a handy box upon his dresser. I'll show him your father's impressive bank account, he'll sell me the stone, and we're off with no one attempting to *flambé* us ever again. However..."

They looked at each other as the carriage made a creaking turn, and Lia's patch of light slid slowly down to her feet.

The thief sighed. "That's not the way it's going to be."

"How do you know?"

"Because it's never that simple. Because the Marquess and Marchioness of Langford picked me to fetch this stone for a bloody good reason, and it wasn't because of my charming personality. That's when you will become too serious a burden, snapdragon. I can't... I can't do what I said I would do and worry about you at the same time. Not any longer."

"You mean, you can't nick it if I'm there."

"You are something of a distraction," he said.

"I'm also bloody useful," she retorted, leaning forward. "I can Turn now—to smoke, at least. I can go places you can't. I can see things you won't. And I can tell you definitively if the diamond you're prepared to buy *or* steal is the one we actually want."

"That's splendid. I'll be certain to remember it as I'm being eviscerated by one of your kinsmen."

"I don't think—"

"Lia," he interrupted, sterner than before, "must I spell it out for you? *You distract me.* The last thing we need is to plunge into the hornets' nest when I can't tear my eyes off you. I need to be clear-minded if we're going to get through this unscathed. I need to keep sharp. But when you're this damned close to me, all I think about is *you.* I think about your mouth, and I think about your breasts, and I think about your pink tongue and your legs wrapped around me. I think about touching you and you touching me—and then I look at you and you're giving me that *look*—yes, that one, just there, as if you want me to kiss you—please stop—" He exhaled on a hiss, tipping his head back against the wood and pressing two fingers to the bridge of his nose. "If you'd like the brutal truth of it, I think I must be the biggest damned fool in creation to have spent last night on the floor. But I did. And I'll do it again if I must. Because we are not going to push this any further than we have."

"Is that right?" she said quietly.

His hand lowered. "You're not going with me to the castle. Any castle. You're not to draw attention to yourself, you're not to go tripping merrily into peril as you seem so inclined to do, and you're *not* going to distract me from my job. If I had an ounce of sense I'd find new transport at the next village and have the coachman turn 'round to take you home."

The carriage hit a rut; Lia grabbed the strap by her head to keep her balance. "But you won't," she said, as the light shifted blue and clear over his face.

He turned to the window and gave a smile to the glass, caustic.

"No," he muttered. "I won't."

❦

There were no actual towns in the foothills nearby. Lia wouldn't have called what they encountered even a village: a collection of thatched-roof dwellings, two taverns, a church, a smithy, and a store for general goods, all of it encircled by a worn stone wall that ate into the hillside. They were directed to one of the larger of the homes in the settlement; it belonged to the village elder. Or perhaps he was the mayor. Lia's grasp of the local tongue was not as certain as she'd hoped.

She'd had years to study her future. Years to seek out the language, the culture of this place. Yet it had happened that finding tutors for what she knew she'd need was not so easy, even in the sophisticated climes of Edinburgh. She'd persuaded the headmistress of Wallence to hire a Bohemian linguist for just three terms. Lia had been his star pupil.

"He says we may rest the night here," she translated for Zane, who was standing benevolently at her side, a husbandly hand at the small of her back. "He says we are most welcome."

But interestingly, for all his flowery compliments, the white-bearded man did not seem especially pleased to have them in his home. He lingered back near the open hearth, standing in front of the woman Lia assumed was his wife—nearly blocking her from their sight—as he nodded and spoke and lifted a hand that made the sign of the cross repeatedly as he bowed in their direction.

He had looked only once at Lia, that moment he had answered his door to find them standing on his front steps. After that he kept his gaze pinned to the hardwood floor or else uneasily upon Zane.

Lia tried her most melting smile. "Thank you so much. Your generosity will not be forgotten."

At that the man glanced at her—a swift, uneasy lift of his eyes before bowing his head again.

"This way," the man said, and led them to a bedroom. *The* bedroom, she realized, glancing around at the plain iron bed and pine trunks and unadorned porcelain basin that held water rimmed with ice.

"Sir, we cannot," she protested, turning to the elder.

"No, no. It is yours for your stay. Please, gentle one"—she thought that was the word he used, although it might have been *noblewoman*—"you honor us. Accept our humble aid."

He seemed truly horrified by her protest, his skin blanching, his wife behind him making a small, distressed noise. Lia looked at them both, then back up at Zane, who offered a droll smile.

"How perfectly delightful," said her false husband, with only the slightest of glances at the cold barren floor.

And it kept like that for days. Every village appeared nearly identical, with clean, whitewashed homes and onion-domed churches, nestled by lakes or frosty streams, and trees climbing mountains to pierce the heavens. At some point they had left Hungary behind for the fertile woodlands of Transylvania, but to Lia the landscape looked the same. The same sheep flocked the hay fields; the same clouds flocked the blue sky. Only the snow changed, vanishing quickly under the relentlessly bright days, leaving the landscape dotted in colors that melted from gold to green to brown.

Every evening they found refuge in one home or another; there was little traffic for inns in these small, nameless places. The thief made his bed at her feet, wrapped in blankets. Lia would stare up at the ceiling as long as she could, fighting sleep, until the dreams would come anyway and drag her down into their depths.

She did not think either one of them was getting much rest.

He was back to riding atop the carriage too.

Lia would wake every morning to find him already up and gone, usually to see about the horses, or the coachman, or the thickness of the mist or the clouds. It was only then, in the privacy of these small, shuttered rooms, that she attempted to Turn to smoke again. It was certainly as much as she dared— smoke might be excused in a house. A full-grown dragon would not.

She was not entirely successful. That first, wonderful time had been so easy. It might have been the passion of the moment, emotions that had swept her along and let it happen. When she tried it now, she found her focus fractured, nothing easy about it. With a great deal of concentration she was able to transform her hair, her right hand and foot. And that was all.

Still, every morning she tried.

Then she would dress. She would greet their hosts alone, accept their bread and good wishes, and carefully attempt to chip away some of the clenched fear that seemed to grip them. However polite she was, however affable, nothing changed.

She left it to Zane to scatter coins upon a table or counter just before they departed. She'd noted how, unless it was absolutely necessary, none of the people here openly touched what she touched.

She was different. She *felt* different, slower somehow, anxious, as if the mysteries of her body were only waiting behind a locked door and the key dangled just beyond the reach of her fingers. The higher they scaled these mountains, the sharper her blood ran, and all her perceptions with it.

Every day now she felt the flash of the *drákon*. It was never clear, never stable; she couldn't seem to pin it to a single place. Sometimes she wondered if the lack of sleep was playing tricks with her mind, but no—it felt real. Usually around twilight, with the sun drained away and the heavens turned translucent, and the first of the stars opening their eyes. It was the time when *Draumr* sang her strongest, a drag of sweet, melancholy beauty that sank heavy through her bones. If they weren't already ensconced in some villager's quarters, she would make a point to have the carriage pull over, to walk the road a moment and breathe in the music along with the thin air until her lungs ached.

That would be when it would happen. The electric warning down her neck, the animal in her waking, searching. If there were clouds she saw nothing else in them; if there was smoke it never openly appeared.

The thief had purchased a hunting knife for her at the last major settlement they had passed, a keenly impressive blade with a slim, leather-wrapped handle that just fit her palm. After much silent debate, she kept it strapped to her garter on her right leg, an ever-chilly discomfort that still made her feel better about what lay ahead.

When Zane inquired, she'd told him what she'd done with it. He'd granted her a sidelong look.

"How do you plan to reach it, if and when the time comes?"

So she'd used the knife's tip to pick apart the seams of the skirts, until she had a pocket-sized hole for her hand in every dress.

"Good enough," he'd said when she'd informed him. "A bit drafty, though, I'd suppose."

She had not answered that. They'd been in bed—well, she was—and his voice, floating up from the floor, had a decidedly sardonic note to it.

She did not retire with it at night. Zane had purchased his own knife along with hers, a much larger one, and she knew that he did keep it close. But perhaps he slept less restlessly than she. Lia would never risk a whetted blade near her face.

On their stops during the day he would show her a few basic moves, the steel in his hand an arc of blinding light, flowing so swift even she couldn't follow.

Under the watchful gaze of the coachman, Zane would slow his hand and show her again what to do. Otherwise he moved like quicksilver in his demonstrations, thrusting, twisting, whirling, his braid a whip that flew straight out behind him. He seemed born for what he did, a human extension of his weapon; she never knew a mortal man could be so fleet. Her own efforts to copy him were clumsy in comparison. But still, little by little, she was learning.

These were the secret seeds of his life. These were things he had learned as a boy with her mother and honed as a man by himself. There was a good reason he was the terror of London, with a price on his head. There was a good reason her tribe perished, one by one, in the worst of her dreams.

Yet the thief had pointed out to her that a knife would do no good against a cloud of smoke. Lia knew it. As she scanned the skies at twilight she knew it, but still, perversely, the weight of it in her hand reassured her.

Someone was out there, watching her, watching them. Amalia was not as defenseless as she seemed.

Come on, then, she would think, searching the heavens. *Come on.*

If she had to wait much longer, the dragon inside her would claw her to pieces.

⚜

On the evening of their eighth day of highland travel, the fine and decorous leader of the hamlet they had entered slammed the door of his home in their faces.

Amalia stood motionless, blinking at the weathered wood. Zane, standing slightly behind her, pushed a strand of hair from his eyes and glanced around the terraced porch.

They were higher than ever in the Carpathian range. The sunset was a blaze of color to the west, gorgeous and unreal, tones so opaque and thick they ran like hot wax down into the horizon. There were pots of wilted herbs drooping along the stairs, and a tabby cat hidden against the turn of the house, staring at them from behind a bush with enormous orange eyes.

Lia lifted her chin. Her hand rose up once more; Zane covered her fist with his fingers before she could connect with the wood, bringing both their arms down together.

"It's no good," he said, as kindly as he could. "It's dusk. We're outsiders. They won't let us in."

She inhaled through her nose, glaring at the closed door.

"Lia," he said, shifting his touch to her elbow. "My lady wife. Let's go."

He drew her with him down the steps, back to the waiting carriage and the gypsy on top eyeing them balefully from over his scarves. The nights were becoming a reflection of true winter, clear and viciously cold; no doubt the man wondered where the hell they would venture next. God knew Zane did.

He'd been expecting something like this for days. He was surprised, in fact, that it hadn't happened sooner. These were not the bored, leisurely aristocrats that had decorated Hunyadi's villa, starved for fresh gossip. These were peasants— by the laws here they were actually still serfs. Their lives would be short and harsh and layered with folklore. No one welcomed a stranger's knock after sunset.

As they walked away, the curtains of a window twitched; a darkened figure pressed against the cloth, watching them go. Zane was about to hand Amalia back up into the coach when a new movement caught his eye.

It was a child. A boy, about seven, hiding behind the rear wheel of the carriage. The boy fidgeted again, his fingers wrapped around the spokes, peering out at them with a pointed, curious face.

With her foot on the step Amalia stilled, then turned. She met the boy's look.

"Buna seara," she said, or something that sounded like that. *"Numele meu este Lia."*

"Jakab," replied the child, inching out from behind the wheel. He was dressed in what could at best be called rags, smudged and barefoot, even with the cold. He rattled back a string of sentences to Lia, who smiled and beckoned him closer with the crook of her finger.

Typically, the youth complied. He was thin and pale and looked like nothing so much as the boy Zane himself had once been, hungry and aloof, slightly desperate beneath his outward serenity. Zane regarded him with narrowed eyes.

"He says we should try his parents." Lia spoke without looking away from the boy. "That they would be glad to see us."

"No doubt. We're a pair of ripe pigeons, aren't we? Foreigners, moneyed."

"No, I don't think that's it."

"Don't you?" He sneered at the peasant child, who watched them openly now with an intensely green gaze. "How naive you are."

"Zane," said Lia. "I think...I think he might be part... you know. Like me."

He turned his face to see her.

"It's a feeling," she said. "Not very strong, but there. Look at his features."

"I am. He reminds me of a drowned rat."

She sighed. "No. Look again."

"What, then?" he demanded, as the light around them darkened and bled.

"He looks like me," she said simply. "Don't you remember? He looks as I did at his age."

"You're not like him," he said at once.

"Don't pretend. Not for my sake." She glanced at him askance; her hair was a woven shimmer in the day's last light, brighter than the heavens. "I remember the past too."

"Snapdragon—"

"It's a chance, I know. But I'd rather see it out than drive on tonight in the dark. Wouldn't you?"

The boy lived in a hut. There could be no other word for it; the roof was straw and the walls were planked wood; the floor was composed of reed mats and swept dirt. There were not actually any farm animals roaming inside, but if the pigs had been gone for less than a month, Zane would have been amazed.

The door was not slammed in their faces here. The door

was swung wide, and the people inside pulled them in with plucking, nervous fingers. The hut contained a man and a wife and three more children besides the boy, who darted around them to clutch at his father's loose shirt.

Lia and the adults exchanged courteous words, the couple bowing and nodding and Amalia smiling in return, her hands a graceful accompaniment to whatever she was saying.

The place smelled of garlic and onions. There was a fire sputtering beside an old inglenook at the end of the chamber; it cast the sole illumination, bright enough to pick out a kitchen hutch, a carved table and chairs, and the wrought-iron cross hanging from a support beam of the wall.

"Look," murmured Lia in English, in the same gracious voice she'd been using for the peasants. "It's the mother. Do you see it?"

He didn't. The woman looked commonplace to him, scratchy blond hair pulled back beneath a kerchief, blue eyes, deep lines around her mouth. She was neither plump nor thin, not tanned nor pale, her gown a wildly colorful mix of embroidered flowers and leaves over felt, a brassy pattern that had appeared on half the frocks of the women they'd encountered in these climes. She was ordinary. He was about to open his mouth to say so when the peasant turned her head, glancing up at her husband—and then he did see. With the light shifting, with her chin lifted . . . her profile held a shadow of Lia's own strange and marvelous beauty.

Drákon.

"Yes," he said, hiding his astonishment.

"It's not much. But she's the one."

"Amalia," he said, as the couple gestured them forward. He curved his fingers around her arm to prevent her from moving, keeping his face a pleasant mask. "Has it occurred to you that these may be the people who played with fire in our hotel? That we've strolled right into their trap?"

"I'm not a ninny." Her own smile remained fixed. "It's not them."

"Because...?"

"Because there's no power here." When he wouldn't release her arm, she deliberately pried his grip from her, following the wife as she urged them toward the table. Zane kept a half pace behind. "The blood is too diluted. It's like... an echo of a song, rather than the song itself."

They sat. The wife brought out bowls and spoons; the husband and two of the children left the hut to see to the gypsy. The boy Jakab and a younger sister remained. They huddled together like sleepy kittens on the inglenook, watching Lia with wondering eyes.

The *drákon* wife served them goulash, piping hot. She sat unsmiling across the table from them both, her hands folded, observing every bite they took.

Lia offered what sounded like a compliment. The woman lifted her brows on a sentence and nodded, then ducked her chin. She said something else almost under her breath; Lia's spoon paused above her bowl.

"What is it?" Zane said, alert.

"Nothing. I've—I've just realized I've been mistranslating a word."

"Not *here is your poison* instead of *here is your stew,* I hope?"

Her lips lifted in a brief, lovely smile. "No." She took another bite, chewed and swallowed. "I thought they had been saying *noblewoman.* To me."

"And?"

"It's not *noblewoman.* It's *noble one.*"

He fished a piece of potato from the bottom of his bowl. "What the devil is that supposed to mean?"

"I'm not sure." Her lashes were lowered; she kept her gaze on her food. "But I imagine it means that these people—that all the people we have encountered in these villages so far—know what I am."

Wonderful.

"This just keeps getting better and better," he said.

"Yes." She blew delicately at the goulash in her spoon. "And have you noticed there are no other rooms here, and no beds?"

⚜

They spent the night together on a pallet on the dirt floor, Zane with his arms firmly around her beneath their blankets, his senses humming, exhausting the hours by hovering between the brink of sleep and hard-awake. Despite Lia's assertion that these were not the people hunting her, he was taking no chances.

The peasant family slumbered around them. Even the Roma had bedded down by the front door.

No one snored. Perhaps no one slept.

He kept her body close for warmth. He inhaled the pleasing scent of roses, her golden head at his shoulder, and let thoughts of sunshine and summer drift through his drowsing mind.

CHAPTER TWELVE

Little is known of what actually happened between the dragon-princess and the peasant who stole her from the bosom of her kind, all those centuries past. We know he was wily enough to thieve the diamond as well, to ensure he would have *Draumr* to bind her by his side. We know he was hungry enough for her to risk his own life to keep her, and ruthless enough to destroy her family when they attempted to rescue her from him.

But what did *she* think, that lovely, lonely girl? Like silent Helen of Troy, we have no records of her thoughts. We know only her actions; we know what mountains men moved for her. The mystery of her soul remains unsolved.

We know she wedded the peasant and bore tainted children by him. We know she remained by his side for many years, raising her family, ensorcelled by the stone.

She had been the prize of her people, cherished and pampered, meant for a royal future. He was naught but a child of the dirt, who did not deserve to even glance into her eyes.

That night she put a blade through his heart, what raced through her mind? When she took the diamond from her husband's body and vanished into the mountains, did she regret her story? Did she fret for her children, left alone and vulnerable to the mercies of humankind? Was it difficult to step into the void of that abandoned copper tunnel? Did she ever hesitate to take her own life?

Perhaps she was merely relieved to have her nightmare ended. Perhaps she focused only on breaking the spell that had enslaved her.

I don't know. I think she was a fool, to wait so long to kill him. I would have done it the very first night, the moment he dared touch my skin. I would have snatched the diamond from him and swallowed it, and then shown him the true, awful beauty of my gilded self.

But I'm not her.

CHAPTER THIRTEEN

Sometime during the oblivion of their twelfth night in the mountains, the gypsy deserted them.

She should have sensed his growing discontent, but he was human, and seldom bothered to look her in the eye anyway. Right up until the night they'd been forced to camp beneath the stars, the gypsy been acting exactly the same: churlish.

Lia had felt a certain sympathy. The constant wind and the cold whittled away at her too. She longed for green England and a soft, safe bed. She longed for silence.

It had been growing more and more difficult to secure accommodations after twilight. The villages this high were scattered; they had spent their days rolling through forests so thick the sun never touched the snow below, and passes so narrow she grew nauseated just glancing out the carriage window at the sheer drop to the rivers and gorges far below.

And everywhere they went now, she was drowning in song.

The Carpathian range was iron and gold and copper; it hid diamonds and silver, salt and coal and quartz, and mines spidering miles through the solid rock as evidence for all these things. She had learned that much in her lessons from school, but not once had she considered the implications: this place was like a drug to her. When she closed her eyes she heard countless phantom melodies in her head, softer, louder, changing as their direction changed. To preserve her sanity she practiced picking out one song at a time, following its tune as it plucked at her, soared, and then grew dim, only to fade back into the mists of her mind. *Draumr* was an ever-present counterpoint to all the rest, always the strongest, always the most beautiful.

And with its beauty, the dreams became more vivid than ever before.

Three days ago, over a luncheon of dumplings and mutton at an alpine farmhouse, Zane had confronted her point-blank about it.

"You've lost weight," he said in English, brusque. "You're not eating, you're wan, and I haven't noticed that you sleep."

"You notice if I sleep?" she asked, looking up.

"I consider it part of my job. Are you ill?"

She shook her head, glancing at the farmer's wife and girl children, kneading dough in a line down at the end of the table, tallest to smallest, like nesting dolls laid out. Lia doubted there was any chance they could understand English, but she knew they listened hard anyway.

Flour from the dough spotted the wood, spurted up in clouds to sift the still air.

"It's not consumption?"

"No."

"Smallpox? The plague?"

"Please."

"Is it love?" he drawled, very dry.

"Do shut up."

"Then what ails you, dear wife?"

"Not a thing."

"I cannot envision which will be worse," he said, flipping back the lace of his cuff to spear a pickled beet on his plate. "Having to return to your parents and say, 'Amalia died of consumption,' or 'Amalia died of stupidity, for refusing to confide in me. Whilst my back was turned, I'm afraid a dragon came and ate her up.'"

Lia's gaze flew to the woman standing just feet away.

"Do not say that word."

"What word?" He smiled, malicious. *Dragon?*

She controlled her voice. "Are you attempting to get us skewered with the carving knife or merely tossed out?"

"Yes, sorry, you're absolutely right. I'd prefer not to be skewered, at least until I'm done with this fine plate of desiccated sheep. Try it, love. A bit chewy, but delightfully piquant." He glanced significantly at the mutton set before her, then back to the round-faced wife. His smile gleamed handsome and bright. "Don't make me say it again."

He watched her as she sawed at the meat, slowly consuming one bite at a time. He finished minutes before she did, sitting back on his bench, sipping the cider they shared from a mug.

The heavy smack of fists striking dough filled the air, muffled, oddly comforting. The odor of yeast was a warm tang on the back of her tongue. Two of the daughters began a lively, hushed conversation; Zane spoke beneath them.

"Bad dreams, snapdragon?" he asked quietly.

She turned a piece of meat over with her fork. "Yes."

His gaze lowered. For an instant Lia dropped her guard; she stared at him helplessly, angry with herself and him, desperate to stop drinking in the sight of his face and throat and the slope of his shoulders, desperate to stop the memories of her blind nights with him from threatening to sweep over her like a black hungry tide—and then he looked up, and she turned her eyes away.

"I could help you with that," he said. "I could help you sleep."

She took a steadying breath. "How?"

His mouth crooked.

Lia felt the animal in her wake at once, its pulse in her blood.

"Herbs," Zane said, going back to his drink. "Our baker friend over there, for instance, has added thyme and rosemary to her bread. Do you smell it? And the mutton was exceptionally overspiced. I'd wager she has quite a store of herbs in her cupboard. It won't hurt to ask."

Her hand ached; Lia was gripping her pewter fork so hard her fingers had gone white. Deliberately, she set it aside. "What do you know of herbology?"

"Only what's of use to me." He shrugged. "A successful businessman learns all the nooks and crannies of his profession. On certain—delicate—jobs, I find it's more profitable to work around a dozing constable rather than a vigilant one. Most of them tend to drink themselves into a stupor by ten, but for those who don't..." He gave a truly wicked smile. "An apothecary shop would be better, but I doubt we have that option anywhere nearby. Still...a little of this, a little of that. It could help your dreams."

"Don't trouble yourself. I'll be fine."

"Yes," the thief said, leaning forward to cover her hand with his own, very briefly. "You will be, because you have me."

It seemed that the woman was also a midwife, most likely

the only one for miles around. She proudly possessed an entire shack of dried plants and flowers, located past the chicken coop filled with hens—which scattered at Lia's approach—and a pen of mournful ewes—which tossed their heads and kept bleating long after she'd vanished from their sight.

Lia didn't even have the words for all the wreaths and roots hanging from hooks or mashed into clay jugs littering the shelves. The thief didn't need the words anyway. With a mixture of flattery and brazen charm, he sidled his way into the drafty shack, opening jars, crumbling leaves between his fingers and thumb, sniffing and occasionally tasting the dust left behind on his fingertips, thoughtful.

The little girls tracked his every move with giggles and more whispers, crowding the doorway and blocking the light, their hands over their mouths. Every now and then Zane would angle a warm look in their direction, and the giggles grew louder.

They left the farmhouse that day with a jug of herbs he had blended himself, which he handed up to her after she was seated in the carriage.

"What am I to do with this?" she asked, still perturbed.

"Unless we can find some hot water this evening for tea, I'm afraid you're going to have to eat it."

"The devil I will." She sat the jug on the seat.

"Language, Lady Amalia." He gave her a sweeping bow. "I fear I've been a shocking poor influence on you."

"You have no notion," she grumbled under her breath as he closed the door between them.

That had been the last day they'd had a hot meal. That evening they'd found a new farmhouse—well before sunset—and then the next morning they were off again... but there was only a single small hamlet nearby, only a few hours beyond the previous one. They'd taken a chance on finding another, but there was none. Instead, at last, they'd sought shelter in what appeared to be an abandoned shepherd's hut.

The Roma lit a fire that sent black smoke pillowing out from the fireplace into the chamber. Cursing, Zane had found a branch to open the chimney; it took the two of them forcing it together to unstick the old flue.

Snow managed to scour most of the soot off their skin, but Lia had spent the rest of the night trying not to cough.

They'd supped on the packet of cold sausages and bread purchased from the last house; she would not touch the jar of herbs. Zane slept as he always did when it was the two of them on the floor: his body molded to hers, his arms pinning her close, her head resting at his shoulder. It was a sexless embrace, at least for him, she assumed. Beneath the sheepskin that covered them, she was hot and uncomfortable and unable to move. When the dreams finally came, she twitched in her sleep like a puppy, distantly feeling his hand sliding up and down her arm to soothe her.

All it did was make the dreams worse.

The next day the villages vanished. As they ambled deeper into the wilderness, they found naught that spoke of people, not even a hint of civilization. No more plowed fields. No mills, or massive rolls of hay dusted with sugar-snow. No grapevines, no wheat sheaths, no cattle or geese or sheep. Only the road, narrow and twisting, climbing nowhere but higher into the purple mountains. Only the woods, hushed and still, as if the birds and deer and squirrels had all fled because they knew she was on her way. Steam rose now and again from the horizon, a sign of hot springs or melt, enormous slow curls dissolving under the sun.

Even the other *drákon* haunted them less and less; the skies echoed with emptiness.

But below, far below, *Draumr* raised her voice in anticipation. They were closer now than ever, and the spell of the song seemed to thrum from the very core of the earth.

So that next night, that twelfth night, they lacked even a shepherd's hut to shelter them, and all the leftover food was gone. They found a clearing beside the road and pulled over, resigned to spending the remaining hours of dark in the wilderness. She had argued with Zane about who would sleep where: he wanted her in the carriage, and she'd refused. She knew from experience the seats were not long enough for comfortable rest, and the thought of spending yet another moment cloistered inside its small space was enough to set her teeth on edge.

The night was arctic-clear. Stars spangled the sky like the glitter of scales and ice. The moon was a rising scythe to the east, paling the heavens in a wide circle from jet to lapis blue through the peaks of the trees.

"You'd prefer it out here?" the thief had demanded, sweeping his hand to the woods. The other hand held one of the oil lanterns, casting mad shadows back and forth. "In the freezing cold? Are you daft?"

"Yes," she'd bit out. "Quite."

"Lia—"

"Take the carriage, if you like it. The cushions stink and the windows rattle. I'm staying out here. In the cold."

So, of course, he did as well. It turned out the gypsy had decided to take the carriage—and everything in it.

There had been no hot water, no water at all save what was in the flask Zane carried that they filled every morning. He had fetched the jug of herbs from the carriage and shaken out a measure into the cup of his palm. He looked at her, his hand held out, starlight glinting along his hair and skin. Lia gazed back at him, unspeaking.

"I can't sleep if you don't," he said frankly, and took her

hand and poured the mixture into her palm. "Try not to taste it. It'll be easier."

Beneath the winking stars she had accepted his dry medicine, washing it all down with a drag from the flask. The flavor of wood and dirt lingered unpleasantly in her mouth.

He'd leaned down and touched his lips to her cheek before turning away, trudging through the snow to help the gypsy with the horses. Lia had sat upon the sheepskin and watched them, shadow men frosted silver, the animals snorting and shivering in their harnesses even though she'd made certain to stay downwind.

Zane had built a campfire. It threw a timid warmth against the chill.

His potion worked well. She was already blinking at the light when he came back to her, pulling her down with him to the sheepskin, tucking over them a blanket that smelled strongly of horse, enfolding her in his arms.

The fire crackled and burned.

"Lia-heart," he murmured, a smoky voice in her ear. "Tell me about your dreams."

But before she could drag her thoughts together for an answer, the shadows billowed around her like the sails of a dark, beautiful ship.

That night, for the first time in years, she slept in perfect silence.

⚜

She awoke alone.

She was aware that she was cold, and the soft something beneath her did little to protect her from the constant chill that seeped up from below. Lia felt heavy and slow, drowsing in the place between sleep and awake, her mind turning over the sensations that began, one by one, to intrude upon her perceptions.

A small wind, stirring against her cheek.

The smell of pine on the wind, and snow, and cold ashes.

The music of the earth, swelling to life.

Draumr. Metals, quartz, hidden diamonds. But something was missing. Something had been taken away....

The yellow sapphire.

Lia opened her eyes. She was by herself in the clearing beside the road of yesterday, and where the carriage used to be there were only tracks laced through the mud and snow. The fire was dead. And Zane, like the coach and the horses and the gypsy, was gone.

She sat up, gathering the blanket around her. The breeze returned and ruffled her hair; she ran a hand over her face, bewildered, and looked back at the prints by the road. They circled off into the dirt and gravel, cutting back over the marks from yesterday.

The wind whiskered through the blue spruce and firs, rushing and fading. Lia found her feet. With the blanket slung over her shoulders, she walked to the embankment where the carriage had been last night. There were the hoofprints of the horses, all four of them. Various human marks, Zane's boots and the gypsy's softer-soled ones, meandering around. But here, just here, it was plain to see how the carriage had turned back to the road, the horses at first walking, then—as she followed it farther down—breaking into a trot.

And pressed through them were the fresher imprints of a man's running steps. Zane, sprinting from behind.

The entire mess swept over the curve of the hill, marking the mud as far as her eyes could follow.

She returned to the dead fire, settling down upon the sheepskin to wait. The forest around her descended into absolute silence. She wished for birdsong, for the breeze to return, for anything to break this idle spell. *Draumr* obliged by lifting in harmony, but Lia was weary of it. She held her hands over her ears and squinted down at the fallen leaves and pinecones, thinking of worms and dirt and the hard winter ache in the air, a sullen pang that pinched along her skin.

Clouds began to brew against the treetops, majestic, heavy clouds that leisurely roiled and ripped themselves apart, only to blend back together in blotchy confusion. It was going to snow again. She felt the promise of it in her every joint.

"Zane," she said aloud, but of course received no answer.

When he trudged back over the hill, it was with a stitch in his side and self-recriminations ringing through his head. He should have anticipated this, he should have known—

But he hadn't. He'd never entirely trusted the Roma, but he also had not believed in the worst of all possible consequences.

He'd awoken to the jingle of harnesses, the soft crump of hooves against snow. The horses were agitated; he felt their uneasy snufflings as if they were standing just next to him. In an instant his mind had pieced together what it meant. He'd bounded up, leaving Lia beneath the blanket, and glared at the sight of the carriage vanishing down the hill into the deceptive haze of a lavender dawn.

That son of a bitch. How had he hitched the horses without waking him?

No time to care. Zane had slept fully clothed; the night necessitated it, and at the moment he was bloody glad for it, because he did not feel the rocky dirt beneath his feet as he ran, and he did not notice the early-morning chill cutting around him. But the gypsy had noticed him, and four horses were swifter than one furious man. With a high *Sep! Sep!* he whipped the steeds into a gallop. The coach—their new trunks, their new clothes, almost everything of use—bounced away down the mountain.

Zane ran and ran, and then slowed to a stop.

It was a lengthy walk back up the road.

She was waiting for him. She sat huddled in her cloak by the burned ring of his fire, her hair mussed to her shoulders, her arms wrapped around her knees.

She'd removed her tapes and hoops for sleeping. Her gown melted around her like a puddle of royal-blue sky.

"I lost him," he admitted, and heard the anger tightening his voice.

Her head tipped; a shaft of sunlight threw a halo around her, much like that endless stroke of time in the tavern when his world had truly first begun to come undone. Her response was mild.

"We need to find shelter. It's going to storm."

It did not occur to him for one second to doubt her.

This was her world, not his.

CHAPTER FOURTEEN

The mining tunnel they found was wet and cold and definitely hewn by man instead of nature. Wooden support beams braced the rock walls; as Zane explored beyond the easy light, he kicked up against the stubs of two pocked tallow candles—no matches—that rattled in uneven circles over to a mound of dirt.

Lia had discovered the entrance. Decades of mossy bracken and uncut trees had nearly concealed it from sight, but she'd felt its hollowness like a sore in the ground. From the depths of the mine small songs still resonated, willing her closer, willing her deeper into their blackness.

She tried to disguise her reluctance to enter by acting as lookout near the opening, but soon she'd have to go in. The forest behind her stretched into clouded, icy shadows, ancient and thick, massive trunks, downy white snowflakes just beginning to fall. Before long the meager path that led them here would be obscured. She wondered if she could find it again. She wondered if she'd even need to.

Lia shivered, her arms closed over her chest, and listened to Zane roam the cavern.

"What was this for, can you tell?" he called, his voice echoing against the walls.

"Gold, I think," she called back to him. "It feels like gold."

He emerged to join her at the entrance, his boots grating against a sea of chipped stone. When he leaned past her to glance at the woods, the wind sucked his hair across his face.

"At least it's not sulfur," he said. "Come in."

"Are you certain it's safe?"

"No." He shook back his hair, impatient. "Come inside."

Inside the tunnel it wasn't precisely warmer, but her eyes finally ceased watering. They walked slowly down the slope of the ground, just until the gloom devoured them both, until the uneven floor became a smooth deception and the loudest sound was a faint trickle of water striking a pool somewhere, caverns below. Then the thief stopped and turned and wrapped his arms around her. Gradually, her shivers subsided.

"Better?"

She closed her eyes and laughed into his cravat. "Not especially."

His face lifted; he rested his jaw against her hair. " 'Tis a small step down from St. James's Palace, I'll grant you."

"Somewhat, yes."

"Almost as drafty, though," he added, thoughtful. "Less ostentatious décor. I wonder where this tunnel goes?"

Lia shuddered. "Let's not find out."

"No. Let's not."

She should move. She knew she should move away from him, she knew she should end this embrace and think practical thoughts, because the winter didn't care if his heart beat warm and he was scented of snow and spice and pine woods. The winter did not care if his arms felt like safety, an anchor amid the black shadows and the white storm.

Oh, but she didn't want to move. There was the sheepskin behind them and the horse blanket, but they didn't comfort her as he did.

"Have you really been inside St. James's?" she whispered.

"Once or twice." His top hand shifted along her back, rubbing a slow circle. "I've enjoyed a few odds and ends the king wasn't using, paintings, silverwork. He's got a Michelangelo bronze of Diana stashed in a dusty corner. I'm considering it mightily for my parlor." His hand stilled. "I'll show you when we get back, if you like."

It was an invitation, one perhaps he hadn't even meant to make, because as soon as he said the words he changed; like the drift of a cloud passing over the sun, he was suddenly darker, and different. A new tension leashed his body as his arms pressed against her; the pulse in his throat became a rush against her ear.

"Amalia," Zane said, but nothing else.

Her hand lifted, tracing his arm, the lapel of his greatcoat, her fingertips coming to rest against the sleek damask of his vest. With her eyes still closed she turned her cheek against his shoulder, breathing him in through parted lips. She drew her fingers downward, following the woven pattern of the damask over his chest to the narrow pocket near his waist. Then behind, where the heat of his body was trapped against his wool coat. She spread her fingers against his back.

He said her name again, hardly audible. His arms were

SHANA ABÉ

still fixed around her. He felt primed as a bowstring beneath her touch.

"You do realize," she said quietly, "that we're going to freeze to death in here."

The thief made a sound, not quite a chuckle. "Is that what this is? The doomed maiden, prepared to sacrifice her virtue"—she turned her face again, pressing a kiss against his shirt; he exhaled very sharply—"at the altar of practicality? How tediously noble of you."

"You have your clichés all muddled. I'm not the maiden but a beast."

"Well, damned if *I'm* the maiden." He set her away from him with both hands at her shoulders and gave her a little shake. Even with the dark, she could see his words frosting into vapor. "Do you really think this is how—that this is what I want?"

"Yes," she said.

"Listen to me, love. This cave is nothing. This storm is nothing. I've been stranded in far worse circumstances than this. We're going to survive today, tonight, and many long nights to come. Save your noble intentions for your future husband, God bless his unwary soul. I have a plan, and a good one. You're going to Turn and guide us out of here."

"What?"

"Turn," he repeated, with exaggerated patience, "to smoke. To dragon. Either. To guide us to the nearest town. And if you happen to catch sight of that Judas of a coachman along the way, you have my permission to eat him."

"No, I . . ." Her hands dropped. "Did you say 'eat him'?"

His voice gentled. "I know you can do this, Lia. I've seen your miracle."

"I've been trying, but—" She ducked her head. "I haven't been able to fully manage it. Not since that first time."

"This seems like an excellent opportunity for further practice."

When she glanced up at him, Zane offered her a smile, one she had seen him make countless times before and for countless different people: charming and impersonal, heartless as a rake. It was his professional look, without an ounce of warmth behind it.

You're going to fail, whispered the dragon inside her. *You want to fail. You want to undo the future, but you can't.*

"Forgive me," he said. "You seem a bit cornered. But we need this very badly. And I suspect that all that's truly holding you back is ordinary fear."

She stood mortified, that he could read her so easily, that he could smile at her like that and her heart still ached. "Oh? Do you know so much about it?"

"More than you'd think."

"You're naught but a human man. You couldn't possibly understand."

He lifted a brow, still smiling. "Liar."

"Cutpurse."

"Runaway."

"Swindler!"

"Coward," he said softly, and she jerked back.

"Bastard!"

"Undoubtedly true." He made a short bow. "But do begin. I'd rather not spend my last day watching your pretty nose freeze black."

She glowered at him, feeling the cold air, and the sharp walls, and the sad, small songs of whatever minerals lay yet buried beneath them.

"I'd like the sheepskin, if you please," Lia said, rigidly polite. "It's easier to concentrate when I'm seated."

The bow he offered her now was polished enough for the

king and all his court. He took up the skin and laid it out for her with a flourish.

"Your very wish, my lady wife," murmured the thief.

⚜

Her hair. Her right hand. Her foot.

Her pump and worsted stocking fell off and she kept them off, because every time she slipped them back on they only fell off again when her foot went to smoke. It was snowing now in earnest beyond the tunnel entrance, a dotted field of pearled light. When they weren't actual fumes, her toes were very cold, even beneath her skirts.

"Relax," advised Zane, seated across from her with his back against the wall. His coat was buttoned up to his chin; his hands were pushed deep into his pockets. He'd recovered his cocked hat at the campsite and had it pulled down low on his head. "Don't consider it so much. Pretend that you're floating in a calm Caribbean sea—"

"I cannot swim."

"Floating along on a midsummer breeze. A butterfly given wings. Everything is effortless."

"So say you," she muttered, rubbing her nose. "It might be easier if you didn't stare so."

"Am I staring? I beg your pardon. It's just that I find the process . . ."

"Freakish?" she suggested, tart. "Unnerving?"

". . . amazing," he finished, and deliberately aimed his gaze down at the rocky floor. "Like you."

She nearly sighed but didn't want to waste the warmth. "Was that a compliment?"

"Sorry," he said meekly, without looking up. "Sometimes it happens. I'll try to contain myself."

Lia felt her lips flatten. Frustration welled up in her once more—it wasn't *working*, she couldn't *do* it, nothing *helped*—

and when her breath hissed out, a small plume of flame ignited in the air, landing upon the sleeve of his coat.

He leapt to his feet, agile as a dancer, slapping out the flame. For the long, astonished minute that followed, they only stared at each other, he standing, she seated, his fingers clasped over the stench of scorched wool.

Zane recovered first. He held out his sleeve to examine it; his voice was even. "I really thought that part of the dragon legend was embellishment."

"So did I." She rose, finding her shoe. "I don't know anyone else who—no one from the tribe has ever..."

"Can you do it again?"

She wiped quickly at her eyes with the heel of her palm, glancing up at him from over her fingers.

There was his smile again, a dangerous thing, handsome and sharp and brutally sensual. "Lia." He crossed to the entrance of the tunnel, where leaves and twigs had blown into corners, and began to toss them all together into a heap. "Do it again."

"I don't know," she wavered, eyeing his pile. The wind shifted, scattering snowflakes along the base.

"Fine. Don't know." He came back to her, took her face between his hands, and kissed her hard on the lips.

She barely felt it at first. She was cold, her mouth was cold, and so was he. He felt like a wall against her. And then he felt like unshaven whiskers. But then...oh, then something between them softened, and his lips became velvet, and her entire being began to warm and sting. She stood on her toes to meet him better, and his arms wrapped around her in a fierce squeeze before letting go.

"There," he said, breathless. "Now. Do it now."

She did not take the time to be angry. With her blood still stinging she looked away from him, toward the stack of debris.

Lia thought, *Fire.*

And when she blew a little breath the flame came once more, floating down to the paper foliage, exploding into light. The snow melted instantly, water, gas, wispy pale filaments that twined upward into nothing.

Zane gazed at the fire, at the pine needles and leaves curling black.

"Well done," he said.

She sank to her knees. He went behind her, crouching down with an arm sliding loose around her neck, and held his lips, chaste, against her flushed cheek.

❧

He did not sleep. He tried. God knew he should be accustomed to the sensations by now: her soft body, her cool fragrance. How her hands tended to wrap over his forearms during the night, her fingers digging in; the small, pretty noises she made as she dreamed.

Her fire was burning well. He'd gathered as much fuel from the tunnel as he could find and then ventured outside for damp tree branches, just to see them through the night.

The branches burned more slowly. They also gave off more smoke; it bubbled at the ceiling before being siphoned off in long white fangs down into the mines below.

The floor was an unholy bed of chips and edges, but he'd done his best to secure her comfort. She slept atop the sheepskin—it was only big enough for one—and the horse blanket was wrapped all the way around her, with just the tail folding over him. He'd lied to her and said he was warm enough from the fire.

Zane followed the shadows shifting and dancing along the jagged tunnel walls as he considered the resources they had left.

The blanket. The sheepskin.

The garments they wore.

His boots, and in them the stack of coins he'd transferred from the valise the night before; he was too canny to store their cash very far away.

His greatcoat, and the bank vouchers from the Marquess of Langford tucked in a pocket.

His picks, in the same pocket.

His dagger.

His new knife.

Her new knife—or so he hoped. Now that he mulled it over, he didn't recall asking her if she still wore it.

The silver flask.

His hat, her cloak, their gloves—and her. Lia. The girl who breathed fire.

But she was no longer a girl. She'd told him so more than once, and for all he wished to God he'd never noticed it, she was right. Lia was a woman. More than that. She was plush and heavy in his arms, she was grace and smoke and temptation, and Zane was wretchedly certain he must be mired in some unnumbered level of hell to be forced to hold her like this every night and bound not to act upon his instincts. Whatever he had done to deserve this torment—and he had done a great many unpleasant things—he was deeply, sincerely, soul-scrapingly sorry now.

She shifted a little, murmuring in her sleep. Without disturbing her he drew up a lock of her hair, very gently, and held it pressed to his face.

He might never see London again. He might never see his home, or taste plum cake, or sip brandy from the best smugglers in Cornwall in front of his carved agate mantel. He might never slide through St. Giles or steal through Pall Mall, inhale the distinctive odor of coal lanterns and whale oil, feel the thrill of an opening lock, or the shimmer of raw silk over his hands. He might never see Lia safe again.

He scowled up at the shadows. Sorry, as it turned out, really didn't help.

His fingers released her hair. He placed his arm over his eyes and commanded himself to go to sleep.

❧

He would wake her. He would say something clever, like: "I have a theory about love, as it relates to itches and distractions."

And her brows would raise in that skeptical, enticing way she had, waiting.

"Scratch the itch, the distraction is gone."

"Is that what I am, an itch?"

"More like a rash. But I'm willing to scratch. If you are."

Dream-Lia would say to him, "That is surely one of the least seductive things a man has ever dared utter to a woman."

"Well," he would reply, still clever, "but you've been cloistered away at your little school, haven't you? How many men could you have known? Perhaps we're all like this."

"God forbid."

"Aye. One of me, one of you." He'd run a finger over her shell-pink lips. "It's really all that's required."

And then he would kiss her. Softly, deeply, using his lips and tongue and all the artful guiles he knew. And even though she wasn't a woman, not really, she would kiss him back. She would make that sweet little moan in her throat, the one that was just the right pitch to send him spilling over the edge of reason. . . .

❧

He dropped his arm. He turned his head to stare up at the ceiling until his eyes teared and the rock crests and smoke all hazed into gray.

"No," the real Amalia breathed, still in her sleep. "No, Zane."

Zane sighed. Very carefully, very slowly, he leaned up on an elbow to examine her face.

Firelight flattered her. She didn't need flattering. She was too beautiful as it was—but with the gold-amber light she became something searingly, magically fragile, the fleeting brilliance of a sunbeam slicing through a cloudburst.

Wife, he thought, and this time the word washed over him with a sensation surprisingly akin to desolation.

She wasn't his. She could never be his.

"Will you?" she whispered, still asleep. "Zane?"

"Yes," he said, and almost from outside of himself saw his fingers stroke back the few bright strands that clung to her brow. "Yes, Lia. I'm here."

It's only to comfort her.

But it wasn't. Even as he moved he knew that it wasn't, another lie, another tally against his soul. His mouth brushed her temple, her cheekbone, her jaw. The loosened strands of her hair caught against his lips and the stubble on his cheek.

Someday, one way or another, they would part ways; they would have no choice. And bastard that he was, he still knew what he meant to have happen next.

It wasn't an itch. It was a sickness. It was poison blazing through him, thinking of her all the time, watching her, touching her, wanting and wanting and wanting until his mind went black.

She turned her face to meet his, her hand lifting from his arm.

He took her mouth that easily. He exhaled all his doubts, let them sift from his body as he placed his lips over hers. And it was just as he'd imagined it, a million fevered times over. It was honey and desperate relief, only better, because her arm came up and hooked around his shoulders, and her chest expanded with his name.

He rolled her on her back. He smelled the cool must of rocks and earth and her, and the smoke from the fire twirling above them. He thought he might still be dreaming—except that when she kissed him she arched taut against him, her legs opening, as if she'd been awake all along and only waiting for him to give in.

He knew all the secrets of her gown. He knew the creamy flesh of her shoulders, the rise of her throat, the poem of her jugular. He knew the dip of her waist, the hard, delicious pink of her nipples. He knew these things as if he knew *her*, every inch of her, because in the feverish dark depths of his dreams he truly did.

She wore no corset. It was easy to loosen her bodice. Easy to pull the stomacher from her waist, to drag his mouth over the satin of her breasts, over the frill of chemise, to close his teeth around her nipple and tug and suckle until the silk was wet and clinging.

She was panting. She turned her head and smoothed her palms across his hair and back, urging him closer. She was adrift in her gown, a warm body cocooned amid feminine ribbons and petticoats, her skirts bunched at her hips, her knees rising.

He felt beyond himself. He felt for the first time in his adult life a shadow of fear in his heart—fear for her, for what he actually wanted from her—and for himself, for what he might do.

Don't think about it. Don't think.

She cradled him with knees and arms. Her eyes drifted open. Her lips parted. The poison for her ate through his blood.

"Do not speak," he ordered, watching her face. He didn't want her to wake; he didn't want her to shape the words that would stop him. "Just feel." Zane found her center, her folds and damp curls, and pushed a finger slowly inside her. "Feel me, Lia."

And he made certain that she would.

He touched her and stroked her until his fingers were slick, until her lashes fluttered closed and she made the soft, restless moan he'd been waiting for, that he recognized from his best fantasies. He freed himself from his breeches and sank into her. She gasped and stilled, her chest rising and falling in short, staccato bursts, and he thought he might die right then from the tight bliss of her sheath.

But he waited. Because she was new to this, she was tender, and some ragged part of him remembered that, for all the hunger raging through him. She was precious. Ardent and throbbing inside her, he would make himself wait.

He dropped kisses along her throat, up to her ear. He caught his breath and dragged his lips over her marble cheek, to her mouth, where she turned her face to his and shaped words he did not hear.

Lia lifted her hips. It wasn't much—a subtle, feminine motion—but like the tumblers turning in a lock, it freed him. He couldn't stop himself now; he pushed deep. He bit her neck and reveled in it, the flowery taste of her in his mouth, the shivers of her body around his. She made a low, keening moan that matched the agony burning through him. He thought he might die with the pleasure of her, lustrous and wet and hot against his skin. Even the shadows along the walls seemed to cower. And it was worth it, every moment, every instant of suffering, because now—

They moved together. They stretched and held and tasted each other as the fire glimmered and they found new magic.

She twined her fingers through his hair with both hands and pulled his mouth to hers, her lips to his, imprisoning him even as he impaled her with his body.

"Lia," he gasped, plunging, unable to stop.

She said something he didn't understand, the flowing language of the mountains, soft and urgent. It sounded like a plea.

"Dragoste tu. Doamne iarta-ma..."

Her ankles wrapped around his hips, taking him deep. She was satin and fire. She closed her eyes and tipped back her head, licking her tongue along his lips. He lost himself at once, just under the spell of her pleasure, her rapture and her flexed beauty, the heat of her burning him to his core. He climaxed inside her, pressing down so hard it had to hurt her, but she only held him closer with a glad, fervent sound. He echoed it, cold white light against his closed lids, bliss and pain and unbearable pleasure wringing through him.

When he could open his eyes again, the world seemed amazingly the same. Shadows still lapped at the ceiling and walls; Lia still lay quiescent beneath him, lush and cushioning, deliciously hot.

He pulled from her, their clothing half-demolished, and smoothed her skirts down her legs as he rolled them both to their sides and drew her back against him.

"Lia-heart," he whispered, hovering with her at the brink of the endless night. His lips met her hair, golden flax against his skin. He felt profoundly changed, a grateful ghost drifting away from purgatory. Everything was new, everything was right.

"I want to marry you," he breathed, and in that moment, he meant it.

She rubbed her face against his shoulder; her voice was a sleepy mumble over the fire.

"Don't be an idiot," she said.

He felt her slide back into the darkness. With the poison lifted from his veins, he followed her nearly at once.

⚜

She was asleep. She knew she was asleep because she was warm, and the sun was shining in molten streamers, and the hills of Darkfrith were grassy and thick with August wildflowers. She was speaking in a relaxed, happy voice with her mother and Joan, the three of them seated on a blanket in the meadow by the falls. They were watching the menfolk teach the children how to fish. Poles stuck up like boar bristles from the line of youngsters. The older ones—Audrey's boys—had done it all before, and their lines whipped straight out into the deep blue pond, spreading ripples to the shore. But it was the first time for most of them, and chaos ruled.

Lia's father pantomimed a quick, flicking cast, and the smaller children tried to imitate it. Rods clicked and tangled, arguments flared. Someone's pole was flung a little too hard and went cartwheeling into the water.

From the middle of the turmoil, she saw Zane shake his tawny head. He waded into the pond, thigh-deep, and scooped the pole back out.

When Amalia looked down, there was a daisy chain in her hands. She remembered now: she'd woven it for their daughter.

⚜

She opened her eyes. The world dawned both prickly cold and magnificently comfortable. She was clasped in a firm embrace; she felt a heartbeat and heard breathing. Her face was chilled. She gazed drowsily at the low, chiseled ceiling of the tunnel, and then at the shadow thrown long across Zane's chest.

A girl was standing over them with her back to the light.

Dark-haired, slender as a nymph, she met Lia's look with eerie pale eyes. She wore no clothes at all. Lia's knife rested flat across her open palms.

Amalia bolted upright. The girl skipped back a step and vanished into smoke. The knife she'd been holding landed with a clatter against the stony ground.

Even as Zane was reaching for her, Lia Turned, chasing the creature out of the cavern and up into the flawless blue sky.

CHAPTER FIFTEEN

She moved because she desired it. She had no body, she had no eyes, but she saw the woods streak below her in a blur of green and white, following the plume of smoke that rose and stretched, thinner than the fat clouds still above them, an improbable spiral of gray that pushed against the wind.

Lia raced after the *drákon* girl. She was gaining too, even as they climbed higher, soaring toward the razor-backed mountains. The trees began to taper off in a low, waving line. Metallic light flashed below her, blinding: lakes bright as coins, rivers feeding them, the fresh snow reflecting the sun and stark long shadows of purple and blue.

The child circled a blockish outcrop of rock, blending for a moment with the lacy filigree of clouds caught at its tip.

And just that easily, Lia lost her. There was no hint of smoke amid the mist, only the faint, distant shiver that told her the girl was still there—somewhere. Lia slowed, pushed sideways with a jet of glacial air, and right as she was about to gather herself for the plunge after her, the girl reappeared. Only now she was a dragon.

Slim as a snake, writhing and twisting, she emerged from the vapor and fell toward Lia. Her wings were folded close to her body; her scales glistened absolute black. Of all her family, of all the tribe, Lia had never before seen a dragon without colors, but this child could have been a thread plucked straight from a nightmare: small and ferociously perfect, only her eyes and her wing tips and the ruff down her neck shining pale, unmistakable silver.

She opened her mouth and bared her teeth. Before Lia could swerve away, the black dragon shot through her, hard enough to leave a hole through what would have been her middle.

It did not hurt. It was strange and unpleasant; for an instant she was aware only of the sky, pulling her into pieces. She tumbled with it, seeing white, seeing azure, another lake shattered with the sun. With a great force of will she drew herself back together, and when she could focus again, the dragon-child was fanning the wind about a mile distant, looping up and down without flying any farther. Her shadow rippled along the mountainside in a slow, lazy figure eight. Her face was lifted in Lia's direction.

Lia realized she was waiting for her.

Turn, she thought, summoning her fiercest thoughts. *Turn, Turn, just this* once *let me do it*—

But she remained only smoke.

It was considered a Gift to linger in this form. Smoke was silky and wily, a sleek, in-between blessing to fully separate their human shapes from their dragon ones. But smoke was also slow, and it blew thin. It was never meant to be held indefinitely, not even under the balmiest of conditions. In Darkfrith, with its rolling green hills and soft inland breezes, the *drákon* shifted in and out of smoke without care.

But here—in an open ocean of a sky like this, with the wind whistling off the bald rock mountains, ripping into her, Lia knew that no matter how much she wanted to catch up with that child, she would fall behind. Nothing was as swift as a dragon in full flight.

She thought of Zane, waiting below her. She thought of the hotel in Jászberény, and the image of the scorched brick around her window, all that had been left of her room.

Lia fought the wind. She curled up and around and swept toward the dragon-girl, who only watched her come, still looping in slow circles. When Lia was close enough to hear the girl breathing, to make out the long black lashes above the bright eyes, the feathered silver lining her neck—the girl Turned. She dropped in a slithery gray plume down to a cliff's edge below them. Lia matched her movements curve for curve, both of them taking their shapes as humans to face each other, standing barefoot in the snow a few feet apart.

The girl's hair was not quite black, and her eyes were not quite silver. And she was even younger than Lia had first thought, no more than thirteen.

The child's hair swirled with a gust of wind, a sheen of walnut brown; Lia's flew up too. The golden ends snapped and danced a bare inch beyond the other girl's body, but neither of them moved. The child stood straight and unafraid before her, framed with sky and light and nothing else, not even clouds.

"*Cine*—" Lia began.

"What are you?" asked the girl, in perfectly accented French.

Lia narrowed her eyes. "*Drákon.* Like you."

"Where is your dragon?" The child lifted a hand. "You didn't take it, even when I challenged you."

"You set the fire in the hotel. You've been following us for days. Why are you trying to kill us?"

"Kill you?" A pair of fine, winged brows rose in what seemed like real astonishment. "Had I been trying to kill you, I would not have failed. You sleep very deeply, you know. Much more deeply than the man."

"Is that so?" Lia took a step toward her now, taller, stronger, anger warming her blood. The child eyed her warily and backed away.

"It was a test, at the hotel. I wanted to see if you were truly one of us. I've felt you for weeks now—you're new. You're different. You look like us and you smell like us. But you did not change to escape the fire, so—I thought I was wrong. Yet here you are." Her mouth pursed. "It's very strange."

Lia gripped the girl's arm. "You burned down the *hotel*—you put lives at risk—for a *test*?"

"They're only Others," replied the child, her ashen eyes unblinking. "What do you care?"

The wind howled between them, harsher than the sun. Slowly, Lia relaxed her fingers. She dropped the girl's arm; her feet shifted and a little ball of snow loosened from the surface. It rolled and rolled down the slope of the mountain, leaving a long, straight trail behind.

"How old are you?" Lia demanded.

"Eleven years. How old are you?"

"Where are the rest of your people?"

Once more the girl lifted her hand, a gesture that encompassed the snow and the sky and the sheer drop to the chasm below. Her expression remained stoic.

Lia released a breath, bringing her arms to her chest. Despite the child's apparent immunity, it was cold up here, it was frigid, and she was going to have to do something about it soon; her bare back and feet had already burned numb. "I've come for a diamond named *Draumr.* Do you know where it is?"

Now the girl blinked, clearly surprised. *"Draumr?"*

"Do you know it?"

"Of course. It's in the mines."

"What?"

"Deep in the mines, the copper ones."

Lia considered that a moment, gauging the light behind the girl's gaze, weighing the probability of truth and lies and what the child had to gain by misleading her. But what she said made sense. It explained why the song had shifted as Lia had traveled closer, sinking like the sun from the sky to the earth.

"Can you take me there?"

"No," said the girl, and grinned.

"Listen to me—what is your name?"

"Mari."

"Listen, Mari. It is very important I find that diamond. I'll pay you, if that's what you'd like. I'll pay whatever you say."

"You're English," said the girl, tilting her head. "Yes?"

Lia nodded.

"I heard you speaking English before. I know a few words. Are you a princess? Are there many like you?"

"Mari." Lia had to clench her teeth to control their chatter. "Will you take me to the mine that holds *Draumr?*"

"Even if I took you there, you would not find the diamond."

"Why is that?"

"Because no one ever finds it," answered the girl, candid. "And if you look hard enough, it will only drown you."

"You hear it too?"

"Everyone hears it. The mountains hear it. The moon and the falcons hear it. Even my husband hears it. But it is beyond us all."

"Your *husband*—"

"If you go searching for it, English, you won't come back."

"Mari—are you telling me you're already *wed*?"

The girl gave her an odd, frozen look. "I must go."

"Wait." Lia grabbed her arm again before she could Turn. "That man with me, the one you're *not* trying to kill. I need to find shelter for him. Can you show me the nearest village?"

Mari shook her head. Her hair whisked out once more, dark against the deep blue sky. "There are no villages up here, not this high, not any longer. The only shelter is over there." And she lifted her hand a third time, pointing. Lia followed her finger. At first she saw nothing but more mountains, shimmering ice, and wispy lilac clouds—but then the wind softened. Something sparkled at the edge of a bleak, crystalline peak. Something glittered, with walls and turrets the color of winter. It looked like a castle.

Lia felt her heart sink.

"You shouldn't take him there," Mari said.

Lia shielded her eyes with her hand and limped a full circle along the cliff, but the girl was right: there were no villages, no trace of mankind around her but a single lonesome road leading up to that peak.

"I have to."

"As you wish," responded the dragon-girl, and without another word dissolved into smoke, floating away.

He was waiting for her in the fresh-packed snow outside the mine. From the sky she could follow the oval of his footprints, winding up against the thicket of spruce, winding back. Smoke from last night's fire still leaked in a trickle over the lip of the entrance.

He recognized her, midair. He'd been gazing upward, obviously searching. As she shifted down toward him he drew himself straight, his hands in his pockets, his face inscrutable. Lia funneled into a woman, once again standing naked and barefoot in the snow.

"Come inside, it's freezing," was all he said, and took her hand to draw her forward.

She might as well have been a pinecone, for all he noticed her nudity.

Her gown and cloak were folded atop the sheepskin, her stockings and shoes placed neatly alongside. The chemise was a sheath of silk piled on top.

"Dress," Zane said. "Hurry."

"Zane—"

"No." He sent her a smoldering look, very quick beneath his lashes, before glancing away. "Dress first, Lia. Please. Or we won't talk at all."

So she did.

⚜

The road was not difficult to discover, now that she knew where to search for it. It was, in fact, the same one they had been traveling with the carriage. There were no forks or branches leading off it, only the whisper of animal paths crossing through, boars or wolves or bears long gone, without even pawprints to break the crust of new snow.

The road was a mire with disuse; mud oozed beneath their every step. Maneuvering through it was often a struggle. They'd had no food for a day and a half, and Lia felt it, even if Zane did not.

Hours passed. The sun hung very close. The mountain

light cut so pure that sometimes it was a relief to close her eyes and feel her way blind—but a rock or fallen bough would always jolt her back to sight. Zane, she noticed, never faltered, not through the muck, not over water. In the sun or by the forest shadow, he only paced her. When she slowed, he slowed. When she stumbled, he held her arm. He leapt over the snowmelt streams like a panther, elegant and swift, turning each time at the other side to lift a hand to her, watching her with his sharp yellow eyes.

Usually she accepted it. His fingers were the only real warmth in the day.

Silence stretched like a bell around them; except for short warnings or observations, they did not speak. She'd already told him everything he needed to know back in the mining tunnel.

She'd described the dragon-girl she'd seen upon waking, standing over them with the knife. She'd explained how she hadn't thought about following her, only done it, how she'd shot up into the sky like a musket ball.

That had won her a smile from him, a genuine one. She'd had to stop and pretend to adjust the frogs of her cloak so he wouldn't see what it did to her.

She'd told him of their meeting upon the wind-whipped cliff top—some of it, anyway. Of how the girl had set the fire in Jászberény as a test, and of the winter castle that would be their only hope of relief.

Zane's smile had vanished by then. He'd stared off into the darkness, rubbing a finger along the stubble on his chin. At last he'd heaved a sigh.

"Bloody hell. I don't see a way around it. We'll have to go."

They'd kicked the fire dead. They'd left the mine without a backward glance, Zane with the blanket and sheepskin tied in a roll over his back—he'd ripped loose the hem of her petticoat for a strap—and half of the money left secure in a pocket of his coat. Lia carried the other half. Just in case.

And the one thing they did not discuss, not in the cave and not in this bright open day, was last night, and what had happened between them. It might have been another fevered dream of hers, except for the faint, smarting soreness between her legs that even Turning had not diminished.

No. He was no dream. That pleasure, his lips, his body inside hers—it had been far too bittersweet to be another dream.

After the tenth or eleventh stream they'd hopped across, Lia stooped to pick up a switch of pine. She shook off the snow as they walked and stared very hard at the tuft of needles sprouting from the end.

She blew fire, and it caught. As usual, Zane didn't break his stride.

"We could make a fortune off this back home," he said casually, not looking at her. "Consider the headlines: *Fire Girl. Breather of Light.* That sort of thing. People will pay a groat to gawk at a talking monkey or a counting horse. You'd bring in at least a shilling. Think about it, why don't you?"

She stripped off her gloves, alternating between cupping each palm against the small crackling flames until the blood returned to her fingers. The scent of burning sap wafted smoky sweet into the air.

"*Roaster of Chestnuts,*" the thief said. "*Heater of Bedpans. No Matches Required.*"

"Would you like to carry it?" she asked him.

He took the switch. Almost at once, the fire snuffed out. She found a new stick for him in the woolly edelweiss fronting the road, and after it was lit he held it out in front of him like a torch.

"You won't get warm that way," Lia said.

191

"No." He still would not look at her. "I've a better notion on how to get warm."

"Actually, so do I."

His mouth tightened. "Lia—"

She spoke lightly, quickly, to cover her embarrassment. "You've changed your mind about wanting to marry me. You're afraid I'll burn down your home. Embarrass you in front of all the other city brutes."

"I am afraid," he said gently, "that you will burn down my heart." He glanced at her askance. "Am I a brute?"

"That doesn't even make sense, you know. Hearts don't burn down."

"That's what you think."

They reached the brink of another wash cutting a sluice through the mud. Zane dropped his branch to the clear water. It sizzled and bobbed, tipping askew with the downward flow. They watched together as it caught in a lethargic spin against the bank, then freed itself, floating away.

"My world is a tinderbox, snapdragon," he said, distant. "It's dangerous and unpredictable, and you are the cinder that could kindle it all to ash."

"Would that be so dreadful?"

He closed his eyes. "Yes. It's all I know."

"Not quite." She waited until he turned to her. "You know me."

His face hardened again, his gaze bright and wary, thoughts she could not read turning behind his look. Lia only gazed back at him. She curled her fingers in the pockets of her cloak and felt the roll of coins he had given her, unyielding against her palm. Then his lips began to curve.

"Isn't this the part where you weep prettily and beg me to change, to give up my evil ways and become a decent man?"

"Who's been reading penny novels? I think you're a decent man already."

He shook his head. "Then you don't know me at all."

She said nothing. She stood in the mud and let the air cloud in front of her, hearing the soft, small rush of the streaming water, the snow melting into raindrops that slipped from the trees, the diamond whispering and yearning below.

Zane picked up a pebble and plunked it into the wash. "Play it out, my heart. What would happen to us? We'd retire to Darkfrith on Papa's reward, and I'll become a dull country bloke, growing old and bored and fat by the fire—when I'm not busy ducking your family, who will *not*, I assure you, find any of this amusing. No doubt they have some eager-eyed, sharp-clawed mate all picked out for you, so I'd be ducking him too. You'd despise me within a year."

"No."

"Then I would despise myself. Lia, all that I am is what I do. I'm not meant for a tame sort of life, to dwell in bucolic splendor. I'm a city rat. I ache for it. I was made for it. And I wouldn't expect you to live as I do. I wouldn't want that for you. But it's all I have to offer."

"Then—I accept."

He brought a hand to his forehead and began to laugh. "It's like being snared in a sugartrap. You won't listen."

"I heard what you said. I'm not the silly romantic you think. I don't want the heavens or the shooting stars. I don't want gemstones or gold. I have those things already. I want . . . a steady hand. A kind soul. I want to fall asleep, and wake, knowing my heart is safe. I want to love, and be loved."

"I do not love you."

"You *are* a good liar."

"I *want* you." He turned and stepped closer to her, suddenly imposing, all humor vanished. His cravat was tied; his hair was braided back; he might have been any English gentleman on any given day confronting her in a wild forest, but he was not. When he moved, he blocked the sun from her eyes. The day flared into a nimbus around him. "I want you all the time, and that's the honest truth. I want to touch you again, I want to be inside you. I want to make you scream, and the hell of it is, I know you want that too. But don't be witless. This isn't love."

She stood her ground. She felt shamed and light-headed and didn't know if it was the sun or him or the lack of nourishment, or if it even mattered.

You will not change the future, the dragon whispered. *You cannot make him care.*

From somewhere far, far away, an eagle let out a single piercing cry, and another one answered it, their calls dying off against the hills.

Zane bent his head. His mouth touched hers, cool and impersonal, the kiss of a courtier, and Lia felt her heart give a painful skip.

"Is this your love?" he asked, his hands rising to her shoulders. His lips traced her cheekbone. "Is this the steady kindness you spoke of?"

Her hands raised too, clutching at the fabric of his coat. She lifted her face and closed her eyes, tilting back into the sunlight, and the world went to red behind her lids.

The coat was one from Jászberény, itchy and coarse, nothing of the smoothness beneath it: the damask vest, his hot skin. But the fact that she knew what waited beneath was enough to excite her. She'd tasted him now. She'd known him, in the depths of the night. His skin was pale without his tan; his nipples were brown; there was an old scar that slashed thin along his left ribs. His arms were muscular and his chest was sculpted. He was a man who used his body as a weapon, and with his every breath, it showed. He tasted like candy, like wine and spice and sugar, no matter what he'd been eating. He moved inside her like a demon, opening gates within her she had not known were there.

She touched a hand to his cravat. She found the knot that held the linen in place and began to loosen it, working a finger down into the folds.

"Don't bother," Zane said. He tore off the sheepskin and blanket, and then the greatcoat and his gloves, letting it all fall to the mud. He yanked at the buttons of his breeches and pushed her hard back from the stream, over moss and ferns and rocks until something hard pushed back: a tree trunk, digging into her spine.

His hat fell off. His hands parted her cloak and dragged up her skirts. His mouth didn't leave hers; she felt his words against her lips as his fingernails scratched up her thick stockings.

"Is that truly what you desire? Love and matrimony, innocence and froth? Or is it this—" He stroked her beneath the chemise. He thrust two fingers deep inside her, and despite herself, Lia moaned. Pressed against her, stomach to stomach, chest to chest, his hand sliding in and out—and in—Zane gave his wicked smile.

"That's what I thought."

His free hand took hers and held it to his shaft. He felt both foreign and familiar, throbbing hot and stiff with his breeches falling open to his hips. She dragged her fingertips against him, exploring his shape, his heat, eager to understand this part of him, eager to know how he tortured her dreams and sent her body into night-sweat agony.

She found his smooth tip and rubbed it, following his ridges, the curves and veins and satin softness, all the way down to the curls at his base. She drew her nails lightly back up, turning her hand, rubbing her palm along his center, very gently, because it made him freeze on a breath.

Zane knocked her hand away. He grabbed her by the waist and rammed into her, and the beech tree sifted snow down around them in utter silence.

He was rough. He was uncouth. He gave her no quarter when she turned her head for a cold, quick breath, but pressed his fingers into her cheek and held her prisoner for his kisses. His beard rasped against her face.

"Scream," he bit out, turning his lips against her throat, his teeth closing on her just hard enough to hurt. He pushed deeper into her, fire and pain, delicious heat and lust that rose through her veins. His words were a hiss against her skin. "Go ahead and scream, Lia. I know you want to."

She buried her face in his shoulder. She felt her toes lift from the earth.

"Lia."

She bit down on his waistcoat. She closed her eyes and opened her throat on a sound that hit the sky more urgent than the eagle's, her body shattering around him.

He caught her to him with both hands, thrusting hard. He was as silent as she was not, a force without words or timbre beyond his ragged breath, the slap of his skin against hers, the sifting of the snow with every fierce push of his body. She felt his release. She felt him spilling inside her, his entire being shuddering, her legs spread wide and every inch of her raw to his touch.

For a long time afterward he kept his cheek to hers, winded, their eyes averted. He kept his hands at her shoulders as he swallowed and slowed his breath.

"That—was stunning. But it wasn't love."

Lia had no answer. Not now. She felt sore and bruised and horribly relaxed, a doll with loosened joints. Her head drooped against his neck; his hands reached up and dragged through her hair, tugging at the coronet she'd plaited tight this morning, his fingers pulling as his palms slid down to her cheeks. She smelled him and burnt pine and fresh water, more intoxicating than any wine.

With his thumbs at her jaw he tipped back her head,

another kiss as his body withdrew. Then he dropped his hands and stepped away. Her dress slithered back down over her legs.

A new noise rattled the forest, not very distant. Horses. The steady squeak of wooden wheels.

Zane shoved his shirt back into his breeches as Lia stepped around the beech to glimpse the road. A coach and four—not their own—was heading down the mountaintop, gigantic brown horses picking their way down the slope, the driver's whip primed high and loose in the wind.

Zane expelled a breath, bending to retrieve his tricorne. "Apparently, my lady, we are expected." He turned around to jerk up her bodice, speaking grimly all the while. "Don't look so calf-eyed. If he hasn't already spied what we were up to, he'll guess it in an instant by the expression upon your face."

She pushed him away, enough to make him stagger. But he only came right back, brushing her loose hair back from her cheeks, dusting snow from her sleeves and shoulders. She reached up and yanked his hat over his ears.

Zane raised it up again carefully, examining her with a critical eye. "It's not entirely your fault, I suppose. No doubt you can't help being so damned ravishing."

She could not think of a single rude response before the coach and four was upon them.

CHAPTER SIXTEEN

The strongest magic, as you must know, is born from the shiny sharp brink of sky and earth. Earth has her roots and geometric crystals; these things are useful for grounding spells, for tempting living beings and bending their fates like a cherry-hot blade to the hammer and forge.

Sky has his planets and orbits and infinite constellations. Sky's magic is transparent, ungrounded, useful for slipping into thoughts, for whispering a name in an unguarded ear, for suggesting alliances and enemies or revealing venom in a cup by the aqua light of a harvest moon.

But only in that bounded, unspoken space where these two realms scrape edges is the purest magic revealed: violent, churning, sparks and comets and whirlwinds, invisible to the human eye. From that place, eons ago, from diamonds and lava and ruby spinning stars, the *drákon* were first thrust into light, which is why we are the apex of all things.

We bleed with the mountains. We ponder with the stars.

Our Gifts are plentiful. We speak to stones. We Turn to smoke. We bend metal with our hands and end lives with our talons. We're clever and subtle like the sky, and feral and potent like the earth.

But dreams are not our natural province. When the Gift of clairvoyance is stirred into the soul of one of our kind, terrible beauties result. Of those few in our history who have grasped this Gift, nearly all sank with it into madness over time. It cannot be an easy thing to know your own future, or that of your kin. It cannot be pleasant to witness the story of the life and death of your tribe before it unfolds.

Under the spell of the mighty Carpathians, with the breath of her creation blowing over her heart, Amalia's Gift splintered. She was given two futures: one dark, one bright, the same mortal lover pulling her two-handed into each.

Every step she took lured her closer to the dark.

CHAPTER SEVENTEEN

The castle was huge. Even from a distance it swallowed the view, commanding the eye with white quartzite towers and rivers of time-melted crystals that bled down the walls. It seemed to cling improbably to the side of its mountain, anchored in some way Lia could not fathom—perhaps by the claws of her dead and buried people: she felt them here everywhere. But beyond the cheerful coachman—human—who had picked them up, there were no other figures to be seen. No footmen, no laborers or dairymaids. The windows of the castle flashed black and empty against their icicled casements. Woodsmoke poured up from unseen chimneys, streamers pointing the opposite direction of the wind.

If the coachman spoke French, or Hungarian, or Romanian, he did not reveal it. He greeted them with a phrase Lia did not recognize and waved them into the carriage with big, open gestures, without climbing down from his seat.

Zane had been standing between her and the horses, studying the man. When the coachman set the brake and made to jump down, the thief lifted a hand, a gesture to hold, and strolled forward to open the door. He helped Lia inside with a speaking look.

Beware. She didn't need to hear him say it. Every nerve in her body tingled.

The coach was far more ornate than the one the gypsy had stolen. It was older too, done up in crimson and brushed saffron, fringed tassels looped from the seats and satin window curtains. There were furs and goosefeather pillows strewn across the squabs, and a small yellow songbird, a real one, in a cage hung from a hook in the ceiling. The bird gripped its dowel with tiny feet, staring at Lia. The brass cage rocked with every bump.

Zane had already overturned the pillows, looking for what, she didn't know. He'd checked the compartments beneath the seats—stuffed with more furs—and run his hands along the walls and cherrywood trim. When he was satisfied there was nothing else to be found, he sat back and looked at her, frowning.

"No hidden perfidy?" she inquired, only half mocking.

"Not yet."

He sat forward and opened a window, letting in the frigid air. He turned around and worked at the latch to the birdcage, tugging it open, reaching a hand inside. The bird never moved.

His fingers were lean and strong. He stroked a finger down the creature's back and pried it carefully from its roost.

With his cupped hands against the sill, his palms opened like a lotus. The songbird fluttered out to the sky, a speck of butter yellow diminishing into the blue.

"Well, that's certain to get us off on the right foot," Lia said.

"An unfortunate accident. The latch was loose. The window was down." He lifted the sash to close the glass once again, shoving at it when it stuck. "It's not my fault they didn't bother to clip her wings."

"She's not meant to survive out there, you know."

"I know." He was watching the sky, or the bird; she couldn't tell which from where she sat. "But I'd rather die out there than trapped in here. Wouldn't you?"

She remembered another bird, another time, in the dark woods, with her brothers and sisters surrounding her. She remembered her fear and her determination, and the fragile life she'd ended in her hands.

Lia bent her head to hide her face, dragging another fur over her legs. "Considering the past few weeks, I'd rather not think about it at all."

"Only a fool fails to contemplate the possibilities. It's better to be prepared."

"Yes. And we've been so well prepared for all this, haven't we?"

"Pardon me for saying so, but it seems *one* of us should have been. Why don't you tell me of your dreams now, Lia? The bad ones."

She hesitated.

"Lia," he said again, dark and smooth, just like those dreams. "Do you think I don't know? Do you think I don't hear you at night? You skim across the surface of sleep. You say my name. Betimes you weep. I'd rather you tell me now our future troubles, and spare me the later."

She lifted her eyes. "I die an old woman. I never visit Tuscany."

"Tuscany."

"Yes."

"What would be there?" he asked, very mild.

"You," she said.

He stared at her. The tassels beside him danced and caught the light in their bright satin weave.

"Did I say we should charge a shilling for your talents? I'm certain we could get at least a full crown."

He'd spoken of the sun in her blind dreams. He'd spoken of the sultry Italian heat, and of the *palazzo* they'd buy as soon as their first child was born.

Zane turned back to the view. "Is the diamond with the prince?"

"No." She waited, but he didn't ask anything else, so she added, reckless, "Don't you want to know where it is?"

It was a long while before he answered. "As long as I have you, I don't need to, do I?" He tapped a finger against a saffron tassel, and watched it as if it held the most valuable secrets on earth.

⚜

No one greeted them at the portcullis, nor at the ancient iron main doors. No one came forward to tend to the horses, but the coachman seemed perfectly at ease with the absence of any help. He guided the carriage along the graveled lane that wound inside the castle walls, slowing to a halt beside a courtyard of frosted grass and alabaster fountains dribbled with ice.

Zane stepped out quickly, the carriage tilting with his weight, and waited almost a full minute before reaching inside for her hand. She joined him on the gravel, squinting.

The castle, the walls, the fountains and snow: all brilliant, blazing white. She couldn't help it; Lia pressed a hand over her eyes, just a moment, to save her vision.

The horses began to snort. Zane pulled her closer by the waist, so close he crushed her skirts, and drew her away from the wheels. The coachman gave them another cheery grin before gibbering something; he touched a hand to his head and snapped the reins. The carriage jolted away, following the lane around the inner turn of the wall.

They stood alone before the great castle, listening to the wind howl. And Lia, turning her head, listened to more than that: she listened to the stone walls and the dirt and to *Draumr,* a songbird trapped beneath her feet.

"Welcome home, little dragon," Zane murmured.

Before she could respond, the iron doors began to grind open, magnificently slow, and between them something bolted from the dark to the light—a pair of dogs, huge ghostly shadows, swift and silent, leaping straight at her.

She had no time to move. She had no time even to flinch. She saw teeth and tongues and very black eyes—and then Zane had shoved in front of her, raising up both arms.

He caught both of them. She couldn't see how he'd done it, only that he had and that the dogs were pinned against him, struggling. He dropped to a knee. His hands were fisted into their necks, buried in white fur. The dogs squirmed and whimpered in his grip, their heads twisting. One of them managed to lick his cheek.

She almost squeaked a breath, and it felt like fire. She caught herself in time, her lips pressed tight, her hands over her heart, and looked wildly at the stranger standing in the gloom beside the doors of the keep.

"My guardians," he called in French, and clapped his hands. "Forgive them. They're brutes."

Zane opened his arms and the dogs bounded away across the courtyard, returning to the other man.

He was *drákon*. She realized it past her pounding heart; a part of her must have been preparing for this from the moment she'd heard the legend of her kind. She felt him before he even stepped fully into the light, a peculiar, subtle current that pushed like a bubble around him, that encompassed the doors and dogs, and the shadows engulfing them. And then he breached the shade from the portal, and the sunlight illumed him in blazing color.

He wore a robe of gold foil and dark teal velvet that spread behind him like open wings, revealing beneath a ruffled shirt and black breeches. His hair was extremely dark—under the sun it lit to nearly indigo, long enough to brush his cheekbones and shoulders. His features were aquiline, his eyes a deep sapphire blue. He was close to Zane's age, Lia guessed, or a little younger, smiling now as he came toward them, his arms lifted, his fingers bejeweled.

He was very, very comely.

And he was not alone. He was flanked by Others, arranged in a human V behind him like geese following their Alpha. And this man, this prince—was definitely Alpha.

"Welcome!" His voice was rich. "Welcome, friends! Excuse my presumption in bringing you here. You were spotted down the mountain, walking alone along the road. I assumed the worst, of course—few venture this high, and no one without transport. Was I mistaken? Have I intruded?"

After releasing the dogs, Zane had not moved except to stand and brush at his coat, remaining half in front of her. But at the end of the other man's speech he shaped a bow, his back straight, his extended arm and leg flexed and graceful. The rope of his braid slid long over one shoulder.

"We are in your debt," the thief said. "You have spared us

some trouble, kind sir. My wife and I"—he glanced back at Lia; she sank into a swift curtsy—"encountered a small misfortune. A minor inconvenience. I beg your pardon for our ill-timed arrival."

"Nonsense." The prince walked up with his entourage intact. "Was it your Roma who absconded with a fully fitted coach?" Zane drew breath and the man smiled again, rakish. "We have your horses in our stables, and the bandit in a root cellar. We are a simple people, perhaps, but not fools. No one believed for an instant the fellow was an Englishman on Tour."

One of the dogs ventured a stiff step past his master's robe, staring at Lia. Zane very casually took her hand.

The *drákon* prince noticed. For the first time, he lifted his gaze directly to hers. "Please." His curved fingers touched his forehead, an elegant echo of the coachman's tribute. "Gentle one. Come inside my home."

❧

The castle was a mirage. It had to be. She was overwhelmed from her first step beyond the doors, slammed with voices, with music, Zane and the prince murmuring sentences, the dogs ahead and the people behind them rustling with taffeta and fustian, their footsteps echoing, the very walls of this place soaring in song.

It was a fortress without but a manor house within. There was nothing rustic here, nothing archaic. The entire place was as modern and refined as the most lavish Mayfair mansion, with Chinese silk and plastered walls and frescoed ceilings, and chandeliers hanging in ice-crystal palaces over their heads. The floors were piled with Turkish rugs; fires warmed every chamber they passed; clocks ticked; dust settled over harpsichords and chinoiserie vases and marble bowls filled with walnuts and figs. The halls were painted sky-blue, or

summer pink, or warm, clean ivory . . . but some of the corridors they traversed had no plaster. Some of the corridors had
only the castle's bare base. Between the quartzite blocks shone
cool, colorless lumps, unpolished and uncut, smaller stones
set within the mortar.

They were diamonds, every one. Lia traced her fingertips
along their bumpy surfaces. If Zane hadn't kept such a firm
grip on her elbow, she might have floated from the floor.

God, this place. She could get lost here. She could remain
lost and be happy about it, as long as she could touch these
walls and hear these stones.

"My lady," said Zane, and she realized he and the prince
had paused in their conversation; everyone drew into a knot
around them. The thief slanted her a penetrating look.
"What would you prefer?"

She lowered her hand. She tried to drag her thoughts back
to what they'd been discussing.

"Tea, I think," announced the prince, decisive. "The
English love tea, I do know that. Tea at once, and then you
may rest. Tonight you will tell me all your tales."

Lia curtsied once more. Zane smiled and inclined his
head, but she saw how his eyes rested cold and pale upon her.

⚜

They took tea alone in the suite of rooms the prince had pro-
vided them, seated silently together before the fire in a pair of
silver-striped wing chairs. Their trunks were carried in by the
human footmen; the tea was served by human maids. There
were diamonds trapped behind these walls as well, hidden,
and Lia sat with her gaze on her clasped hands, letting their
notes wash over her, smelling hot sugar and baked cloves and
curling her toes in her shoes.

Zane handed her a cup. From somewhere inside the castle, a harp was being played. Its melody blended with the

stones—with her yellow sapphire—swelling and falling, mournful and delicate.

And behind the wall to her left, sly as mice, were the prince and four Others. She'd needed no special Gifts to know they were there. It was a child's game to pick out their scents, their heartbeats past the wainscoting and quartzite, and she couldn't imagine why a *drákon* man wouldn't realize that. Perhaps he did. Perhaps it was a test of some sort, to see what they would do.

Lia accepted her cup. She locked eyes with Zane and lifted her chin to the wall; he answered her with a bare nod. He was the one who had found the listening holes drilled through the flowers of the wallpaper in the first quick, stolen moment they'd been left alone.

"Out from the frying pan," he said in English, and tried his tea.

It was excellent, she knew. Everything was excellent, the tea, the vanilla crepes and syrupy little cakes flecked with shaved almonds. She ate as if she hadn't taken food in weeks, not days. When the platter was empty, the servants arrived with another, this one heaped with fried pastries and sour cream, and apples dusted with flakes of real gold.

She drank her tea and listened to the harp and the diamonds and the small shifting noises of the dragon-prince. She turned her head and gazed out at the sky beyond their windows, hazing slowly into a turquoise sunset.

Zane had already searched his trunk for his weapons and found them all intact.

She'd never dreamed of any of this. She did not know what would come next.

⚜

The great room was enormous. At last the ancient roots of the castle became apparent, because the chamber was long and narrow with arrow-slit openings high above, letting the dusk slant through in thin blue pieces, braziers and candelabras illuminating the medieval shields with painted crests fixed upon the walls.

Dragons writhed on the shields. Crescent moons. Six-pointed stars.

The main table was fashionably new, mahogany. The service was china with gilt, and miniature peacocks and columbines painted over and over in exact sameness. The table was set for four, although besides the prince and themselves, there were only serfs in the room.

The prince's name was Imre, his family the Zaharen. He'd laughed as he introduced himself, by all appearances abashed that he had not thought to do so before.

He shook Zane's hand—in the course of the introductions, Zane had elevated them from lord and lady to earl and countess—and bowed over Lia's. He gave no indication he'd spent half the afternoon spying on them.

Behind a lacquered screen in their bedchamber, Lia had changed into her lemon-yellow gown. She wanted to be visible, brash, a distraction enough to allow Zane in his plain gray coat to melt into the night if need be.

The fireplace at the end of the hall was large enough to roast oxen. Prince Imre's chair backed against it, so when he sat, the high, carved wood kept a corona of flames. His pair of white dogs sprawled nearby. They were panting from the heat, their eyes following Lia with jetty interest.

"We don't receive many visitors, especially this time of year," Imre said. His gaze flicked to the manservant nearby, who stepped forward with a decanter of wine. "But of course, *you* are the Englishman on the Grand Tour, and a very intriguing one, if I may say so. I find your face far more credible than the gypsy's! That reminds me"—he watched the servant tip the wine into his goblet, the decanter mouth held high, a narrow

golden-green stream splashing neatly against the crystal—
"what shall we do about your thief? Shall we hang him?"

In spite of herself, Lia started. Imre fixed her with a laughing look. "I'm joking, of course. We are not so uncivilized, my lady, even here. But in these mountains, in the passes and steppes, our laws are sacrosanct. He's a Roma and so born a savage. If I let him loose, he'll only steal again."

"Some thieves may be redeemed," she said, as the servant drifted toward her glass.

"Do you think so? You have a tender heart, well paired with your beauty. I fear you're much too kind. But I shall leave him to your mercies. He's your thief; I will do with him whatever you say."

She did not for an instant glance at Zane. "Let him go."

"Alone? In the winter woods?"

"Give him a nag. Give him blankets. My lord will compensate you."

Imre tapped a riff against the table, his mouth quirked. "Anything else?"

She thought quickly. "Matches. Candles, and a cloak. Enough food for a week."

A rimmed bowl was placed before her. She did not look down to see what it was; it smelled like cold strawberries. She held Prince Imre's blue gaze and would not blink, not even when the fire behind him began to hurt.

"A noble heart as well," he said eventually, very soft. "It's fortunate for me you're not *my* wife, Countess. *Zaharen Yce* would be overrun with the dregs of mankind within a month."

"Indeed." Zane sounded bored. "You should see our little estate in the country, Your Grace. She's already commissioned a parish school and a workhouse, for all we've been wed just under a year."

Lia picked up her spoon. The bowl held a soup, although it still smelled like fruit.

"A noble heart," repeated the prince, nodding. "Most becoming in a lady." His voice raised slightly. "Don't you agree, my love?"

From the doorway at the far other end of the hall, a new figure approached. It was a woman, garbed in gold and emerald, similar to the colors of the robe the prince had worn this afternoon. But this was a gown, a *robe à la française*, shifting and flowing, elaborate and modish in a way that Lia's simple lemon frock could never be.

Candlelight glimmered over her face. She wore a topaz choker about her neck and a matching butterfly in her powdered hair.

It was Mari.

The dogs began a deep-throated whine.

Imre stood; Zane followed suit. Lia remained in her chair, staring, as the girl—not a woman—glided forward and lifted her hand to the prince. Both dogs climbed heavily to their feet.

"May I introduce our guests? Lord Lalonde, Lady Lalonde, I present my wife, the Princess Maricara."

The girl acknowledged them each with a curtsy. Her face was powdered too, her cheeks rouged. She lifted kohled eyes to Lia and spoke in a solemn voice.

"I'm late. I apologize."

"Not at all," said the prince, as one of the footman pulled back her chair. He flashed a beaming smile around the table. "We've only just begun."

CHAPTER EIGHTEEN

It was the most delicious and unpleasant meal he'd ever endured. Zane had dined with all manner of evil before, thieves and murderers, rapists and cutthroats, and he'd felt more comfortable in their company than he did seated in this luxurious prison of a chamber, reminded with every glance that he was the sole person at the table who didn't have another life involving scales and smoke and wings. That—hell, that he was the sole person at the table.

This princess could only be the dragon-girl Lia had told him about. Zane was practiced at hiding his true face, but Amalia was not. Days and nights he had spent with her, waking and sleeping; he was attuned to her now, to her every breath and movement, the tilt of her head, the fall of her hair.

When Imre's wife was still four chairs away the light had crossed her face and Lia had shivered—slight, swift, a fractional disturbance in the air that passed from her to him, and he knew what it meant.

The girl was a dragon. He would have figured it even without Lia's reaction. The complexion, her face, her bottomless eyes. She did appear older than the child Lia had described, but Zane had spent too many years learning Darkfrith not to recognize the *drákon* in their human disguise. It was how he knew that, despite the dogs, Prince Imre of the Zaharen was one of them as well.

He'd not yet had a chance to discuss any of it with Lia. He regretted that, but they'd not been significantly alone since the woods. A man who spied on strangers behind walls was a man wallowing in something far beyond ordinary suspicion. Zane had no desire to provoke him into defense.

He had most of his weapons back. He had his training, and his nerves. But now he had something more precious to consider than just his life.

From the corner of his eye she was amber and yellow with winsome flushed cheeks. She'd threaded ribbons through her hair that shone with the firelight. She sat a little forward in her chair for the meal, alert, mostly silent. Her plates were being taken away still nearly full; she'd hardly eaten. But she was listening, he saw that. She was following his story. Good.

He'd stuck with their fiction about the Tour, since the prince seemed inclined to accept it. He'd woven in riches for good measure and a family seat in York. He droned on about tenants and wheat and the varying qualities of English wool, and all the while the prince nodded and ate and asked vague questions, and no one said a bloody word about *Draumr*, or the *drákon*.

Lia had told him already that Imre didn't have the diamond. No sense in stirring the waters. The sooner they could skip this place, the better. Thank God the Roma had been clumsy enough to get snared.

At the end of the meal Imre caught his wife's eye; she looked back at him tranquilly. Like Lia, the princess had not spoken except when directly addressed.

"I trust I won't offend you," announced Imre, turning to Zane, "if I suggest we forgo the English custom of separating the ladies from the gentlemen for port. Maricara and I, we seldom follow the strictest rules of society." He shrugged a little. "Perhaps because there is seldom anyone here to mind. My lord, my lady, will you join us for dessert abovestairs? I've something I'd like to show you both."

Abovestairs was not another parlor, or an armory or solar. With the dogs trotting ahead, Prince Imre took them up a new labyrinth of halls, up stairways that were at first marble, and then limestone, and then wood. They climbed and climbed, Lia at his side with her hand resting lightly atop his, the prince and his wife leading, and just when Zane was reassessing the moment, was considering the location of his dagger and the speed with which he could reach it, the prince stopped at a landing.

"Here we are at last," he said, and pushed at the narrow door before him.

It opened without sound, revealing a rectangle of fireglow and stone.

It was a balcony off the rooftop, wide and open, with two towers behind and a terrace deck that jutted out over the vast drop down the mountain below.

There was a table in the middle, set with sweets and champagne. There were braziers glowing and liveried footmen waiting against the wall with their hands behind their backs. And beyond all that, there was nothing but stars.

The night absorbed them from their first step, midnight blue seeded with silver, a river of light scoring the vault above their heads: sparkling and infinite, vanishing against the peaks of the high mountains.

He heard Lia make a small noise of wonder. She walked forward, all the way to the edge of the terrace, and stood with her face to the wind.

It was impressive, he had to admit, the contrast of heaven and earth and the starlight polishing everything from the Carpathians to the castle elfin silver. Below them stretched air and the dark descent of the mountainside—and up above was only air. He couldn't glance straight up for more than a few seconds at a time, in fact; it dizzied him, an uneasy sensation that crawled along his senses, that warned he might tumble free from the terrace and fall backward into the sky, lost in the thicket of stars.

The prince joined them, handing a glass of champagne to Amalia, then to Zane.

"Inspiring, is it not?"

"Yes," agreed Lia, warm. "It's extraordinary."

"I'm pleased you like my little surprise. The snow has ended, the clouds have blown west. Tonight turned out especially well." Imre lifted a hand for his wife. She walked forward silently, standing at his side. "Shall we indulge in a game?"

"What manner of game?" Zane asked instantly, before Lia could speak.

"One of the imagination." The prince smiled at Lia. "Imagine this, Lady Lalonde. Look out at my realm and imagine you are not quite what you seem to be. Imagine you are something else entirely, a creature who might spring from this balcony and swoop upward, following the wind as far as you can go. Imagine—you are a dragon."

Lia fell very still.

"This castle, all these lands, were said once to belong to the dragon-people of the mountains, did you know that? No?

It's a well-known tale out here, but perhaps not in England." Imre tasted his champagne, his hair glossy blue, his expression thoughtful. "Legend holds they built this castle themselves. For generations they defended it, guarding their home and their blood. But despite their magnificence, there became fewer and fewer of them, until there was but one left. He died alone, many years past."

Zane switched his glass from his right hand to his left. He flexed his fingers, an instant from the dagger at his waist.

"Yet it happened that this last pure-blooded dragon was not actually the *last* dragon. There were others, you see, spread throughout these valleys and slopes, dragon-people of tainted blood, not pure. Would you like to hear how they came about?"

"Yes," said Lia, facing him squarely.

"It is a boring story," declared Maricara. "I've heard it too often. I'm cold. I wish to go in."

"By all means," replied the prince, and bowed to his wife. "We shall join you soon, my dear."

The girl curtsied again. As she was rising, Zane thought he saw her dart a last look at Lia, her face a starlit mask, but then she'd turned and walked off. She circled wide around the pair of plumy white dogs; two of the footmen accompanied her inside.

"They were known as the *drákon*, these creatures. They ruled this mighty land, and very well too, at least for a while. But they had a secret weakness, one they did not wish anyone to know. It was a mystical blue stone, a diamond. And the diamond's name was *Draumr*."

Zane set down his glass. He meant to watch the prince, to follow the man's eyes and his hands, to be ready—but he found instead that he was watching Lia. Her expression was suddenly wiped as empty as the princess's had been: wooden, polite, her hair drifting free from its coils to toss about her face.

"Once, you see," said Imre, "there was a princess...."

Time slowed down. When Lia's hair moved, it was a silky, languid motion. When she blinked, it was like she was sleeping, like she was drifting between dreams and awake.

Zane heard about the princess. He heard about the stone. He heard about the peasant boy who'd shattered the rigid, icebound rules of the *drákon* and used the dreaming diamond to steal the bride he wanted. About their children, and their deaths, and the diamond lost to the copper mines, and he looked at Lia, awash in starlight, and thought, *She knew.*

She knew.

And all at once everything *he* had not known, everything he hadn't been able to puzzle together, made a dark, lucid sense. Why Rue or her husband hadn't come themselves. Why Lia had risked tribal punishment to steal away. Why she stuck with him like a burr no matter how he'd tried to shake her off; her evasions; her restless dreams. She was steeped in magic herself, a child of dragons who could close her eyes and peer into the future. She had seen what he could not. And he'd bet his life it wasn't Tuscany.

A diamond to control the *drákon*. A diamond, a physical thing, that would allow someone—*anyone,* even a common thief—to take command of the most god-awful incredible beings on the planet. To have them do whatever he willed.

It was more dizzying than the stars. It was...perfect.

In that slow-moving dream on the castle terrace, Amalia turned her face to his. Her eyes were deeper than midnight, her skin silver-blue. She gazed up at him without words, without acknowledging the prince or the story or anything else but him.

Zane smiled at her.

"My lady," exclaimed Imre at once, taking up her hand, "are you well? It's only a legend, I promise you! I meant it as a pleasant trifle, a little history of my home to enliven the night." He snapped his fingers at a footman, who hurried forward with more champagne. "Pray do not concern yourself over it." The prince held out her glass; bubbles fizzed up to the brim. "There are no such things as dragons, after all."

❧

She did not remember what she said to excuse herself. She left Zane and the prince standing at the precipice of heaven without her, a footman at her heels as she descended the stairs from the terrace, moving from cold air to cool as the door was shut behind her.

She'd forgotten about the dogs. They'd rumbled as she went past but she had not slowed, and before they could do more than that, she was inside the castle again.

It seemed darker here than the night. There were lamps, but their flames were so dim, she could hardly see where she was going. But she had to go—she had to walk. She could not stand beside Zane for another instant and witness that awakening upon his face.

She was glad now that her dreams had been blind. She was glad she'd never before seen that chilled hunger as he looked at her, that wolfish, glimmering calculation.

At the foot of the marble staircase Mari awaited her. She stood with a hand atop the banister, gazing up at Lia with her striking clear eyes.

"Leave us," she said to the footman, who bowed and backed away.

Mari crossed to a doorway and allowed Lia to enter first, latching the door behind them.

It was a music room. There was the harp Lia had heard

hours ago, golden and silent in a corner. There was a pianoforte at the other end of the chamber, and chairs and a carved ivory folding screen. The rug was latticed with roses and lavender, the walls were apple-green. Lights glowed from frosted-glass sconces. It was a feminine place, peaceful and pretty, as genteel and contained as the night outside was not.

"Do you play?" Mari indicated the harp, and crossed to it when Lia shook her head.

"I do. I've learned." She plucked a few notes, then stroked her fingers over the strings, releasing a waterfall of sound. "I never told him we'd met. He doesn't like it when I leave the castle. I hope you didn't mention it."

"No."

"Are you still going to try to find *Draumr*?"

"Yes."

"Why?"

"I have to. I'm meant to."

Mari gave her a sideways look, gray ringlets framing her face. "Many have thought the same. They all perished. I can tell you what it's like. You go down there in the mines, you fly or you walk, and the song beats in your head like a kettledrum until you can't think any longer. Until you're mad with it, and you have to leave or else lay down and die. It won't let you have it."

Lia sat upon a chaise longue and dragged a pillow to her lap.

"And even if you found it, Imre would never let you keep it," the girl continued. "He's jealous of us. He'd steal it from you as soon as he found out."

"Jealous?" Lia repeated carefully. "Why?"

Maricara strummed a new waterfall. "He's powerless. Couldn't you tell? *He's* the last of the pure-blooded *drákon*—he's the one from the story he was telling you. But he was born without the Gifts. It's why he took me from my village, even though I was just a serf. It's why he's welcomed you into his home. He can see us, and he can touch us. But he cannot *be* us."

"He said it was a game. He said it was a legend."

"Yes," said Mari flatly. "The game is that he is toying with you. He enjoys it. But he knows what you are. He knew the moment he first saw you, just as he did with me. I'm the only female alive who can transform—at least I was, until you. Are you truly wed to the Other?"

"Yes. Are you truly wed to the prince?"

"Yes." Her fingers found a descant, floating soft and sorrowful through the room. "But he would divorce me, I think, for you. He wouldn't have to wait for children then." Another descant. "I wish you weren't wed."

Lia squeezed her pillow. "I wish you weren't either."

Maricara gave up her standing tune and took the stool behind the harp, spreading her skirts. She leaned forward, her white arms stretching, and began a new song with her cheek pressed to the gilded frame.

"They'll come down soon," she said under her music. "When will you go for the diamond?"

"Tonight. I suppose—tonight."

"It's dark now. It's cold. Better to wait."

"I don't think I can."

"Why?"

Lia was quiet for a moment, listening to the tiers of the song.

"I dream the future," she said finally. "It's a Gift. And in my dreams, my people are destroyed. My home is abandoned. My husband is my enemy. And it is all because of this wretched diamond."

"Then you should kill him," said Mari, calm. "It's why you came here, yes? You can't let him have it."

"I know."

The girl's fingers skimmed a heavenly scale. "Shall I do it?"

"No."

"You love him."

Lia tried to laugh; it caught in her throat.

"You do," said the princess. "It is unfortunate."

Lia stood up with the cushion in her clenched hands. "You will not harm him. Do you understand me? You will not touch him."

Maricara bowed her head. "We'll see."

"I swear to you, if you—"

"What's it like, to be in love?" Mari's chin lifted; she stared once more directly at Lia, painted and pretty, not a cloud behind her gaze. "The servants speak of it when they think I can't hear. I only wonder."

Lia turned around and tossed the cushion back to the chaise longue. She found that she didn't have an answer to Mari's question. She couldn't say what she'd heard her sisters always say, *It's thrilling,* or *It's bliss,* or *He makes me so happy.* She raised her head and swallowed the strangeness in her throat, walking to the fireplace, to the pianoforte, pressing a finger against the honey-buffed wood.

"It is," she said at last, "the most terrible feeling in the entire world."

And she meant it.

"Yes," the girl agreed, examining her face. "I think it must be."

"If anyone is to kill him, it will be me."

"As you wish."

The song concluded. Maricara's hands lifted from the strings for only a brief moment before she closed her eyes and began the same piece again.

"Perhaps none of it will come to pass. They're only dreams."

"Not mine. They come true. They always come true. And no matter how I dream it—he's always the one who ends up with *Draumr*. He's always the last one to hold it in his hand."

"If you kill him," said the child, practical, "he won't hold it at all."

"Then it would just be someone else, wouldn't it?"

"Mayhap. It's been lost all these centuries. It could stay lost."

"No." Lia went back to the fire. "It won't stay lost, because I'm going to get it. And then I'm going to destroy it."

"You think you can change the future?"

"I don't know." She shook her head. "I have to. I have to try."

"Countless lives have been sacrificed seeking that stone. My uncles and grandfathers. My older brother."

"I'm sorry for your loss." Lia held her hands to the flames and spread her fingers, watching the heat pink her skin. "But it doesn't alter anything. My people know it exists now. Zane knows it exists. They'll never stop searching for it. But I'm the one meant to find it. *Draumr* wants me to find it."

"How do you know?"

"It told me. It's always been telling me."

❦

Zane was not a man susceptible to flights of florid imagination. He was cunning; he recognized that about himself. He was intelligent. He was intuitive. He had the gift of invisibility when necessary and a quicksilver tongue that had gotten him out of more disasters than one. He was not soft, not romantic, and not gullible. One of his very first memories was of being taught by a black-haired prostitute with pocked skin and no teeth—her name had been Dee—how to rub dirt in his eyes hard enough to make himself cry. He had been five, the cloying hook in a wiry gang of street children; as soon as he'd managed the trick, he helped lift his first purse from a drunk skinner. At the age of seven he was doing it alone. At ten he was the leader of his own ragged gang; they'd squatted in a tottery ruined warehouse by the docks, sharing quarterns of gin and roasting rats for supper when the days had gone lean. Most of the windows had been broken out by stones or birds. He'd spent those first years of his life smelling the Thames, day and night, silt and manure and rotting fish.

He'd never dreamed. He'd worked. He hated the warehouse, so he schemed for a better place. He hated the taste of rat, so he'd found Clem, who fed him meat pies and puddings in exchange for copper coins and snuffboxes. He hated the effects of the gin—the loss of dominion over his own body—and so stopped drinking it.

Prince Imre's diamond tale was so tragic and far-fetched it was better suited for a nursery than a starry night among French champagne and adult company. The street urchin inside him wanted to laugh at the mere notion of it. But Zane was more than that child. He was grown, and he'd seen and touched wonders that would have sent an ordinary man into spasms of denial.

He never dreamed; he did not dare. But he watched Lia Langford walking away from him across the terrace of the cold, glinting castle, heard the click of her pumps against the hard stone, her skirts trailing wide, her head bowed, the nape of her neck revealed, and he was gripped by a desire so strong he nearly couldn't breathe.

If he had that stone...if he held the diamond...then there would be no stopping his dreams. Not any of them.

And the boy who had chewed upon rats to survive thought:

She could be mine.

CHAPTER NINETEEN

She waited for him in their sitting room. She waited a very long while. The longcase clock down the hall struck half past two, and still he did not come.

There was no one now behind the walls. She made certain of that; she opened her ears and her nose and took in the silence behind the wallpaper flowers. There were no Others keeping watch. The prince was somewhere else, far else. She felt only dimly his presence within the castle. Far stronger was Mari, secluded in another wing, alone and unmoving. And Zane...

She cast out her awareness and encountered nothing of him. He would not have left, not without her. But she was used to his presence now, to the warm energy of him, his quiet strength. Perhaps it was the chorus of diamonds surrounding her—among all the Others, she couldn't find him.

And he did not come.

She was too restless even to sit down. Lia paced the connected chambers, passing the canopied bed and the rosewood nightstands and the washbasins painted with vines and blue larkspur. She crossed to the windows and looked out at the harsh lucent night and realized Maricara was right. She should wait.

As smoke she couldn't carry anything with her into or out of the mines; she would be truly alone. Assuming she could even find the right entrance to the right tunnel, she'd have no light, no clothing, no guide but *Draumr*'s beckoning. She'd likely freeze before finding it. Everything she'd accomplished so far would have been for naught. The diamond would still exist. The threat to her people would still exist. Only she would be gone.

She lifted a hand to the pane in front of her, pressing her palm to the glass. It was bitterly cold, drawing the heat from her body into a mist around her open fingers. She held it there as long as she could stand, thinking, *This is what it's going to be like inside the earth.*

When she turned around again, Zane was standing beside the bed, watching her with a half-lidded gaze.

This is what love was to Amalia Langford:

It was to carry a secret in your soul for all your days and nights, a secret so heavy and terrible it changed you, made you smaller and more frightened than anyone you knew, a secret so harrowing you couldn't share it with anyone, not your family, not your private journal or closest friends.

It was to know that the man who had captured your heart would also capture your future, relentless, absolute. To always wonder if he was truly friend or foe. To realize that if you spoke your secret aloud to anyone of power—to your father, to your mother, or the council leaders of your kind—the best and worst you could hope for was that they might actually believe you.

And then the man you loved would be put to death.

No trial, no judge or jury. Just...killed. And he would never even know why.

All because of you.

"Tired?" he asked, in that gentle tone that revealed nothing.

"No." She tucked her hands into her skirts. "Where have you been?"

"Exploring."

"This late?"

"Darkness," Zane said, "is surprisingly helpful when entering locked places. It's what I do, Amalia." His lashes lowered at her expression. "It's why I'm still standing here tonight, having this conversation with you. If there are rooms I cannot see, I always prowl. Every night."

"You didn't at the villa."

"I did, but you slept through that one. Why did you think *Madame* Hunyadi was so eager to be rid of us the next morning?"

She said, shocked, "Did you steal something from her?"

"No, I refused something from her." He gave her a look, then crossed to the bedpost, propping a shoulder against it. "It was quite a night for my sense of worth. She found me in her husband's extremely dull library, a book of German poetry, I believe it was, in hand. I've a feeling she was pacing outside the door, waiting for any handy fellow to wander by. Yet it so happened that my affections...were otherwise engaged."

"But—you never told me. You never woke me."

He lifted his gaze straight to hers. "I don't trust anyone, Lia. I never trust anyone. It's how I've survived all my years." He gave a lazy smile. "Another something we have in common, I suppose."

Her lips bowed. Everything she wanted to say to him, everything she wanted to confess, remained trapped in her throat. She couldn't open her mouth to utter a word.

"I'm glad you're awake." Zane pushed off the post and strolled toward her, scented of night and torchsmoke, more beautiful than she'd seen yet, coiled grace and tawny hair, his face clean planes and lines that glowed with firelight. His shoes made no sound across the floor. "I'm not much in the mood for sleeping either." He lifted a hand and brushed his knuckles against her cheek; his eyes followed his movement, a sliding touch that skimmed from her lips to her jaw to her throat, his fingers spread along her collarbone. With his hand warming her skin, his gaze angled to hers through his lashes, pale yellow masked dark.

"You weren't going to tell me about *Draumr*, were you?" His other hand came up. He wrapped a tendril of gold around his finger. "Devious little dragon. We're definitely better paired than I thought."

She felt the beginnings of despair sink runners through her heart. "Promise me that you won't use the diamond against me."

"Against you?" the thief murmured, and touched his lips to her forehead, feathery, fleeting, cool as the air.

"Against my family," she said. "Against my kind."

He said lightly, "It's only *against* if one resists. What if I use the diamond for something you'd like?"

"You don't need *Draumr* for that." She caught his wrist in her hand, pulling away to see his face. "Promise me, Zane. Please."

He unwound her hair. He looked up and then away from her, staring out at the starry distance just as she had done.

"No," he finally said, without a trace of inflection. "I do not promise."

She pressed back against the glass. "I won't take you to it."

"Won't you?" His eyes glanced back to hers as his smile returned. "Allow me a bit of conjecture, my lady." With a sudden deftness he left her, walking back to the bed. "I think your dreams have had nothing to do with sunny Tuscany. I think they have to do with you, and me, and this most enthralling diamond we're about to recover. I think I somehow end up with it whether you take me to it or not." He began to unbutton his coat. "You dream the truth, don't you, Lia? How spot-on am I? You asked me about this once, years ago. It's rather embarrassing that I've only just now recalled it." The coat was tossed to the edge of the bed, pale gray across the violet-and-slate-patterned counterpane; it slid slowly to the floor. "I don't claim to be a prophet or a mystic. The vagaries of fate have never much interested me. But *you*... you interest me, Lady Amalia. Everything about you interests me. Why is that, do you suppose?"

Lia did not drop her gaze. "Because you are in love with me."

"Is that what this is? I see myself in you, I know that. Your thoughts, your moods, your eyes—I see me. And I never realized that either, until tonight. Is that love, then? I fear I must rely upon your greater wisdom, my lady. It turns out I have no experience with the subject."

She shook her head, frustrated; his tone was sardonic but his expression was not. He was taunting her and he was serious, but she couldn't tell which he meant more. She couldn't tell anything any longer—that damned prince and his damned stupid story, ruining everything—and it was like a long, winded free fall, frantic, pinwheeling. Everything was changed, everything was dark. She felt trapped and afraid, and the person she wanted most in the world to comfort her only stood nearby, idly removing his garments.

He took off his waistcoat, his shoes, and unlaced his shirt, his bare skin gleaming. In his breeches and stockings, he lifted his arms and pulled the tie from his hair. His muscles worked; the fire threw silken shadows. Without meaning to, she let out her breath.

Zane looked at her askance—a hot, merciless look. "Shall we examine the notion further? I've an excellent idea how."

He dropped the tie to the floor and undid his breeches, one button at a time. He stepped out of the last of his clothing and turned to her fully, allowing the firelight to reveal him. He was lean and tanned and aroused, unashamed. His hair brushed halfway down his back.

She felt panicked. She felt desperate. She could not look away.

He lifted a hand to her, palm up, waiting. Her blood sang and the dragon in her burned, but she did not move.

"Lia-heart," her true love said. "Nothing either of us can say will change this night. No amount of hand-wringing will end our story any sooner or cast our fates any differently. Tomorrow we can be enemies, if you like. Tonight we can be the very best of friends."

Over her pounding pulse, she heard herself say, "You're bloody practical, aren't you?"

"Hazard of my profession. Come here."

She closed her eyes, fighting this, fighting the want and the fear and her aching need for his touch.

His voice went smoky. "Lia."

She felt herself begin to crumble, little pieces, small as miller moths, winging out into the unknown. She took one step toward him, and then another.

And then she stepped into his arms.

⚜

She was rumpled a little, perhaps from their time outside. Her hair was still falling down, strands pulling loose from their pins, and her cheeks were stained, just faintly, from the wind or the fire's heat. He found that in these small, unkempt details she became more real to him, less a creature he knew by myths than the woman he had slept beside, and shared his body with, argued with and admired and lusted after with black hopes and a blacker heart.

For all the tint in her cheeks, she was cool when she came to him, flowers brushed with frost; he felt the chill of her through her clothing and brought his head down to hers, to rest his cheek on the loops of her hair.

One by one he removed the pins, feeling for them, tugging them carefully free. He enjoyed the sensation of weighted locks unwinding through his fingers, darkened gold, as the pins pattered down to the floor like tinny rainfall. She remained motionless for it, her eyes closed, until finally the last coil was undone and he put a finger under her chin to tip her face to his.

Her lips were as chilled as the rest of her, chilled and tender soft. She kissed him back but only just, tentative. He felt hot and alive and hungry for her; with her very reticence she inflamed him. Her arms had slid up to rest around his shoulders. He put his own around her waist and turned her to the bed, breathing against her skin, easing her backward until her legs bumped the edge.

"My word, an actual mattress," he murmured. "How exotically different."

She smiled, just as he'd hoped. He scooped her easily into his arms, clambering atop the covers on his knees. The mattress was thick and very soft; he lost his balance at the end and they landed flat together, his chest over hers, her hair a ripple of wheat and honey tossed across the linens, her brown eyes wide.

He bent down and kissed her. He kissed her eyelashes and her brows, and the tip of her nose, and the corners of her lips.

Her palms stroked up his arms to his bare back as he found the underside of her jaw and behind her ear—she began to laugh without sound, hiding her face against his shoulder.

"It tickles," she whispered.

So he did it again, just to feel her laughter shaking him, then dragged his mouth harder against her, tasting her neck, more serious, and her breathing grew quicker and her hands more restless down his back.

Her gown was combed woolen, soft, but not as soft as her skin. He held his cheek to her chest, finding her heartbeat, her breasts, and turned his mouth to her there—snowy skin and the stiff edge of her stomacher, a few layers of cloth and wire and bone all that lay between his flesh and hers.

Zane took his time remedying that. He discovered her shape, the corset that bound her, the hidden ties that cinched her waist. He tasted Brussels lace and her, inhaled the scent of Lia—no cosmetics, no powder—and it was so delicious and drunkenly sweet he felt he could swim in her forever, here in this bed, in her arms, her head back and her closed lashes dark and smudged against her cheeks.

He didn't know if this was love. Surely whatever love was, it couldn't be finer.

With steady hands he loosened the ties and then the stomacher. He found a nipple, luscious and pink, and suckled until she was gasping, until her hands threaded through his hair and her figure writhed beneath his. He knew her like this, his marvelous dragon; his teeth bit her gently, and she said his name, a catch in her throat. She was musk and succulence, her arms outflung. She helped him shuck off her gown.

He didn't wait. He drew his tongue between her breasts and down, over the curve of her belly—lush, soft, delightfully rounded, and he bit her there too—to her thighs, to the warm amber curls between her legs, his own hair trailing dark along her white skin.

She did not protest. He'd expected her to; she was young, and she was new to this game, and he knew for a fact she'd never been with anyone else. But she only stilled beneath him, her body tense, the muscles of her legs and stomach flexed and smooth and feminine, so lovely he had to taste her again.

He found her place. She kept her taut serenity; he heard her breathing, softly agitated, and his own, and his heart, and the muttering fire. He dug his fingers into her buttocks and nuzzled her and kissed her and thought, *This is love,* because his body was a firestorm set to kindle, and still he pleasured her until her gasps became the shape of his name.

He adored that. He adored her willing body and her wanton mind and the broken, breathless sound of his name rising from her lips.

"I'm here," he said, lifting up to his elbows, plunging into her.

"Don't stop," she said, her fingers in his hair, tugging. "Please, Zane."

"I won't."

She stretched beneath him as he filled her, she turned her head. He murmured words in her ear that meant *yes,* and *that,* and *oh, God, that again.* When she turned back to him he tasted salt on her cheek. It checked him, enough so that he framed her face with his hands and slowed. She bit her lip and closed her eyes, her lashes squeezed to a straight line, beaded with tears.

"What is it?" He was caught between her pain and his own release, trying to focus. "Am I hurting you?"

"Yes." And when he stilled, instantly appalled: "No— don't. I don't want this to end." Her body arched. He went deeper as her legs opened, and when she spoke again her voice was broken, more hushed than a whisper. "I love you so much."

She pressed her face to his neck.

He hovered above her, dazed and delirious. Too late—
she'd spoken and he'd already stolen her words, lifting her
face and holding his lips to hers so she could not amend them
or take them back. They belonged to him now.

She loved him.

He moved once more, his hair drifting over his shoulders
to brush against her cheeks, her lips parting. Her lashes lifted,
and she gazed up at him.

Something inside his chest unlocked—wildly, slowly, a
peculiar sort of melting. He was lost. He was the thorn and
the thistle, blown upon her breeze. He felt, strangely enough,
staring into her eyes, like *he* was going to weep.

Zane had told her the truth before. He didn't truly know
what love was; from the corners of his soul, he could barely
guess. He'd loved Rue with a boy's infatuation, and as a man
he'd loved the thrill of his life and power and hard-won luxury. He'd loved his home, and peaches and scones, the heavy
hush of London fog and outwitting the law and his rivals.
He'd loved concepts and he'd loved things. But her, so brave
and rapt beneath him...

But this...

He was naught but her will. Zane gave her his body and
his seed and everything else of value to him: things he had no
names for, reflections of himself he'd kept quiet and hidden,
fear and hope and unfurling desire. He gave her all he could,
including her climax—shuddering and gorgeous around
him, a delicious throbbing that sent him splintering beyond
stark bliss—and when it was over, when he held her lax
and drowsing in his embrace, he mouthed the words to her
that she could not see, and that she could not hear. It was all
he dared tonight, strangers in a castle, strangers to this land,
their future a great black question mark and an ending he
could not foresee. He bent his lips to her ear and said without
breath:

Lia-heart. Little dragon. I love you too.

And with her cradled at his side, Zane stared up into the darkness. He knew what had to come next.

⚜

She awoke alone. Again. Only this time she was in a bed that swallowed her in feathers and ticking, and she was actually warm and quite comfortable. The morning light was crisp and sharp, a blinding flare through the beveled panes that sliced into the room, picking out colors and shadows and the tapestry cushions on the chairs, the hues of the cloisonné pitcher atop the nightstand: enamel blue and glass green and pearl, flower petals shaped from wires of gold.

Zane.

She closed her eyes and searched for him, her arms spreading to either side beneath the empty sheets. She smelled sunlight and sweet biscuits, and hot chocolate. She sensed diamonds and dogs and Others, and—

Lia opened her eyes and sat up. She wasn't alone after all.

"He's gone," announced Maricara, seated in a corner by an oak coffer. The chocolate scent was coming from the service set beside her, a silver pot, napkins, two saucers and cups. The biscuits were iced pale pink. "Imre took him to the mine hours past. You truly do sleep deep."

"Imre...?"

"I told you he was toying with you. He knows your husband can touch *Draumr* without consequences. And he knows exactly which tunnel leads down to it. I showed him last year."

Lia stared at her, trying to wake. "Zane *left*?"

"Your *husband*," replied the girl, biting, "claimed this morning to believe in dragons and legends. He said he was sent by the English *drákon* to fetch the diamond, because he is the only one who will be able to return *Draumr* to daylight.

They have an augur who foresaw it—I assumed he meant you." The princess was dressed in orange brocade, silhouetted in light, her face smooth and grim beneath her powder. "Imre desires the stone; we all do. But he's never gone all the way down to it. The song is too maddening, so I can't show him where it rests. He's sent Others after it, but they always get lost. Some never come back. So over breakfast they made a pact, the two of them. The prince will deliver him to the nearest tunnel to where the diamond lies, and the Earl of Lalonde will find it and bring it up."

"Why—" Lia's voice, tremulous and too high, cracked. She cleared her throat. "Why would he do that?"

"The earl said that in exchange for Imre's help, he would sell the diamond straight back to him—for hardly more than what your own people would pay. I did wonder what the English had decided it was worth, but I was listening behind the walls at the time. They moved off, and I was not in a position to ask."

Lia flipped back the sheets. "You've got to show me where they went."

"It's probably too late," said Mari. "If the earl has found the diamond by now, Imre will have already killed him."

"Oh, my God."

The girl's eyes narrowed; she sent Amalia a speculative look. "You'll be a widow then."

Nude, uncaring, Lia ran forward and towed Mari out of her chair. "Take me to them right now!"

A frown creased the girl's forehead. She turned her face away. "I'm sorry. I've been forbidden."

Lia gritted her teeth. *"What?"*

"Do you think I'm here because I love the prince?" Maricara tore free, her voice throbbing. "Do you think I enjoy his company? He holds my family in his fist. He is the master of this land, Giftless or not, and he has an army of

Others behind him. Most in my village can't transform at all, not to dragon or smoke. He paid money for me and my parents profited, but the real reason I stay is because I have a younger brother. I still have a father and a mother. And Imre controls all of us. He told me I couldn't show you the copper mine. The last time I disobeyed him directly he had my mother flogged. I won't do it again."

She stood in a beam of light that slashed ocher across her gown, breathing hard. The powder was already fading from her hair. Despite her paint, she looked her age then, small and thin, her lips trembling. She wore a necklace of ornately worked gold that seemed too heavy for her chest.

She's just a child, Lia realized. Skinny, afraid. Just as Lia had once been.

"I was supposed to serve you this when you woke." Maricara indicated the pot of chocolate. "It's drugged. You're supposed to sleep until they return." She sent Lia a beseeching look. "Perhaps you didn't want cocoa this morning, but I cannot leave this castle. It's all I can do. Do you understand?"

"I understand." Lia went to the girl and pressed a hand to her shoulder. "Stay here. I can manage alone."

Mari grasped her arm. "Don't let him kill you."

"I won't."

The window was ancient but the latch was not. She turned the lock and pushed against the hinges, bathed in sunlight, inhaling the mountain air.

"Go east," said the princess behind her.

"Yes," replied Lia. "I know."

She Turned to smoke. She twisted out the window and into the open sky.

CHAPTER TWENTY

For the first time in her life, *Draumr* whispered to her, *I'm ready.*

And with that message came the music, always the music, thick and heady, drawing her in a straight line to a pair of lonely mountaintops and then down, down a tapered chasm that widened into a gorge below, a river of green ice moving with winter sluggishness around boulders and decaying logs.

The mountains were hollow. She felt it, the bitter channels that burrowed through them, connecting in warrens of wasted water and ore, splitting off again.

Draumr called, *Yes! Here!*

But she didn't need the stone's guidance by then. Very few paths cut through the firs and austere pastures; a parcel of men gathered along one of them, standing outside a square, gaping hole in the mountainside.

Lia shot toward them, very fast. A few looked up and pointed, but she was too high, too swift. She passed them in a gray arrow, soaring straight into the tunnel.

There were lanterns set about on the ground, picking out the lines of an old iron track. They showed her the narrow confines of the mine, the flaked rock and inky depths. There was a rope snaking alongside them, descending into the unknown. Lia followed it.

The air about her grew close and humid, cold enough to freeze crystals into the wooden beams and along the chipped walls, arabesques of light in glittering crevices. As smoke the cold meant nearly nothing to her; she could still slice through it, she could still maneuver and duck and turn. But she began to wonder what it was going to be like when she had to Turn back.

Don't think about it. Just get that stone.

The rope kept on, occasionally lit by those lanterns. She was moving quickly, so quickly that when she passed Imre he barely had time to glance up at her—but he did. The tunnel was tight and she could not avoid him: he lifted his hand to her, the cuff of his coat falling back, his fingers opening a wake through her center as she flew past.

Damn it. She floundered, swirling, struggling in her velocity to pinch herself back together. He vanished as she fell down another level of the mines, and the diamond's song shuddered through her, the notes pitched sharp and painful. She clouded against an empty shaft, hanging there until the ache began to weaken.

The rope dropped straight downward. The glow of another lantern rose up like hellfire from the bottom of the earth.

She slithered down. *Draumr* echoed in widening waves,

bouncing back off the vertical tunnel, doubling, tripling, louder and louder, and Lia understood what Mari had been trying to tell her: to go farther would be madness.

But she did.

Zane was with the light, in a small landing littered with rocks and the rusted remains of a toppled cart. He was staring up at the shaft she was descending, the rope wrapped in coils around his arm. He was breathing frost, his hair pulled back, his eyes narrowed. He wore heavy boots and gloves and a fur coat and hat she had not seen before—all courtesy of Imre, no doubt.

"Amalia."

She did not stop. She hardly slowed. *Draumr* sucked her down past him and she let it, almost floating. She was ahead of him now. She was going to win. She was going to reach the diamond before anyone, take control of her destiny, and save her people and the man she loved, and if *anyone* tried to stop her—

But she had forgotten something important. Something she'd known, and had forgotten.

It was a peculiar limitation of the *drákon* that actual sight was necessary for the Turn. The sages said that for every Gift there was a balance, and for Turning it was this: all surroundings must be visible. Without sight, this Gift was gone. The surest way to constrain her kind was with a blindfold or a hood. It was used as one of the harshest punishments in Darkfrith, on runners or the particularly wicked. A very few offenders were offered the choice between permanent blindness or death. Most chose death.

As a *drákon* who could not Turn, Lia had never deeply considered it. Her world had been smaller, and far more human. When her brothers and sisters put their heads together over tea or backgammon and compared their limitations, Lia had only sat apart, watching them, thinking, *So, so lucky…*

It happened that a pitch-dark cavern eliminated her sight. As the last of Zane's light faded behind her, Lia found herself gathering, a raincloud set to descend. Before she could control it, she Turned back into woman, staggering against the uneven floor.

She fell to her knees. She scraped her palms. She caught herself against a wall—she thought it was a wall—and knelt there, panting, the utter darkness wrapping around her.

Draumr showed no mercy. The song was a hammer inside her head, thunderous and unremitting; her skin went to gooseflesh and her body began to clench. She staggered to her feet, using the wall to guide her upright. She took a step forward and sank calf-deep into glacial water, the cold so fierce that for a full second she didn't even feel it. And then—

She began to stumble ahead, one hand still tracing the wall. Nine hitched breaths—long enough to numb her to her knees—and she was out of it, climbing atop a pile of chipped stone, hugging her arms to herself, bowing her head.

I'm here, here, here, Here, HERE, HERE—

The diamond wasn't far; the song was screeching through her in something close to agony. Surely it was nearby, not even in another shaft. She took a blind step forward, and then another. On her fifth step, she splashed down into a lake.

Perhaps it wasn't a lake. It felt like one. There was no bottom, no sides. Only water. And she could not swim.

HERE, HERE, HERE—

Draumr rested at its bed, she was certain of it. Lia flailed and struggled, finding her head above water for a few precious seconds—enough to gulp a lungful of air—and sank again. She lost the feeling in her legs and fingers. She lost all direction. She held her breath and let gravity steal her weight, controlling her panic. Pressure at her ankles, solid stone: she had reached the lake bottom.

She bent down. She stretched out her arms. With her

lungs burning, she crept and crawled like a crab, searching, following the song—she was so near—

But it had taken too long. She ran out of air.

Stupid, stupid—and too late. She tried to push up against the bottom, but it wasn't enough to break the surface. She was being pressed thin in the icy water, suspended, and no matter how she fought, there was no longer any up or down. There was only black liquid, and *Draumr* retreating into silence inside her head, the opposite of her booming heart.

. . . here . . .

With the last pulse of the diamond, Amalia succumbed. The air left her body in a rush of gently rising bubbles.

Something grabbed her by the neck. She was jerked upward—tugs and pulls. Then she could breathe again, and the something turned out to be an arm clenched around her, and a solid man at her back.

She made no noise beyond purling water as Zane hauled her to a precipice of rock.

"Get up. Get up there! Goddamnit, Lia, wake up—"

He climbed out first, dragging her after him. She rolled onto the stone and retched. She was coughing, freezing, and Zane was hanging over her with his hair dripping onto her face.

"Lia!"

She realized that she could see him. There was a lantern chucked sideways in a pile of gravel—the same pile she must have mired through before; there were her footprints—its light spitting and threatening to die. But she could see him. The space of the cavern, huge and ominous, chunks of rock and ore glistening. The rough face of the lake—God, it was a lake—still blackly chopped, his coat and hat tossed at its brink.

His palms chafed her cheeks. His lashes were wet, he was scowling and saying words she no longer heard.

Lia Turned. She rose up in an arc and poured herself down to the lake, pushing hard at the thicker water, forcing herself beneath the surface skin.

Smoke was not meant to divide heavier elements; it took velocity and focus and great determination. It took desperation and *Draumr* singing her on. But she knew now where she was going. She would get as close as she could, Turn to woman, reach the diamond, and bring it back to the air, throw it somewhere high where Zane could not reach, Turn again—

Just a few feet under, the water pushed her back into her human shape. She kicked downward, sinking again into the frigid depths.

She felt, rather than heard, the impact of Zane's body striking the surface. She felt him above and behind her, moving more swiftly than she.

Zane, of course, could swim.

But *Draumr* wanted *her* to win. She knew it. It was what kept her falling into blindness, and silence, and pressure, until there was only the diamond again in her head.

HERE HERE-HERE-HERE-HEREHEREHERE!

And there it was. Even through silt and the baleful black waters it shone, a spark of pale blue, a call and a cast of light that drew her forward. Her arm reached out. Zane was on top of her.

From the edge of her vision she saw his hand, his movements barely perceptible yet matched to hers so perfectly it was as if they had rehearsed it, a slow water dance, their fingers open, their wrists straight, trajectory and purpose exactly aligned, and only the split-second advantage she had over him, the fact that she was a foot lower, meant her fingertips touched the diamond first.

Lia closed her hand over it.

Pain exploded through her, instantly, horrifically. In a

storm of silt she thrashed and screamed, her fingers clenched around *Draumr,* and she could not let *go,* she wanted to let *go* but her fingers would not open again—

❧

Rue was in her garden at dawn. She enjoyed its early-morning hush just as much in the winter as in the full bloom of summer. Winter brought its own gifts, holly berries, dried grass that crushed beneath her feet as fragrant as straw. She enjoyed the notion of the world tucked asleep, of the plants holding their lives curled tight and safe inside their stems, waiting for spring.

She walked alone this morning, a bengal shawl about her shoulders, witnessing the salmon-pink light lift into blue. Behind her slumbered the gilded cage that was Chasen, holding *drákon* servants and her husband and two of her children. This early in the day, only the restless and the chambermaids were up.

Something sparked overhead, not a dragon. She looked up and caught the tail of a comet, a blaze of fiery gold streaked across the heavens, widening and fading, a thousand fireflies falling to earth.

For no reason at all, it sent a needle of panic through her heart.

Amalia, she thought.

The marchioness let loose her shawl. She picked up her stylish skirts and ran back to the manor house.

❧

She Turned to dragon. Right there beneath the lake, writhing in silent fury. As a dragon Lia released the stone, pushing past the human man who bobbled at her side, using all her might to erupt up into the cavern, fountains of water streaming from her wings and neck and scales. She smashed into the ceiling, unstoppable, slapped along the walls, still scream-ing without voice. True dragons made no sound; she only smacked, over and over again, against the confines of the hol-lowed rock.

Another man stood watching at the mouth of a tunnel, a tiny black figure edged in light. She howled toward him, Turning to smoke only at the last instant, raging out past him toward fresh air and sky.

❦

She'd struck his head with her tail. He'd thought it was her tail, but it could have been a wing, or a leg—it was enough to disorient him, to leave him floating too long without breath or measure. In his daze he thought he saw the diamond drift-ing past him from where she'd dropped it, rounded blue light, a crystal star trapped with him in these dark waters. He reached for it and missed, his fingers sweeping across nothing. The light faded.

Zane grimaced and swam after it. He would have to breathe soon, it was hurting too much, but if he looked away from the diamond now he'd likely not find it again. It was too dim here, the waters too deep. It might take weeks to search the lake.

He did not have weeks. Judging by what happened to Lia, he had barely minutes.

He began to curse in his mind, every filthy word in every language he knew, mild oaths, dirty ones, the crudest street slang he hadn't let himself use in years, all distractions to the fact that his body was dying, that his lungs were collapsing, and soon he'd have to give it up or give up his life, because he couldn't find it, it was gone, and he was done, he was exhaling—

There. There it was, a glint of blue. With a last surge of strength Zane stretched for it—and got it.

His legs worked. Pressing his lips closed was the most heroic thing he'd ever done in his life, because every part of him was clawing for release, for breath, for *air*—

The water broke around him. He sucked in a mouthful of lake with the air and coughed it back out, still wheezing, still grateful, and fumbled his way over to the ledge he'd found for Lia. He forced his body to the rock, rolling, dragging his legs from the water, his ears ringing and the light from his lantern beginning to die.

But . . . there was a diamond in his hand. It was heavy and even colder than the atmosphere. When he could, he lifted his arm and squinted at it, a smooth, uncut stone, breathtaking even without facets, sending a buzzing nearly up his arm.

He had the strangely random thought that since *Draumr* was here, the dead princess would be too. In his exhaustion he sent up a prayer for her, just a few words, as the water streamed from his clothing along the rubbled stone, leaking around him in puddles and dripping back into the lake.

Thank you.

"Thank you," echoed a voice above him, but in French. "You've done what I could not. I appreciate it. I admire your courage, my friend. Almost I regret to kill you." The prince stepped into view, smiling, a pistol leveled in his hand. "Almost."

"Stop," Zane croaked, and again felt that buzzing in his fist. The prince paused, then shook his head.

"It's no good." He began to creep down the sharp slope of the entrance, raining pebbles upon the mound that held the lantern below. "One of the discrepancies in my blood, I think, but *Draumr* won't work on me. Yet I have no doubt it will do very well for your wife and mine. I'm quite eager to meet my new English family."

The Shadow of Mayfair had a bounty of three hundred fifty pounds upon his head, and that was only because he'd been diligently bribing the deputy mayor not to make it more. He'd been imprisoned twice and walked out both times with a fresh cadre of men at his back. He owned watchmen and magistrates and three quarters of the shares of a very respectable textile factory to cover his tracks.

He was not entirely credulous.

There were weapons hidden about him, small deadly things concealed on his body, in his clothes, none of which he could reach in time. But in all his plans, in all his calculations, Zane had been certain the conditions of the tunnels were too humid for gunpowder to ignite properly.

He'd been wrong.

He hurled the diamond at the lantern just as Imre fired. For a fleeting second the cavern flashed white with the spark of the pistol, then dissolved into pitch.

CHAPTER TWENTY-ONE

She flapped through the air, circling, aimless. She was the wind and the sun; in her turns and loops she discovered her own beauty: her body was amethyst and cobalt, the deepest heart of the sky. Her wings were pearl. Her tail was barbed with gold, and so were her claws.

She snarled at the wind. She devoured it. She twisted up into the heavens and celebrated herself, her sovereignty, and the world below shrank small and unimportant.

She soared above mountains capped with snow, and walled villages hugging sunken valleys. She ringed the clouds and studied the sun and considered rising to it, to eat it too, but there was something stopping her... there was something singing to her far, far below....

Lia turned an eye to the earth. Smaller beings trembled. They hid in their burrows and hoped she would not discover them, that she would not bother to look. And it was their good fortune that the song rising up to her was more compelling than the hunt. It called her name, her human name, and although she had left her human self behind, there was an ember in her heart that lit in response, that wanted to answer it.

Amalia. Come down.

No, she thought.

Come down.

And even though she didn't want to—even though she was free and untamed up here, commanding the sky—she tucked her wings close to her body and began a spiraling descent, marking a white stone castle as her center, tightening her circles until the walls and towers winked at her in ripples of quartzite, until the man and the girl standing in the inner courtyard followed her with upraised faces, waiting.

From somewhere else on the castle grounds, dogs began to groan and then to wail.

She landed in a skid, her talons raking through the gravel, knocking over a fountain at the end of it with a contemptuous flick of her tail. The alabaster basin hit the ground and cracked apart.

"Change back," commanded the man, unmoving.

She inhaled. She closed her eyes and reined in her magnificence. She Turned into woman, standing cold and alone.

Faces watched from behind the castle windows. No one stirred.

The man glanced at the girl, who walked forward and draped a mantle over Lia's shoulders, closing it at her chest. The girl's eyes were bright and very clear.

"Beautiful ladies," said Prince Imre, observing them with

his hands in his coat pockets. "My ladies. We'll go inside now."

The mournful baying of the dogs followed them all the way in.

⚜

The worst aspect of a shoulder wound, Zane considered, was not the blood soaking his shirt and sleeve to clammy coldness, or even the pain that stabbed hot pokers through his veins. It was that, even with a tourniquet, it made his arm useless, and climbing extremely damned difficult.

Still, at least Imre hadn't hit him in the leg. Climbing up mine shafts with a leg wound would have been impossible.

So Zane climbed. It took him hours to escape the mountain. Hours to find another way out of the tunnels besides the way Imre—and, he hoped, Imre's henchmen—took.

After being shot he had, quite sensibly, rolled back into the lake. At least it had seemed sensible at the time; Imre still had his gun and surely the means to reload it. But the nearest bright light was a tunnel away, and unless the prince could see in the dark—Zane sincerely hoped he couldn't—reloading would be tricky.

Let Imre think he was dead, or close to it. He had no problems sinking below the slick surface of the water, floating without noise. The cold had numbed his wound. He'd hardly felt anything at all.

Imre had rummaged around for a few minutes and then left. Zane floated a few minutes longer, listening hard, but there were no further sounds disturbing the cavern beyond his own breathing and the subtle lapping of water against stone.

It had taken far more effort to escape the lake again than it had to roll into it.

He thought of sea monsters lurking beneath waves. He thought of Lia, of metallic coils and open wings, and dragged himself out.

His coat was where he'd left it, the fox-lined hat too. He fished the candle and phosphorus matches one-handed from a pocket—thank God Imre hadn't discovered the coat—and let the slight, wispy bend of the flame show him which way the air drew.

It also showed him that the diamond was gone. He found the smashed lantern, and that was all.

Bloody good aim, he'd thought hazily, and began to climb.

Hours. He imagined her wounded. He imagined her bleeding, as he was. He imagined her supine with Imre above her, his hands on her white skin, and he staggered along a little more quickly. Occasionally he worked without the candle to make it last; he had ten matches. Nine chances to get it re-lit. He tried to use them only at forks in the tunnels.

He didn't know when he began to realize that the small glow of his flame wasn't the only light source before him. The walls began to gain texture and shape. The air lost its deadened scent.

He heard a bird warbling. His tunnel ended in a chink of daylight, a pile of fallen rocks that showed an opening hardly larger than his face. He put his eye to the hole and looked out at a sun-dappled forest, at a tiny bright songbird, butter-yellow, perched on a pine bough dead ahead. The bird looked back at him, falling quiet. It hopped sideways a little on its branch, fluffing its feathers, then began singing again.

❦

In a small, quiet corner of her heart, Lia observed what was happening to her. She felt the hands of the Others as they helped her dress. She heard their whispering voices,

Romanian words she could not quite understand, but it hardly mattered because they were talking about her, not to her.

She felt the daylight on her shoulders as they bound her into her corset. She smelled the outside on their clothing, chemical roses from the rouge on their cheeks, coffee and dairy on their breath.

She lifted her arms as they fitted her with the deep-green bodice, the lace scratchy against her breasts. She gazed out the windows of the bedchamber and thought, *Turn.*

But she did not. She didn't really even try. Prince Imre had handed her cordially to the human maidservants and commanded, "Let them attend you," and that's all she wanted to do.

The dreams had not offered her sight, but she had it now, and with *Draumr* a low, agreeable swirling in her head, everything about her appeared softer, mistier; a sheen of water separated her from the room and the women and everything harsh. She stood alone behind it, admiring the play of light, distracted and happy and at peace. She was back beneath the lake; she had never left the lake. She did not need to swim, because drowning turned out to be so sweet.

Except for that one little corner.

The canopied bed had been made up since this morning. There was no indication anyone had ever slept there; even the pillows were smoothed. And but for the lingering caress of his scent, there was nothing left in this chamber of Zane. Only her belongings remained, her trunk and gowns and two pairs of buckled shoes.

The women placed rings on her fingers that were not her own. They touched perfume to her throat that she did not know. She admired the view and let them comb out her hair, and curl it, and sift French powder down to her scalp.

That unknown corner of her began to bleed, but her body remained passive. Despite her secret heart, she was content to sit until Imre called for her again.

⚜

Like the palace in Óbuda, there would be no stealing into *Zaharen Yce.* It was a fortress before anything else, with a single entrance that he knew of, and that a guarded gate and portcullis, as formidable as any Norman stronghold dotting the hills of the English countryside.

He approached it openly, keeping a hand pressed to his shoulder under the gray fur coat. He greeted the men who poured out to intercept him—bewigged footmen and a few fellows more serious than that, reminding him greatly of Hunyadi's guard. Before they could touch him, he informed them he had news for their master, *drákon* news, managing to imply through his tone and the lifting of his bloodied palm that should any one of them feel the need to prevent him, it would be on their heads.

Zane was escorted inside.

The courtyard looked as if it had seen a tussle. There were deep furrows scoring the driveway, and at least one fountain and an urn toppled and broken.

He'd seen marks like that before. Five claws, four feet. A dragon had skidded to rest here since he'd ridden out this morning, and he had a damned clear idea of who it would be.

He knew from his prowling that *Zaharen Yce* had a ballroom. He hadn't lingered there last night; empty ballrooms echoed uncomfortably and usually held little of interest. Yet today, for some reason, it was where the prince had decided to take his supper.

It was a tower chamber, huge and round, chilled from the slab marble walls that alternated from cream to smoky blue and the Roman pillars that touched a frescoed ceiling at least three stories high. The fresco was of planets and stars and silver-painted beasts. Gauzy curtains shot with gold draped the windows, framing treetops and mountains and that endless deep sky all around. The late-afternoon light slanted in, cool and drifting; the white sparkling floor was devoid of any rugs. Dancing here would be akin to dancing atop the clouds.

There was no hearth, no furniture at all save the table at the end, where the prince sat in a throne chair, platters of food and drink before him, a crystal vase of jasmine adding fragrance to the air. Flanking Imre on either side were the princess and Lia.

It wasn't a ballroom. Zane realized that now. The floor, the stars, the vaulted ceiling: this was a place designed for the convergence of dragons.

One of the footmen hurried ahead, his heels striking hard at the stone. He approached the prince and bowed and muttered, but from the instant Zane had entered the chamber, Imre had not taken his eyes from his.

Zane offered a smile, insolent. He'd intended insult and hoped for surprise. He thought from the prince's rigid expression he'd managed both.

The footman bowed again, and Imre dismissed him with a nod. Zane had not stopped walking, outstripping his reluctant escort. When he was near enough to make out the embroidery on Imre's oyster-gray lapels, he halted.

"You are dripping blood upon my floor," observed the prince.

"My apologies. It is the unfortunate consequence of being shot."

"Indeed." The prince's black brows lifted. "You might have done me the favor of expiring before reaching my halls."

"No," said Zane, and with an effort that cost him dots in his vision and a cold sweat down his back, he completed a sweeping, perfect bow. "I fear I'm never so couth as that."

"So I see."

As he raised from the bow, Zane risked a look directly at Lia: her pallid face, her slumberous eyes, her lips dabbed red and her hair ivory-white. She gazed back at him impassively, her hands folded in her lap.

"I'm going to make the diamond a pendant, I think," said Imre conversationally, tapping light fingers against his vest pocket. "It's too large for a stickpin and too heavy for a ring. Don't you agree?"

"That's how I plan to wear it, Your Grace. I must applaud your taste."

"And I your bravado, though no doubt it grows tedious over time. Lady Amalia informs me you're no earl. In fact, you're not even a lordling. Best of all—you're not wed to her."

"Not yet. We'll be remedying that very soon."

Imre sat back in his chair and began to laugh. "You *are* bold, peasant—or else simply a madman. Why in God's name would you return here? Was a bullet in your body not message enough?"

"I've come for Amalia, and for *Draumr*," Zane replied peaceably. "I won't be leaving without them."

"Pity I don't have my pistol on me. Ah, well! Lady Amalia, how are you feeling? Are you quite rested, my dear?"

"Quite," she said, her face turning to his.

"Excellent. Then listen to me, please. I want you now to Turn into a dragon and slay this man before me. Try not to damage the walls."

Lia glanced back at Zane. She was his and not his, changed since the last instant he had seen her—not from scales to flesh, but from something soft and real and earthly to something else: jewels and gold, rice powder and cool sparkling eyes. She was more gravely beautiful than ever. Her head tipped as she gazed at him, as if he puzzled her, only slightly, a small conundrum that warranted merely the pucker of her lips and a downward sweep of chocolate lashes.

He loved her. The thought that she was going to be his kept him standing upright even as the blood slipped from his fingers.

"Still you smile!" exclaimed the prince. "A madman, just as I thought."

"No." Zane curled his fingers into his palm. "It's just that I know what you don't."

"Oh? Have you some magical spell tucked up your sleeve? Some wizard's potion to stop a dragon in her tracks? I'm all agog. Pray, do tell."

"No spells, no potions. Nothing so dramatic. What I know . . . is the future. And you're not in it."

Imre's expression hardened. He took the diamond from his pocket and clamped it in his fist. "Amalia. Kill him."

She rose to her feet. She stood behind the table, a perfect gentlewoman with smooth powdered curls and ebony lace rucked at her sleeves.

"Lia," Zane said. "My heart. I don't want to fight you."

"I rather think you don't," agreed the prince. "She's about to have a significant advantage. Lady Amalia. Obey me, if you please. Now."

Her eyes closed, opened again. Her cheeks were bloodless, her breathing slowed. The moment spun out, shining, delicate, and Zane thought, *She won't do it, she won't*—

"Zane." It was a whisper. And then, with a cheerful tinkle of falling rings, she Turned, smoke, sinuous shape rising to the air and coalescing down again, and he was looking at the other side of her, a creature so bright and gorgeous it nearly hurt to see, shimmer and color and very long claws.

Behind the table, Imre picked up his wineglass. The princess never moved.

A lovely woman, a lovely dragon; he'd seen them like this, the *drákon* of Darkfrith. He knew their ripples and turns, their long lashes and grinning fangs. He knew their lethal grace, but this was Lia, his Lia-heart, and when she turned her head and fixed him with eyes of molten gold, he did not flinch. When she swept her tail toward him, a blur of gilt and violet-purple, he skipped back a single step, and it was enough to save him.

She's not serious. She's not truly serious.

Her head whipped about, iridescent blue scales, a silky ruff framing her face. She lunged at him, snapping her teeth, and missed him by a hairbreadth. He leapt once more, truly leapt, a shade too slow, a pitch too awkward, and like lightning she struck again, this time whirling to connect the thick of her tail with his left leg.

He heard the bone snap. It didn't hurt; there was no time for that. He fell to the floor and tucked his body into a tight tumble, instinct taking over, moving him away to swift safety. He reeled back to his feet amid dizziness and more blood and couldn't seem to find a certain balance again.

There was a scarlet handprint on the floor from where he fell. His shoulder was afire. He hobbled and turned his back to the blood and thought of all the sly weapons he still possessed: Knives. Picks. Wire-thin blades meant to carve up a heart beneath rib bones, or slice out an eye.

He wouldn't use any of them. She wasn't going to kill him. Despite his leg and his shoulder, there was no force on earth that would make him act against her.

Lia spun about, striking the table with one impressive white wing, tipping it over in a great mess of shattered china and jasmine and spilled wine. The prince jumped back. The princess still did not rise, not even when the broken vase ruptured flowers and water at her feet.

Lia narrowed her eyes at him, every inch of her bristling.

She drew one curved golden claw slowly across the floor in front of her, leaving a scratch mark an inch deep.

Zane began to rethink his strategy.

⚜

Someone beyond the lake was controlling her muscles. Someone beyond the lake sang a chant in her ear, *Obey me, obey me, obey.* She was the song, she was the melody and the harmony, the clever death that swept up and down through the score, sideways, bending, a *chanson* that lifted wings and air and forced the human man battling her to duck small and fling himself hard away.

He had no sword. He had no gun. It hardly seemed fair to kill him, but the hot scent of his blood filled her nostrils, and that was exciting. She'd already wounded him, and that was good.

He spoke her human name.

Lia!

Something cold stirred in her heart. A worm; a doubt. Something as deep as sinew and marrow protested, rusting her in place. It forced her to pause, to examine the man limping before her, returning to her despite the fact that she was about to take his life.

He lifted his eyes to hers, his lips pulled taut, his hair spilling over his shoulders and down his coat. He held up a bloodied hand to her, keeping his weight on one leg.

And then . . . she remembered him. The sight of his hair, long hair—too long for a man—the glint of honey and of sable, blond and richly brown. She knew that color. She knew his face. His set jaw. His yellow eyes.

Yes. She'd known him all her life.

She had a sapphire because of him. She had a dream, many dreams, and a family and a home—because of him.

Lia saw him in a different place, a land of green hills and

gentle streams. A land with ponds, and children, and fishing poles that struck circles into flat water.

She shook her head. She glanced wildly around the foreign room and felt herself begin to shrink inside.

"Snapdragon." The man was not so hardy as he appeared; he listed sideways and dropped to one knee, his skin beaded and pale. Blood had splashed a circle of red raindrops around him. He looked very ill.

She Turned to smoke. She Turned to woman. Beyond the placid lake someone thundered her name, and she put her hands to her ears, crouching down, rocking in place, not listening.

No, no, no—she'd rather drown, she'd rather die—

A hand met her shoulder. The man drew her to him with one arm, this mortal man, smelling of sweat and fox and fresh blood, clasping her to him with a faint, faint noise in his chest.

All the water smothering her fell away in a silent rush. She flung her arms around his neck. She pressed her face into his hair and felt Zane's rough inhalation.

"I'm sorry," she was gasping, "I'm sorry, it wasn't me, oh, God, what happened? I'm so sorry—"

"Hush," the thief murmured, his arm very tight. "Sweet girl, I've got you. Hush now."

The *drákon* prince lifted his voice in time with *Draumr*'s dark tune.

"Lady Amalia. For every second you disobey me, there is a knife stabbing you in the heart."

She took a long, shuddering breath—and felt the blade sink into her.

"It hurts you like fire. It scorches your skin. You're burning, Amalia. You must kill him to stop the pain."

Her throat closed. Her eyes teared. Her fingers clenched and her head fell back and she could not breathe.

"Fire, Amalia. All you have to do—"

Zane said urgently, "Lia. Don't listen."

She was blistering. She was smoking. She twisted against the hard floor and felt her flesh begin to melt. Zane's hand at her shoulder was a smoking iron, crisping down to her bones.

"Lia! It's not real!"

"But it is, my lady. End it. Turn to dragon. He is nothing to you. You'll be whole again."

So here was the other side of the lake: a sheet of fire. Here was an aspect of *Draumr* she'd never even imagined, that it could be used to set her nerve endings alight, that it could whisper, *Burn to ashes and embers,* and she would.

"Destroy him, Amalia, and the pain will cease."

Zane was trying to stand. "Damn you! Stop hurting her!"

She ripped at her hair; she couldn't scream. She could only shake her head, over and over, not even managing a moan.

From a very great distance, she heard the prince sigh.

"Maricara. Finish it."

A chair was pushed back, scraping the stone.

Lia found her voice. *"No."* The word came hoarse, broken with rage. It sounded inhuman, an animal voice, but it was hers. "I'll kill you. I won't let you."

Traitor, sang the diamond. *Burn merry, a merry burn. . . .*

⚜

Maricara moved to obey like a mermaid beneath the sea. She was slim and lissome; it was one of the reasons she made such a fine dragon. She glided in front of her husband in the orange brocade gown he'd picked out for her this morning, her arm reaching up, the supper knife firm in her grip. She struck him deep beneath his third rib; he was tall and she was not; she could not reach much higher than that.

Imre stared down at her with an expression of astonishment. She felt, interestingly, absolutely nothing. His hands closed hard over hers, jerking her close, so that her skirts swept his legs and her chest met his belly. Red ribbons spurted over their joined fingers; the diamond blazed hot against her skin. But it loosened his grip on her and she jerked back, stepping into a tangle of jasmine stems.

For a long instant her husband stood alone, his blue eyes clear, his handsome face blanched. He swallowed and pulled the knife free, frowning at the blood-smeared metal.

"You didn't say how," Maricara said, as the prince collapsed to the floor.

⚜

Draumr rolled free from Imre's fingers. It didn't roll far; it wasn't round, only rounded, and the force of the man's hand striking the floor sent it off with a small, chinking rattle that was the only sound Zane heard beyond the prince's breathing and Lia in his arms, panting tears upon the floor. It came to rest at the feet of the princess.

She seemed not to notice the diamond, or anything else. She stood cool and blank above her husband—but with a sudden sob, her face crumpled into tragedy. She dropped into a squat, as inelegant as any street waif, and buried her head in her hands. A choked, high-pitched moan pushed past her palms.

The prince lifted his arm. He touched the hem of her skirts.

She kicked free of him, scrambling back, and the diamond went rolling again. It bumped into the overturned table and caught against a cluster of white flowers.

Lia turned her head.

In the space between one heartbeat and the next, Zane realized what was about to happen. She still lay beside him, her body cold and nude and unbroken. She did not shift, she did not tremble, but he felt her intent as surely as if it had been his own. As his heart reached its next beat, she Turned to smoke.

He was a thief, a rat, an urchin. He did not think. He did not pause for judgment. He lurched to his feet and pitched after her.

She should have reached it first. She was a misted rush that zoomed toward the table, a silky gray cloud that began to draw into fingers, into a figure, inches from *Draumr,* and he was none of those things.

Zane gave up his uneven dash. He lunged chest-first to the floor, skidding with the slippery fur coat into a banner of light, his good arm outstretched. Black pain roiled up through his brain, but beneath it, behind it, the icy heft of *Draumr* smacked into his palm. Lia's fingers covered his a bare instant too late. They slammed together against the table, and the pain inside him lit to blind agony.

"No," she cried, anguished, and tried to pry open his hand. She was very strong.

Zane managed a winded gasp. "Stop. Lia, stop!"

And she did.

When the black suns faded from his vision, she was seated like a statue over him, one leg tucked under her, her head lowered and her face hidden. Her hands still covered his.

Something wet struck his wrist. He crawled up to an elbow, dragging the length of his coat and his useless leg, and then to his hip. He used the table behind him to support his back.

The double doors to the chamber opened. Voices rose; a swarm of men began to clip forward. The gauze curtains beside them twirled gold in their wake.

"Princess," Zane rasped. The dragon-girl lifted reddened eyes to his, her cheeks streaked with kohl. "Get rid of them. Verbally," he added hastily, as Maricara found her feet.

She gave a command in her foreign tongue. A few of the

men pressed on and she sharpened her tone, lifting an arm to point at the door.

The body of the prince was half obscured by the table. If any of the servants could see it, they did not linger to ask questions. The men bowed and backed away. Maricara raised her voice to add something else, and the doors closed quietly behind them.

Then the girl only stood quiescent, a puppet awaiting the next pull of her strings. Lia had not yet moved; her head was still bent and her arms wrapped around her shin. Her skin peeked cream beneath the burnished curtain of her hair.

Zane groaned. He tried to slow his skipping heart, waiting until he could breathe normally again before opening his hand to examine the blue diamond. He *was* a peasant, unskilled with mystical things, but God's truth—he felt the power he cradled, felt its buzz and shine and the promise of all things bright and dark.

He could have anything. Sixty thousand pounds, ultimate power—whatever he wanted, whatever the *drákon* of Darkfrith could give him. Or steal for him. He could be the greatest thief of all time; he could be richer than the king—

Softly, almost imperceptively, Lia gave the smallest of sighs.

Zane glanced at her, then lifted the diamond closer. *Draumr* dazzled his eyes like a cold full moon, like a secret drop of unholy sky.

The moisture on his wrist had been a tear. He rubbed it away absently on his thigh, and as if the scratch of the fabric had reminded him of it, the pain from his broken leg washed up into a great greasy knot inside his throat.

"Shit," he muttered, squeezing his eyes closed again. "Shit. Lia. Maricara. Find anything flammable and put it in a pile at my feet."

He heard them moving, Amalia's soft treading and the

swifter steps of the princess, and when he could see again there was a colorful mound of skirts and table linens and damp jasmine beyond his boots.

"Not the dress," he said, and Lia lifted it out, shedding flowers.

He dragged himself straighter. "Is there any wine left in the bottle?"

"Yes." Maricara brought it to him. He took a generous swig, and then another, and then handed it back to her. "Pour the rest on that pile."

It was a Bordeaux, a damned good one. It stained the white holland and stone in a wave of deep maroon.

"Snapdragon." She was standing at his side. All he could see was her leg and hip and the glinting fall of her hair, curving gently above the pretty arch of her buttocks. He shifted on his good hand, dragging his body sideways to get out of the way. "Set it afire."

She walked to the pile. She lifted her hand to her mouth as if to blow a kiss, but instead, a small, perfect flame hit the air, falling sideways to catch at the edge of a napkin. The fire began to crawl along the cloth.

"Right." Zane gritted his teeth and dragged himself forward again, trailing blood. He waited until the flames were taller, until the flower stems curled and the smoke lifted black up to the high, painted ceiling, and then he tossed *Draumr* in.

⚜

For an infinity, she did nothing. Lia really couldn't quite comprehend it: *Draumr* was in the fire. Zane had pitched the diamond—his fortune and her future—into the fire.

It landed amid the folds of the tablecloth, glowing like a blue heart to all the dancing orange and gold. Its song lifted dulcet and pure, still beckoning. The smell of scorched linen singed her nose.

She sank to her knees. From a music-filled distance, she saw her hand reach out.

"Don't." Zane shoved back her arm. "What's the matter with you? I thought this is what you'd want."

"You can't burn it away," said the princess from behind them, her voice muffled. "It's a diamond, not a piece of coal."

"I'm well aware of that."

The linen began to crumble apart. The diamond kept its blue glow.

"Lia." He waited until she glanced back at him, her face pale, distracted. "I need you to remove my boot. The right one. Don't touch the left."

She came to life. She knelt before him and ran her hands down his left leg, finding the break in his femur, his swelling skin. Her fingers were light as butterflies, and misery throbbed with her every stroke.

"I did this. I'm so sorry."

"Yes," he snarled, his head banging sharp against the table. "But, the *boot*."

"Use this." Maricara handed him an elaborately decorated pump, the buckle made of lapis and heavy gold. "It's new. There's a steel rod down the center of the heel."

He'd hurled *Draumr* against a glass lantern, and it hadn't suffered so much as a nick. But even diamonds had fractures. All it took, he knew, was the proper application of stress and force. He'd watched stolen gems the size of hailstones cut into tiny pears and rounds by the best hands in the business. He'd seen grown men weep from an unlucky fracture in a priceless ruby or sapphire; even the most skilled of jewelers couldn't predict a perfect facet.

Clearly, smashing something to bits only took a bit of willpower.

Zane used a spoon to roll the diamond from the ashes. He lifted up the pump and brought the heel down hard on the heated stone. The impact jarred him all the way up his spine. The wound in his other shoulder broke open.

Nothing else happened. Lia made a low moan.

He hit it again. Three times.

On his fourth strike, the heel broke off the pump, and *Draumr* skittled back into the flames.

He swore under his breath. He reached out, reckless, and snatched up the hot diamond, throwing it as hard as he could against the wall.

It burst into splinters, a shower of pale blue shards and light falling back to the floor. Both women cried out.

Zane looked at Lia, his fingers singed. She stared back at him with her hands over her mouth.

He said, "I'd make a ring of them for you, if I thought you'd have me."

And then, most unfortunately, he passed out.

CHAPTER TWENTY-TWO

A full day spun by.

Lia kept watch over Zane in a wing chair beside the bed, listening to the unnatural calm that had taken hold of the castle with the dawn, keeping her senses bright for any hint of coming trouble. She ate little, and slept even less.

But so far, they had been left alone.

She sat in the slow-shifting light and passed the time by deliberately considering which had been worse: watching the prince's physician dig out the lump of lead from Zane's shoulder yesterday, or having to help the man set the broken bone.

Zane had been awake for the bullet, his eyes fixed on hers, his skin very gray, paler than the sheets of the bed. But his lips kept a grim, narrow smile. He did not look away from her face. She'd held his hand and tried not to speak, because she wasn't sure what might come out. Apologies, babbling love talk and nonsense. She didn't want to break down and weep in front of the physician.

Sunlight crawled along the woven colors in the rug. She decided that setting the leg had been worse. Lia wouldn't trust the footmen to handle him—she didn't trust the physician either, but couldn't see a way around that—and so she had held his ankle and Maricara his shoulders, and the physician placed his hands on Zane's thigh and told them how to pull.

Zane's eyes had rolled back in his head; his body fell slack. She'd been biting her lip with the effort not to cry out and was glad he couldn't see it.

And that day had finally passed.

The death of the prince had rocked the castle society to its foundations. There had been true panic at first, the serfs converging and a rumble of ugly unrest rising through the halls. Lia had felt it, Zane had felt it. Last night, Others with rushlights and torches had assembled outside her windows in the courtyard below, and Lia had only stood at the glass in her blood-spattered skirts, watching the people, wondering if a dragon breathing fire in their midst would force them to retreat.

But then had come the princess. Maricara, young, glassyeyed, who had done nothing less than save Lia and Zane and perhaps all the tribe of Darkfrith as well. Maricara strode out alone into the night, into the thick of those torches, and raised her treble voice and commanded obedience.

By then Lia had the window open. She stood listening, and watching, and knew that with the candlelight behind her she could readily be seen.

Perhaps it was the notion of two dragons in their midst. Perhaps it was only that they were used to complying. But Lia thought that mostly it was the cold living flame that was Mari, pushing the restless back into their quarters, using will and daring and some God-given audacity to face a horde of Others who had lost their Alpha—to a girl-child not yet in her teens.

The serfs had gradually dispersed. The body of the prince, Lia knew, had been taken to the chapel.

She wondered if Imre would find peace in his heaven. She remembered the flames eating her skin and hoped not.

Maricara had glanced up at the window where Lia stood and Turned to smoke in front of the stragglers, probably just for extra measure. Lia had stepped back and let the girl Turn back beside the bed.

Mari touched a hand to Zane's forehead.

"No fever," she noted, as if she had not just prevented what promised to be a revolution.

"No." Lia remained where she was. A pair of ladies in the courtyard scooped up Mari's shoes and the empty orange gown, hastening back inside the castle. "The physician said the bullet wound was clean. What will happen to you, Mari?"

The girl shrugged without looking up. "Nothing. I suppose I'll make my brother the new prince."

"You can do that?"

Now the crystal eyes met hers. "I can do nearly anything. This is my haven and my world. Imre truly was the last of his kind, but the people will still want a male to lead. Papers can be easily forged to name him Imre's heir. Better my brother than some new master. It will help placate them, at any rate."

"How old is your brother?"

"Seven years."

"You'll have a while to reign."

"Yes," said the girl, and flicked her hair from her shoulder with a thin, graceful wrist.

"We'll stay as long as we can," Lia said. "He can't travel yet, and you might need...extra persuasion on your behalf."

"Yes, do."

They gazed together at the sleeping figure in the bed, his arms lax above the sheets, his face drawn in angles and shadows, still far too pale.

"So you're not married, after all," mused Maricara.

"No. And neither are you."

Silence descended. The candles flickered, very faintly, with the draft from the window. Behind walls, behind doors, the Others stirred and muttered.

"Is there a cleric for the castle?" Lia asked.

"Imre disliked having God so close. The cleric lives two villages down the mountains. It's about a three-day ride." The girl's lips curved in a smile. "Less, of course, for smoke."

⚜

Around two in the afternoon, Lia fell asleep in the wing chair. She hadn't meant to sleep, and in fact had chosen the chair specifically for its hard horsehair base. But sleep had come anyway. She had no dreams.

When she opened her eyes again, the sunlight had shifted from the rug to the bed. The fire had smoldered out and remained dead cold. The candles had burned down to stubs. She twitched the blanket she'd found a little higher over her shoulders and shifted in her seat to check on Zane.

He was watching her. He lay very still; the light slashed hard and clear past the canopy curtains, brightening the sheets, catching in his hair, fringing color along his dark lashes. A corner of his mouth quirked.

"Hullo," he said, husky.

"Hullo."

"You snore."

"I don't!" She pushed the blanket from her lap and sat forward.

"Only a little. Very ladylike snores. I found them charming."

She shook her head, her fingers at his wrist. His pulse felt stronger today, and a measure of warmth had returned to his cheeks.

He blinked slowly, gazing around the room. "Did we win?"

"For now. I'm afraid we might have a slight uprising on our hands, but not to fear. There's an eleven-year-old girl on our side, so I'm sure we'll do fine. The physician left you this." She picked up a glass of clouded water, a layer of white powder settled thick at the bottom. "I've tried it, and apparently it's not poison. Would you like it now?"

"Dear me." He regarded the glass. "Are things that bad?"

"For a despot, Prince Imre was apparently far more popular than he deserved."

"Let them come," Zane said, again with that slight dry smile. "I can do amazing things with—" He cut short and jerked his hand free. "My picks. My tools." He began to struggle to sit up. "Where the devil did you put them?"

She pushed him back firmly. "Yes, I'm quite well too, thank you for asking. Look there." Lia opened her hand to the top of the rosewood nightstand. "This was everything we found on you. You *are* an arsenal, aren't you?"

His eyes scanned the weapons laid out—slight things, deadly things, metal and bone and wire—and finally relaxed back.

"I like to be prepared."

"So you've said. I do wonder what this might be." She dangled a heavy brass key from her index finger.

His smile grew drier. "The key to my heart? No? Very well. I sometimes find that it's more, ah, expedient to deal with shortcuts."

"A skeleton key. That *does* seem like cheating."

"I hardly ever use it," he said, defensive.

"That's all right." She replaced the key on the nightstand. "I'm not above a few shortcuts myself. I've sent for a cleric."

Zane took a breath. "Oh."

"I thought that I should, since you're already helpless here in bed. You're quite at my mercy."

"I know that," he said in a strangely flat voice.

"And there's something else." She reached into her pocket for her handkerchief, balancing it on her knees, very carefully untying the knot. Inside the wrinkled linen sparkled the remains of a legendary diamond. She placed it on the bed beside him and stirred her finger through the splinters and dust.

Like moonshadows, like fairy song, eerie notes lifted and faded.

"There's nothing much left for a ring," she said quietly.

"Did I say that out loud?"

"You did. And I won't let you steal it back." Her eyes lifted. "Zane. What you did—" She lost the words. She felt the tears from before threaten again and had to look away so he would not see.

"Lia-heart." His hand moved, his fingers lacing through hers. Through the haze in her eyes he was prisms and color, but his hand felt firm and strong. "I would have forsaken a thousand diamonds to save you. Ten thousand—well, perhaps not *ten* thousand." He squeezed her hand, and his voice roughened. "I would have done anything. Don't you know that?"

"No." She wiped at her cheeks with her other hand.

"Then you haven't been paying close attention. I love you. Even more than gold and dreams, I love you. It seems insane you haven't realized it. You *were* the one who first informed me of it."

"I broke your leg," she said, and dropped her head to the covers.

She remembered that moment from another life; her hunger, her excitement. She'd been glad to hurt him, glad to be stronger, and larger, and faster. It shamed her more deeply than anything she'd ever known. It frightened her.

"There is another heart in you," Zane said, after a time. "Not evil. Not bad. Just another heart. I understand that very well. You weren't under your own control. You cannot blame yourself. I don't."

"I'm sorry."

"Don't apologize for being true to your nature. Not to me. I'm hardly a model of upstanding virtue. I respect the dragon. I respect the woman. Amalia, my sweet, thief that I am, I love both your hearts."

The fabric beneath her cheek was growing damp. Zane gave her fingers another squeeze and let go; she felt his palm begin to stroke her hair.

"However . . . you *did* singe a perfectly fine coat of mine, if you'll recall. You're going to need a new stone for a wedding ring, and no doubt I'll feel compelled to shower you with gifts over the years just to remain in your good graces. I fear you're going to be a very expensive wife." He gave a sigh. "And to think I could have had sixty thousand pounds to begin it with."

Lia turned her face and spoke to his hand. "My dowry is thirty-five." She waited, then looked up at him. "A year."

His brows climbed. "You're joking."

"I would never joke about money with a notorious thief. Just imagine, in a mere two years you're at a profit."

"How I adore a woman who does mathematics in her head."

"I can forge signatures as well."

"Splendid. Exactly the bride I've been hoping for."

She stood. She leaned over the bed and pressed her lips to his. He let her, reclining back luxuriously, his eyes drifting closed and his hand sliding up her arm. She drew away only when both of them were short of breath.

"I think you should come over here," he said. "It's a very large bed. Very lonely."

"I think you're mad." But she did it anyway, crossing to the other side of the mattress, climbing up to him with her skirts hitched to her knees. He followed her progress with bright yellow eyes.

"Aren't you warm in all that mess? Wouldn't you prefer to shed a few layers?"

"It's cold in here, Zane."

"Not beneath the covers."

"I admire your ambition. But I believe I'll stay as I am."

She settled down by his wounded side, finding his plait, curling the tip of it back and forth inside her palm. He turned his head to see her better.

"They won't accept me," he said, matter-of-fact. "You know that. And they're right. I'm not good enough for you."

"We'll talk them 'round."

"Silver-tongued as I am, love, I find your family a bit formidable. Perhaps it's all those teeth."

She stroked the plait against her cheek, closing her eyes. "Then we'll go to Tuscany. We'll live in caves in the South Seas. We'll swim the warm tropical waters—you'll have to teach me how. Zane, they *will* accept you. They will love you because *I* love you. And that's all we need to make clear to them."

She was granted his profile, masculine and sharp except for those long, sunlit lashes. "Do you?" he asked, in that flat voice again. "Love me?"

"Of course." She bunched the pillow beneath her cheek.

"You haven't said it before."

"Oh. Pardon me." She paused. "I thought I had."

"Well, just that once. Under extraordinary circumstances."

"I love you." She sat up and tugged at his braid until he glanced back at her. "I love you. I've loved you since I was little. Asleep or awake, I love you. Do you believe me yet?"

"Not quite." He caught her wrist in his hand and hauled her closer, ignoring her protests. He cupped his palm against her nape and lifted his mouth to hers, another kiss, ruthless and hard and delicious. She balanced over him, finally sinking to brace her elbow against his pillow, as he nipped and sucked and drew at her lips.

She did what she could for him. She kissed him in return. She lost her breath and both her hearts, and finally Turned to smoke and back, so she could lay atop her gown and the blankets and feel his hand upon her bare skin.

⚜

Much, much later, Lia whispered, "I don't snore."

And the thief angled his gaze warm to hers, offering his lazy smile. "Aye, love, but if you did, I'd still treasure every one."

Letter to the Marquess and Marchioness of Langford
Chasen Manor, Darkfrith
York, England

13 January, 1774

Gentle Sir and Madame,

Forgive my presumption in addressing you. Enclosed please find a communication from your daughter the Lady Amalia, currently an honored guest in my home. She writes to assure you of her good health and happiness and that of her husband, Zane Langford.

I wish to inform you that they will both be welcome here for as long as they may desire. You need not worry about the serfs or any rumors that may have reached your shores. Our situation is quite secure.

Perhaps one day we shall meet joyfully in person. Until that day, I remain,

Your faithful servant,

The Princess Maricara of the Zaharen
Of *Zaharen Yce*
Of the *Drákon*

EPILOGUE

If you were to close your eyes and dream of heaven, what would you dream?

Angels and golden scepters, perhaps. Halos and hallelujahs. Winged beings soaring, singing amens to the pristine clouds.

When I close my eyes, I see nearly the same thing. But there are no angels flying, and the clouds are not white. They're storm clouds, dark and violent and viscous. The creatures that tear through them have wings of scales, not feathers.

They duck and turn through the turbulent mists. They watch not the heavens but the earth, with brilliant jeweled eyes. They do not search for angels. They scrape the skies and search for glory.

There are so few of us left. Even with the discovery of the English *drákon*, we number so few.

Draumr is destroyed. The couple who holds its ruins are on their way back to England. One is blessed, one is not.

Together they have conquered the myth, and I confess myself still amazed.

But I...I wait here. I quell the serfs and listen hard every night to the voices that sweep to me atop the winds. Soon I'll have to leave too.

My brother is young and not quite as clever as I. But I think he will do.

The future charges closer and closer, a rousing thunder in my sleep.

I hope the English like black dragons.

ABOUT THE AUTHOR

SHANA ABÉ is the award-winning author of nine novels, including *The Smoke Thief*. She lives in the Denver area with five surly pet house rabbits, all rescued, and a big goofy dog. Please, please support your local animal shelter, and spay or neuter your pets.

Visit her website at www.shanaabe.com